FALLING FOR MY SECRET BILLIONAIRE

SECRET BILLIONAIRES
BOOK TWO

BELLA MOONDRAGON

For Sonya

CONTENTS

CHAPTER ONE

BREE

DID OLIVIA JUST SAY COCK-CUTERIE?

"You can even get it engraved with your name on it. Wait. I'm going to send you a picture."

My phone dings beside me. I open the text from my best friend and see the picture she sent. She did, indeed, say cock-cuterie.

"Is that made out of bamboo?" I ask, bringing the phone closer to my face to get a better look.

My best friend nods on the video call pulled up on my laptop where it's sitting on my coffee table.

"It has to be wood," she says, emphasizing the "wood" part.

"Of course, it is." I roll my eyes at her cleverness.

Olivia cackles with laughter, tossing her head back so her blonde curls tumble over her shoulders. "I love it," she says. "You have to have one for your bachelorette weekend."

"It seems like a lot of commitment. What am I supposed to do with a penis-shaped charcuterie board after my bachelorette party?" I ask.

"What can't you do with it? That thing deserves a place of honor in your kitchen. Maybe even your china cabinet. Right next to your Thanksgiving gravy boat," Olivia says. "I will require a cheese assortment every time I visit."

"I'm sure Trevor will be thrilled with that." I laugh at the thought of my future husband's reaction. "Wait, why don't you have one?"

"I just discovered it. I expect one for my bachelorette party. I prefer a script font for my name," she says.

"Nothing says class like your name in script across the balls of a cock-shaped cheese board," I tell her.

"If I don't have elegance, who am I?"

"And speaking of elegance, the napkin samples came in today." I smile, knowing she'll be excited.

"That was fast."

"I know." I reach over to the box sitting on the edge of the table and pull out the stack of samples. "I'm really glad I ordered the full range of greens and pinks. It's amazing how different the shades are when you see them in person. I wish you were here to compare them with me."

"I do, too. You'll have to bring all your planning stuff with you when you come for the party in a couple weeks."

"I don't want to steal your thunder." I exhale loudly.

Giggling, she says, "Just don't stand up on the table and do a slideshow presentation about the proposal and show off your planning binders while people are toasting us, and we're good."

"Damn. That was exactly what I was hoping to do." I laugh, too.

Changing the subject, Olivia asks, "What are you wearing tonight?"

"Oh! I wanted to run that by you. I have a couple of ideas, but I'm not sure which one I want to go with." I pick up the computer and start toward my bedroom. "Come with me."

I set the computer on my dresser and gesture to the three dresses I have laid out across my bed. Coordinating shoes sit on the floor beneath each.

"I can't really see them. You're going to have to actually put them on," she says.

With a sigh, I tug off my T-shirt and yoga pants, grabbing the first dress and dropping it down over my head. The shimmery black fabric skims over my hips and stops a few inches above my knee. I pick up one of the shoes I chose to go with it and hold it up so Olivia can see it. "Maybe?" I ask. "I'm just not sure about the black."

"A little black dress is classic," Olivia reminds me. "But you have to think about the pictures."

"Exactly," I say. "I don't know if that's really the look that I want immortalized from tonight. Let me show you this one." The second dress is longer than the first and the pale pink color feels airy and romantic.

"I love that one." Olivia lets out a romantic sigh. "And it's longer so it won't look like Trevor is trying to peek up your skirt when he's down on one knee. Show me the third one."

"This one is kind of the wild card," I tell her. "It might take me a second to get into it. Hold please."

I take off the pink dress and pick up what looks like a scrap of gauzy lavender fabric.

"Oh, no. You got one of those infinity things, didn't you?" Olivia asks.

"They look amazing when you tie them right," I tell her, wrestling with the long pieces of fabric meant to create the top of the dress.

"When you tie them right being the operative concept here," she says mockingly. "I don't know if the best choice is a dress that requires supervision and an online instructional video to get into."

"Just give me a second."

I manage to twist the straps a few times and get them looped around the back of my neck then tied around my waist. Olivia's flat expression judges me from the computer screen. "Your boob is going to come out," she warns.

I look down and notice I am about an inch and a sneeze away from displaying my nipple. "We'll go with the second one."

Getting back into my regular clothes, I carry the computer into the living room, plop down onto the couch, and pick up my binder and flip it open.

"What are you doing?" she asks.

"I just thought of a question I want to ask when I start touring venues," I say. "I've been trying to write everything down so I don't forget when I'm actually there."

"You're not thinking about anywhere other than Maple Valley, are you?" She tilts her head to the side with that judgy look on her face again.

"Of course, not." I roll my eyes.

It's been a few years since I moved away from my hometown where I grew up with Olivia, but I haven't even considered having my wedding anywhere but Maple Valley. I finish jotting down the note and see her glance at the time on her screen.

"All right, I've got to run. A couple of Brandon's coworkers are coming over for dinner, and I still have to get to the grocery store to buy the cake I'm going to put in his grandmother's glass stand and shamelessly claim as my own. You better call me with every single detail." She gives me a pointed look.

"I will. Love you."

"Love you more."

I look down at the picture of the penis board on my phone one more time and shake my head, laughing as I close the screen. I'm still grinning as I close my planning notebook and head for the bathroom for a long bath to get ready for my date tonight. My cheeks ache from how much I've been smiling the last few days. I can't help myself. Olivia and I have been dreaming of being engaged together since we were little girls. We used to plan out elaborate joint weddings with matching dresses and towering cakes covered in pink roses and sugar pearls. Now as adults, we've given up the thought of actually sharing our ceremony, but getting to plan together has already been the happiest time of my life.

And let's be honest. I would totally still have a joint ceremony with her. I could probably forgo the matching wedding dresses.

I fill the tub and pour in far more bubble bath than the measly single cap the bottle instructs me to use. Stripping out of my clothes again, I sink down into a mountain of frothy bubbles that make me feel like I'm floating around in whipped cream. The thought makes my body tingle. I reach for my pouf and catch sight of my left hand and its bare ring finger. I dip it into the water to wash away the bubbles and hold my hand up to look at it, envisioning a diamond sparkling there.

All right. So, here's the thing. I'm not actually engaged.

But I'm also not the star of one of those women's network movies where the woman concocts her perfect man to impress people and then gets caught; my lack of a ring is just a technicality. Trevor and I have been talking about our future for months. Just a few weeks ago, we went to a jewelry store under the guise of looking for a birthday gift for his mother, but he ended up browsing the rings and even asking me which style I liked. Tonight is our three-year anniversary, and I know in my bones he is going to propose.

I don't know where he's bringing me or what he's planned, just that he's going to pick me up in a couple of hours. I haven't heard from him today, which tells me he's busy putting together something really special. Olivia is convinced he's going to spring for a photographer to capture the moment, so I have to look perfect. These are going to be the pictures we look back on for the rest of our lives.

Just the thought makes me let out a little squeal and sink beneath the bubbles *Pretty Woman*-style.

After a long soak, I switch to a shower. I'm blow drying my hair when I hear my phone chirp to let me know I have a text. It's from Trevor, making my heart leap a little bit.

Be there about half an hour early.

If I wasn't already most of the way ready, I would probably be aggravated, but I'm too excited. Finishing my hair, I start my makeup, smiling into the mirror as I resist the urge to try the elaborate sculpting techniques from the online tutorial I watched earlier. I tell myself I'd like to be one of those women who can transform themselves into looking like they were just peeled off a magazine page, but the truth is I just don't have that kind of skill. I still look pretty good sticking to the basics.

Twenty minutes later, I've just managed to get the tiny clasp on my favorite necklace to close behind my neck when I hear Trevor knocking. A lot of our friends think it's strange that after three years we don't live together, but I like it this way. There's something romantic about him coming to the door to get me for date nights, and I like not sharing my bathroom. I'm going to have to get used to it soon, though.

I open the door with a wide grin and throw my arms around Trevor's neck.

"Happy anniversary!" I say happily.

"What?" He takes me by my hips and guides me a step back away from him.

He's wearing jeans and a T-shirt from his college that I've tried to throw away on multiple sleepovers. My head tilts to the side as I take it in.

"Did you bring clothes to change into?" I ask. I look down at my dress. "Or should I change? You didn't tell me what we're doing tonight, and I just thought maybe I should look special." I give him a coy smile, but Trevor's expression doesn't soften. He hasn't moved from the doorway, and my heart starts to beat faster in my chest.

"I didn't realize tonight was our anniversary," he admits.

"What do you mean? You said you made plans for us," I remind him.

"I know I did, but it wasn't ---" He lets out a sigh and shakes his head. "This isn't going the way I wanted it to."

"What isn't?" I glance behind him at my neighbor who has just come out of her door across the hall. I take Trevor by the arm and tug him the rest of the way into the apartment, closing the door behind us. "Come in. What's going on?"

"I wanted to see you tonight because we need to talk." A sharp V forms between his eyebrows.

Little lights start flashing at the edges of my vision. He didn't just say that. He did not just say we need to talk.

"What do we need to talk about?" I ask.

But I know what's coming. He didn't know it's our anniversary. He isn't here to whisk me away and propose. He's here to break up with me.

"I think we need to call it quits."

My mouth falls open slightly. "Call it quits? We've been together for three years. This isn't a pickup basketball game. What's going on?"

"We don't want the same things, Bree. We're at different places in our lives, and I just don't see us getting on the same page. It's better to go our separate ways now than keep on dragging this on."

I blink a couple of times, trying to get the words to make sense. "When did you decide this?"

"A few weeks ago," he admits.

"A few weeks ago, we were looking at engagement rings," I point out.

"And that's what started it," he says. "I saw how you were looking at those rings, and I knew I should be feeling something, but I wasn't. Then it started sinking in that people are expecting us to get married and settle down, have kids, be adults."

"We are adults." I fold my arms beneath my chest.

"But I'm not ready for any of that. Not with you."

Holy shit. There it is.

"Get out," I say, fighting my tears. I don't want to give him the satisfaction of seeing my mascara run.

"Bree, I want–"

"I don't care what you want. Not anymore. Get out." I walk around him to open the door and point out into the corridor. "Now."

Trevor looks at me for another second, then walks out, leaving me alone in my perfect engagement photo dress, completely humiliated. I close the door behind him just as the tears start.

Happy fucking anniversary.

CHAPTER TWO

Malcolm

"Shit," Preston mutters, watching the golf ball he just hit follow an arc through the sky and then land far closer to us than I think he anticipated. "I swear they gave us a defective bucket." Preston is a good friend and someone I do business with quite often. Most of the time, our business is handled on the golf course or the driving range.

"A bucket of defective balls?" I ask. "That sounds like my company's executives meeting."

Preston cringes and searches through the bucket like he's looking for a ball that somehow looks or feels different from the pile of others that are exactly alike. "Speaking of which, how is all that going?"

"The defective balls? I'd have to get a doctor's note to answer that." I chuckle.

"The meeting," Preston says. "The issues with the hotels."

Letting out a sigh, I twirl the club I'm holding. "It's just the same bullshit. Reservations are down. Loyalty isn't like it used to be. Guest satisfaction has dropped. Staff is leaving for other companies so retention rates are lower. But isn't that everything, everywhere? How many business owners have you heard recently complaining that their numbers aren't good, and customers aren't loyal anymore? And that keeping staff is impossible?"

"I mean, yeah." Preston sets his selected ball down and takes aim. "I've heard that from some people. But didn't your biggest competitor just open up ten new hotels in the last year?"

"They still don't have as many as I do," I point out.

I'm immensely proud of the collection of hotels I inherited from my grandparents and have grown into a hospitality empire. Most people don't know I am at the helm of the entire enterprise. I'd rather people not be aware of the extent of my wealth and power. Even the people in my company who do know that I'm fully in charge were required to sign an NDA restricting them from revealing my identity. It makes my life easier that way.

"No. But that might tell you something. They're obviously not dealing with declining popularity and have more than enough staff to go around." He takes another swing at the ball, and it goes barely further than the first.

I'm not entirely sure why he insists on us coming out to the driving range so frequently. Neither one of us is great at it, and I quickly grow bored of standing in the bay smacking balls out onto the artificial grass. It's marginally better when we actually go out to a course. At least then I get to ride around in a golf cart and see something different at each hole.

"I've been offering the best in luxury hotels and resorts for years," I remind him.

"But maybe that's just it. You haven't changed."

"Why should I change something that's always been the peak of the industry?" I adjust my grip on the handle, wishing he'd let me have a turn.

"Because everything around you is changing," Preston says. "Have you ever stopped to consider that some of it might be about the company culture itself?"

"What do you mean?" I ask. Since when is he such an expert on my company?

"You know you're one of my closest friends. I don't say this as an insult. But you have to admit you're pretty disconnected from everybody around you."

Irritated, I turn to look at him as he's digging in the ball bucket again. "What's that supposed to mean?"

"You have no idea what it's like to not have the entire world at your feet. You don't really understand your employees or the people who stay at your hotels, so maybe you don't really understand what it is that they really want. Or need. You're the one running the company, but you don't really get what matters to them. That might make it hard for you to see what could be changed to make things better." Preston shrugs, trying to soften the blow.

My eyebrows arch as I try to digest what he's just said. He's always had an insight I've lacked, especially when it comes to reading other people. "You think I'm disconnected?"

"You have private suites in your hotels in every major city in the country and several around the world. They were made to your exact standards. And if you don't have a hotel somewhere you want to go, you just rent out a house."

"And?" I ask.

Preston chuckles and goes back to his bucket of dysfunctional balls.

"Just something to think about, buddy." He settles on another one, hits it, and cringes when it lands about forty feet from us. Not what he was aiming for.

Later, when I get to the restaurant where I have reservations with my best friend and his fiancée for dinner, I'm still feeling kind of pissed off about the conversation with Preston. The hostess at the podium smiles at me when I walk through the door. I'm here often enough that she knows my face.

"Hi, Mr. Barrett," she says. "How are you this evening?"

"I'm well, thank you, Ruby. How has your day been?" I flash a genuine smile at her and watch her face light up.

"I can't complain," she says in a flirty tone.

I've always hated that phrase. It seems like it should mean that everything is fine, and the person has nothing to complain about, but it comes across like there's something stopping them from actually telling the truth.

"Good to hear," I say anyway. "I have a reservation."

"Of course." She picks up three menus. "I have your regular table ready for you."

"Have my friends gotten here yet?" I ask.

"Not yet. You're the first."

She steps out from behind the podium and gestures for me to follow her. We weave through the restaurant to my preferred table in an alcove toward the back. It gives me privacy I appreciate whether I'm here with other people or just don't want to be watched eating alone. I thank Ruby and slide into the booth, looking at the day's menu she handed to me.

The waiter shows up with my regular drink, and I order a few appetizers for the table. I'm browsing the entree options when I hear Brandon's voice.

"Already getting started without us?" He chuckles and nudges me in the shoulder.

I grin and stand up to give him a hug, pounding him on the back.

"You should have gotten here sooner." I step around him and open my arms to Olivia.

"Hey, Malcolm." She steps into my embrace. "Sorry we're late. Brandon was primping."

He fluffs his hair and gives a half shrug. "Coming to a swanky place like this, I had to make sure I looked good."

"Looking fantastic as always." I guide them into the booth. "I ordered some appetizers, but check out the menu. It sounds great tonight."

The waiter appears back at the side of the table to get their drink orders and then the plates of appetizers arrive. I select a few bites from each of the platters and put them on my own plate. Brandon and Olivia follow suit.

"How is the wedding planning coming?" I ask.

They glance at each other and smile like just the mention of the wedding makes them giddy. In the decades I've known Brandon, I've never seen him as happy as he has been with Olivia. I've never been one to look for my own happily ever after, but seeing the two of them together could make anybody believe in it.

"It's going," Olivia says. "There're still a lot of details to get in place, and some of the big stuff still needs to be decided. Brandon is dragging his feet on the catering."

"It's the one thing about the reception I really care about." He shrugs and finishes sliding an appetizer into his mouth.

Olivia doesn't even pretend to be offended. "It is," she says. "He can't decide which menu he wants."

"I will get it figured out." Brandon gives her a reassuring look. "We still have some time."

"Please don't let that become your mantra during planning." Olivia narrows her eyes at him.

"It will be fine." He looks at me. "How was golfing this morning?"

"It was golfing," I say. "But you know, Preston really pissed me off. We were talking about how the hotels aren't all performing as well as they used to, and some of the employees are leaving for other companies. I told him most of the chains are having similar problems, and he pointed out that the Creative Hospitality Group has been expanding and not having those issues. Then he said he thinks it's down to the company culture and that I'm disconnected from my employees and guests."

I wait for their reaction, expecting some sympathy or outrage. Instead, they both just stare back at me.

Brandon slowly chews a bruschetta. "Oh," he finally says. "Is that it?"

"What do you mean, 'Is that it?'" My eyebrows knit together as I stare at him.

"I mean, you are kind of disconnected," he says. "I thought you knew that."

Tipping my head to the side, I study him for a long moment to see if he's serious. "No, I didn't know that," I finally say. "What do you mean I'm disconnected?"

"You have no idea how normal people live their lives." Brandon shrugs. "You don't even know how moderately wealthy people live. You can't wrap your head around it."

Shaking my head, I scoff. "So I'm disconnected from the two of you, too?"

"That's different. I've known you since I was a little kid. We didn't know we were all that different. It didn't occur to you that my family worked for yours and that's why I was hanging out at the hotel all the time. We know each other too well for either of us to care about any of that. But the truth is, you don't have any concept of what other people's lives are like or why certain things would matter to them," he says. "You would have no idea how to live the same way your workers do."

"Yes, I would!" Offended, I wipe my hands on my napkin, done with the appetizers.

"I think I feel a challenge coming on." Olivia giggles, trying to break the tension. She glances over at Brandon.

He gives her a little grin back. "What are you thinking?"

Looking at me, she says, "I challenge you to live on the wage of your lowest-paid employee and with only the benefits your company provides them." Her lips curving up in a smile.

"For how long?" I ask.

With a shrug, Brandon says, "Six months."

They both look at me with mischief dancing in their eyes.

"Starting when?" I fold my arms across my chest.

"We'll give you a couple days to get ready." Another chuckle slips from Brandon's mouth.

Olivia rests her elbow on the table, propping her chin on her hand and lifting her eyebrows. "What do you think?"

These are two of my favorite people in the world. Who are actively trying to screw me over.

I could just say no. I could tell them that I'm perfectly happy with the way I live, and I don't need to prove anything to anybody. But I'm not going to. I've never been one to back down from a challenge, and Brandon knows it. Picking up my glass, I hold it up toward them. "You're on."

CHAPTER THREE

BREE

I am now convinced that whoever decided to start putting Halloween candy out on grocery store shelves at the beginning of August was going through a breakup. Nobody needs enormous bags of tiny chocolate bars sitting around their house two months before any trick-or-treaters will be coming to the door except somebody who has just had their heart ripped out and stomped on. It really is the ultimate marketing ploy.

I don't even bother taking out the pumpkin bowl I fill for the children who live in the building every year so I could at least look like I was preparing for the holiday. Nobody can see me walking around my apartment in my baggy clothes, the candy bag tucked under my arm like a security blanket. No one has been here in the last two weeks and probably no one ever will come here again. Because I'm going to die alone.

And when I do, the pink dress will probably still be balled up in the corner of my bedroom where I threw it after Trevor left. I hate seeing it there, but I also haven't been able to bring myself to pick it up and hang it back in my closet. It's just a reminder of what it felt like to look at the door slammed closed behind him and try to wrap my head around what had just happened. I went from comparing shades of pink for wedding reception napkins and discussing the finer points of phallic servingware with Olivia to wondering if I could put my phone through a shredder so I didn't have to go through the humiliation of deleting a gallery full of pictures of us together.

It completely knocked me on my ass, and I haven't been able to get out of my funk. I tell myself that two weeks isn't enough time to mourn three years of the relationship I thought was going to be it for me. After all that time of thinking of Trevor as The One, with the capital letters and everything, I couldn't just expect to hop out of bed the next morning, Disney Princess style, and forge ahead. But at this point, it'll take a friendly woodland creature doing an interpretive dance to snap me out of this. And maybe to help me clean up my apartment, too.

Where are the mice with the brooms when a girl needs them?

Dropping down onto the couch in my living room, I stare at my computer sitting judgmentally on my coffee table. I need to get some work done. I haven't been able to concentrate on it, and deadlines are rapidly approaching. At least the notes that are piling up have taken up the space in the corner where my wedding planning binder used to sit. That got unceremoniously tossed into the dumpster in the middle of the night so I didn't have to look at it anymore.

I know at least one neighbor saw me make my trek to the trash, and I can't help but wonder what she was thinking as I stomped across the parking lot in my pajamas to fling a binder and box of napkins samples into the dumpster. But honestly, I don't care. Go ahead and make my moonlight meltdown your Tuesday evening ladies' wine-and-whine gossip fodder, Barbara. I did what I needed to do.

I've poked a couple of letters on the keyboard, and I'm willing the rest of the article to just appear, when my phone rings. I pick it up and sift through the candy bag next to me in search of something with caramel.

"Hey," I answer.

"You sound perky," Olivia says.

"That's me," I say, finding the elusive candy bar and unwrapping it. "Just bubbling over with enthusiasm for life over here."

"Well, you should be," she says. "I can't wait to see you this weekend."

And then it hits me. This weekend. Her freaking engagement party. Since this isn't a video call, I have the luxury of making a face and doing an undignified little flail in response to remembering the party looming at the end of the week. I managed to completely block it out of my thoughts, but now I not only have to deal with it, I have to get ready for it in just a couple of days.

"I can't wait to see you, either," I say.

That's the truth. It's been months since I've seen my best friend in person, and I could really use a hug and some quality time. I just wish I didn't have to face all the wedding stuff and be right up close and personal with the world's happiest couple. But it's not like I can miss her engagement party. The maid of honor skipping out on something like that is generally considered bad form. I really don't have any other choice but to pick myself up and be there for Olivia.

"When are you getting into town? You're coming early to help me get everything ready and keep me from losing my ever loving mind with all the family around, right?" she asks.

"Of course, I am," I tell her. "I'll probably hit the road Thursday late morning or early afternoon so I can get there, and we'll have all of Friday before the party."

"Hit the road?" she asks. "You're going to drive?"

"Why not?" I ask.

In my mind, the road trip is the perfect opportunity for me to roll down the windows and blast some self-indulgent angst music while justifying a constant stream of salty junk food.

"It just seems like a lot of hours on the road for you to only be here for a couple of days. I bet you could get a really cheap flight that will get you here faster," she says.

There is a little hint of pleading in her voice, and if I know my best friend, which I do, she is already on every travel site she can think of looking for a last minute ticket.

Ten minutes later, my flight is booked, and I'm staring at my confirmation number, dreading the trip. It's been a long time since I was back in Maple Valley, and I thought this time I would return with my shit together and a fiancé to introduce to everybody I left behind. Instead, I'm showing up alone and miserable. Fan-fucking-tastic.

I might not care what Barbara and her gaggle of grown-up mean girls are saying behind my back as they chardonnay themselves into oblivion while brandishing hot glue guns in the name of pursuing Internet craft hack stardom, but the same can't be said for the people back home. Not only are their DIY skills on point out of necessity, but they've known me my whole life. They watched me pack up and leave, eager to see what else the world had to offer beyond the tiny town I grew up in. And I know for a fact they've all been following my relationship with Trevor since we went social media-official.

I cringe. Cyrus McGuire probably already told everybody I called him to set up an appointment to tour the wedding pavilion he built on the edge of his apple orchard. Damn it.

No matter how many times people tell me I don't need to be at the airport so far in advance of my flight, I can't bring myself to cut it any closer than breezing through the terminal three hours before takeoff. Getting caught up in a crowd and witnessing somebody completely losing it on the TSA agents that once resulted in a frantic sprint toward my flight that was nowhere near as cute as it is in the movies was enough to scare me straight. I'd much rather be that person who shows up at the gate before the gate agent does and sits alone watching the planes come in than deal with the stress of barely making it or risking missing a flight.

So when I wake up Wednesday morning to rain pounding down and visibility at what I think meteorologists technically refer to as jack-shit, my travel day is not off to a great start. I already did most of my packing yesterday, but I still have to take a shower and get ready before packing up my toiletries and makeup. I'm in the middle of trying to get my cosmetic bag to fit into my carryon when Olivia calls me. I put the call on speaker so I can leave the phone sitting on the bed.

"Hey," I say.

"So there's a slight change of plans," she says in a perky voice that says she knows I'm not going to love hearing that.

"What's going on?" I ask.

"We're not going to be able to pick you up at the airport," she says. "It's Brandon's boss's birthday, and everybody at the office just decided that they need to go out for drinks. All of the wives and husbands and everybody are going to be there. It's a big thing, and it's kind of understood that nobody can skip it. Are you mad?"

"No," I tell her. "I get it. Have to keep the boss happy. Especially since Brandon is after that promotion this year. I'll just get a rental car. It's no big deal."

"No," she says. "You don't need to do that. I'll have a ride waiting for you."

"It's really fine," I tell her. "I can just book a car."

"It's already taken care of," she says. "This little hiccup is on me, and I am not going to put more stress and expense on you. Just get here, and I'll see you at dinner tonight. Have a great flight."

Thunder crashes overhead, and I close my eyes, taking a deep breath. Perfect.

Getting to the airport isn't too bad, but as soon as I approach the main terminal, it's like everybody around me has forgotten how to drive. Sitting up as high in my seat as I can and leaned close to the windshield, I try to navigate cars shifting in and out of lanes, following far too closely, or drifting back until it looks like they are making space for an eighteen-wheeler to cut in. By the time I almost miss the entrance to the parking garage, I'm already too close to the time of my flight for comfort.

The seemingly never ending line of cars parking means I have to circle around through several floors before I finally see the elusive little green light that promises an empty parking spot. I make my way directly to it, only for somebody to swing in from the other side, nearly causing me to smash into them. The sound of the rain lessens the volume of the string of expletives that streams out of my mouth, but I would not be surprised if at least a few of the other drivers hear it. Pulling away from the stolen spot, I continue the climb up the levels until I finally find another spot and manage to make it in.

I'm not going to remember where I parked when I get back, so I snap a picture of the nearest marker, grab my bags, and head for the terminal. The storm that followed me from my house hasn't had any impact on the flights, miraculously, so mine still says on time when I speed walk past the board on my way to the boarding pass kiosk. Apparently, everyone who is flying on the same airline as me has gone to the kiosks at the same time, and it is another twenty minutes before I have my pass in my hand and make a beeline for security.

"Boarding pass and ID?" the agent at the podium asks when I finally make it through the line.

I hand him them over, and he narrows his eyes as he scrutinizes my ID.

"Did you know that your ID is expired?" he asks.

"I know it expired a couple of weeks ago, but I got a replacement..." My heart sinks. "That I left in the envelope on my kitchen counter."

Mother fu---I hate Trevor. I'm blaming him for all of this.

"Weren't you aware that you need a valid ID in order to board an airplane?" the agent asks.

My teeth grit together so hard I think they might crack. I force a smile so I don't scream.

"I am aware of that," I tell him. "It was a mistake. But I really need to catch this flight. What can I do?"

He lets out a sigh that sounds like I have just burdened him far beyond his job description and walks away, carrying my boarding pass and invalid ID with him. He talks to another agent, who looks over at me with an equally withering look, and I can feel the line of people behind me starting to plan a revolt. The second agent takes my documents from the first and makes eye contact with me, giving me a "come here" gesture with one hand.

I step out of the line and meet the agent on the other side of the podium.

"You're going to have to go through an enhanced security screening," she tells me.

That sounds ominous, but I don't really have a choice in the matter. I've got to get on the plane. I agree, and she brings me to the center of the screening area. Reaching for my bags, she looks me up and down.

"Anything in your pockets?"

I am wearing a pair of yoga pants and a tank top with flip-flops.

"What you see is what you get," I tell her.

She is not amused.

"Shoes off," she says, putting my bags on the conveyor belt.

I put them into the bucket she offers me and send them through the machine along with my bags. It seems like I'm just going through the same steps I would if I was in regular security until I go through the full body scan and come out the other side to see another agent unpacking my carryon. Beside her, another is doing the same to my backpack. Everything from my cosmetic bag to my neon green lace thong panties ends up spread across the counter for the world to see.

"What's this?" one asks, holding up my cylindrical plastic toothbrush holder.

I really want to tell her it's a vibrator. Just for the hell of it. But I highly doubt it would be the most shocking thing she's ever discovered in a bag, so I don't bother.

"My toothbrush," I explain.

She puts it through another scanner that shows everything up on a giant monitor beside her. My cosmetic bag is next. Then my toiletries. As the rest of the passengers who were behind me in line slide past, I watch the agents take every second they possibly can to go through my bags. Finally, they determine I am not attempting to smuggle anything dangerous onto the flight and usher me to the end of the row to repack everything. When I'm finished, the first agent meets me to ask me a series of questions I'm sure are intended to confirm my identity. All I can think as I rattle off my social security number, address, birthdate, and another rendition of why I don't have a valid ID is that it seems if I was really trying to game the system with fake identification, I would at least make sure it had a valid expiration date.

At last, the agent decides I am safe to fly, and I have my boarding pass back in my hand for another sprint to the gate. This time, I'm hauling ass with purpose. The pre-boarding I paid extra for has already started, and I get to the gate just in time to join the line. I flop down into my window seat with exactly zero sense of calm and relaxation.

This is for Olivia. This is for Olivia. This is for Olivia.

My mantra gets me through the rest of boarding. As it turns out, the woman seated next to me has chosen today as the day to confront her lifelong fear of flying by hitting the skies solo. As we taxi down the runway, I'm afraid she's going to pass out right beside me.

"That wasn't so bad," she says when we've finally touched down.

She smiles at me as if she hasn't just spent the entire flight repeatedly clenching her claw-like fingers around my arm, sure we were going down. Grabbing her bag from the overhead compartment, she shuffles down the aisle and out of the plane. I follow behind her and soon learn the friendship we forged miles above the earth has continued beyond landing.

"What brings you to Richmond?" she asks, falling into step beside me as we make our way through the terminal.

"I'm actually on my way to Maple Valley," I tell her.

"I've been in that area. It's beautiful," she says. "On vacation?"

"I'm here for my best friend's engagement party." I force a smile.

"That's wonderful!" she gushes. "How about you? Are you married?"

"No." My smile fades.

"Engaged?" she asks.

"No." I try to walk a little faster in hopes that I'll lose her in the crowd.

"Seeing someone special, then?" she asks.

"Nope. It's just me."

"Oh," she says, sounding distinctly pitying. "Well, that's all right, honey. You just keep your chin up. You'll find him."

I make a face toward her that I hope looks like another smile and not the snarl I'm feeling and bolt for the doors leading outside. A small sense of relief hits me as soon as I see a man standing a few yards down the sidewalk holding a sign with my name on it. At least I can finally see Olivia and this day from hell can end. Somehow, it doesn't help that the driver she sent is gorgeous. I walk up to him and point at the piece of white poster board he's holding, trying to ignore his startling blue eyes.

"Bree Connor," I say. "That's me."

"Nice to meet you," he says. "I'm--"

"Is this your car?" I ask, cutting off the small talk and pointing to a tan four-door a few feet away from him.

"Yeah," he says.

"Great." The trunk isn't open, so I go stand beside it.

"Let me get that for you." He walks around to the driver's side.

The trunk pops open, and I put my bags in. He doesn't make a move to come and close it, so I shut it and walk around to the back door.

"You can hop in the passenger seat," he says.

I am so not in the mood to have this guy try to bump up his tip by flirting with me.

"Thanks, but I'll just sit back here," I say, pulling out my phone to text Olivia and let her know I've landed.

He gets behind the wheel and glances around at the jam of cars trying to get away from the airport. "Looks like we might be here for a bit. How was your flight?"

"I'm sorry, I'm sure my friend didn't specify a quiet ride when she ordered it, but it would be great," I say.

I notice a hint of a smile come to his lips, but he holds his hands up like he's surrendering and sits back.

"Got here," I message Olivia. *"Wait until I tell you that horror story."*

"Oh no! I hope it wasn't too bad. Did you find Malcolm all right?"

Malcolm? How often is she using rideshares that she knows this guy by name?

"Malcolm?"

"Yeah. Brandon's best friend. I've told you about him. I asked him to come pick you up."

You've got to be fucking kidding me.

My eyes snap to the rearview mirror where I see him staring around, drumming his fingers on the steering wheel as if he's listening to music in his own head. Letting out an exasperated sound, I wrench off my seatbelt and get out.

"You could have told me you aren't a rideshare driver," I say, getting into the passenger seat with embarrassment burning my cheeks.

Malcolm shrugs. "You didn't seem like you were too open for conversation."

The cars ahead of us finally thin out, and he pulls into line.

"Who holds a sign with a person's name on it if they aren't a driver?" I ask.

"Someone who has never met the person they are giving a ride to," Malcolm reminds me. "And when was the last time you had a rideshare driver put your name on a sign?"

Crossing my arms over my chest, I turn to look out the window, not looking forward to the rest of the drive to Maple Valley.

CHAPTER FOUR

Malcolm

I HAVE NEVER SEEN OLIVIA'S BEST FRIEND IN A GOOD MOOD, BUT SHE IS sure as hell adorable when she's pissed off.

Looking across the car at her glaring out the window, I can't help the instant attraction I feel toward her. She might be extremely difficult, as she has already proven, but there's something about her. I keep wanting to look at the tendrils of honey colored hair that have escaped the bun on the back of her head and are framing her face or the perfect way her leggings and tight tank top mold to her curvy body. Even the sour expression on her face has my attention. If they weren't drawn tightly into a frown, those pink lips would probably be soft and plush and her narrowed eyes are a vibrant green that at this moment could probably cut glass but that I find myself wanting to see softened.

We are only a couple of minutes out of the parking lot of the airport when she lets out a sigh and rolls those eyes.

"You should have taken the other way," she says. "It's a lot faster."

"This is the way I always go," I tell her.

She searches the dashboard of the car. "Don't you have a GPS?"

"No, not built-in to the car" I tell her, "Would it make you feel better if I pulled one up on the phone?"

"Not particularly, considering you're driving," she says, rolling her eyes. "It's fine. we're already heading this way."

She reaches forward and fiddles with the air conditioning vent. I know she's probably not getting as much cold air as she would like on the steamy Virginia August evening. The lack of an integrated GPS is just the beginning of the issues I'm having with my current vehicle. Part of the challenge I accepted from Brandon and Olivia, the aging sedan was the only thing I could afford on the tiny amount of fake savings they allowed me to start my experiment with. I found it online and paid for it in the middle of a parking lot with a handful of cash in an awkward transaction that felt far removed from every time I've gotten a new car. There was no perpetually-smiling salesman sitting in the passenger seat beside me on a test drive touring the town or long presentation about the various amenities and features. I didn't fill out paperwork. It was a spin around the block to prove the engine worked, a handshake, and it was done.

But I needed something that would fit in with my new lifestyle and this was what was available. I just hope it will survive the next six months.

The drive from the airport to Brandon and Olivia's House in Maple Valley feels a lot longer with Bree's stony silence beside me. Olivia asked me if I could go pick her up because Brandon and she weren't going to be able to, she said it would be a good opportunity for Bree and I to chat and get to know each other. That is not happening. Instead, Bree continues to stare out the window for the entire drive and only turns her head to look at the front of the car when she tries to adjust the air conditioner again.

She looks as relieved as I feel when we pull up at Brandon and Olivia's house.

"Thanks," she says, opening the door and climbing out. I get out and she stares at me. "You're staying?"

"Olivia invited me to stay for dinner," I tell her.

Bree looks like she wants to say something, but before she can, the front door to the house opens and Olivia steps out. She lets out a squeal and rushes down the steps toward us. Bree throws her arms open and the women jump on each other, hugging tightly.

"I can't believe you're here," Olivia says happily. "It's been forever."

"It would have been sooner if we hadn't gone the scenic route," Bree says.

"Well, you made it. Where are your bags?" Olivia asks.

"In the trunk," Bree says.

"I'll get it," I say, opening the door to pop the trunk.

She grabs out her bags and heads for the door without saying anything. I shake my head as I close the trunk and follow behind the women.

"Brandon's in the kitchen," Olivia tells me.

She leads Bree toward the living room at the back of the house and I detour to the kitchen where I find Brandon making drinks.

"Hey, buddy," he says.

"Hey," I say. "How was drinks with the boss?"

"A lot of fake laughing and toasting to random things," he says.

"So, essentially an audition to be one of the big guns," I say.

"Pretty much. And holy hell do I want to be one of them. I will fake my way right to the bank," he says.

I cringe. "Probably shouldn't throw phrases like that around when you're with them."

"Yeah," he says. "I'll work on it. Anyway, thanks again for picking Bree up at the airport. I know it's not exactly the most fun use of an evening."

"No problem. Consider it part of my best man duties."

"At least you had a chance to get to know Bree a bit. I can't believe the two of you haven't met before. She's great, isn't she?"

"She's definitely something," I agree. "Speaking of her, though, I'm assuming she doesn't know much about me?"

"What do you mean?" he asks.

"She just didn't seem surprised by the car I was driving."

Brandon grins. "Oh, you're asking if she knows about your alter ego."

"Well, technically this is my alter ego. I'm asking if she knows about my real identity. Jeez, that sounded dumb."

Brandon laughs as he finishes off the drinks and sets them on the kitchen table. "Your secret is safe, Batman. I asked Olivia if she ever told Bree about you, and she said she mentioned you in stories but never told her anything. She figured she wasn't supposed to. So all she knows about you is what she's finding out this weekend."

"And what happens after the six months is over?" I ask. "I mean, I have a feeling I'm going to see her again at some point."

"So, we'll tell her," Brandon says, as if this situation is completely normal. "It's not like you want her to know that your last name should actually be Fitzpatrick and you're the heir to the Fitzpatrick Hospitality empire."

I started using my mother's maiden name when I was younger, wanting to go through school and early adulthood without the weight of my inheritance on my shoulders. There was never any escape from people knowing I was wealthy, but I didn't have to grapple with people already knowing who I was just by hearing my name.

"You know I hate when you call me an 'heir,'" I complain. "It makes me sound like I should be a prince or something."

"I know," he says with a wider grin. "But I love it."

"You love what?" Olivia asks, coming into the kitchen with Bree.

"You," Brandon says, reaching out to take his fiancée into his arms and nuzzle her neck.

She smiles and rolls her eyes at the same time. "Yeah, I know that's not what you were talking about. But I'll give you a pass because you're too damn cute for your own good."

"Always works," Brandon says, popping a kiss on the side of her neck.

"Is everyone ready to eat?" Olivia asks. "I'm starving."

"Me, too," Bree agrees. "The woman beside me on the plane wouldn't stop talking long enough for me to even get a snack. The flight attendant just walked right past us."

"She sounds like a trip and a half," Olivia says as we sit down at the table. "I do feel kind of bad for her, though. That first flight when you are afraid of flying has to be awful."

"True," Bree says. "At least I wasn't trying to get any work done on this flight."

"What do you do?" I ask her.

Olivia hands a basket of bread to Bree, who takes a roll and hands it along to Brandon.

"I'm a freelance content creator," she says without elaboration.

I have a sudden vision of her doing one of those viral dances in a skimpy outfit. I don't think that's what she's talking about, but I wouldn't object to seeing that content.

"Is that something you've always wanted to do?" I ask, getting the bread and adding a roll to my plate.

She looks at me for a silent beat, those incredible eyes cutting into me.

"Absolutely. I distinctly remember my kindergarten teacher telling us all to draw a picture of what we wanted to be when we grew up and I drew a freelance content creator," she says flatly.

There's another beat and Olivia laughs a bit too intensely for the situation, then shoots a raised-eyebrow glare toward Bree. She lets out a breath.

"What do you do?" she asks, obviously putting some effort into sounding friendly.

Unfortunately, I'm not sure how to respond. It hasn't been part of the discussions when Olivia, Brandon, and I talked about my challenge. It somehow didn't occur to us to come up with a cover story. I couldn't exactly tell her that I own a network of hotels and resorts across the globe. I look over at Brandon, then back at Bree.

"I work in hospitality," I tell her.

It isn't a lie, though technically at the moment I'm not doing anything. I took some unheard of vacation time to get settled into my temporary life and hang out with Brandon. I'm supposed to be relaxing, but I can't stop wondering what's going on at the company without me there at the helm every day. I want to think that I can depend on the executives to handle things while I'm gone, but the truth is I'm just not that trusting.

I'm expecting a follow-up question from Bree, but instead, she looks over at Olivia.

"So, what's on the docket for tomorrow?" she asks.

I look over at Brandon with raised eyebrows and he gives me a little shrug. Olivia says something that makes Bree laugh and the sound goes right to my gut.

How the hell could this woman be so infuriating and yet so intriguing at the same time?

CHAPTER FIVE

"Are you absolutely sure you don't want to stay here for the weekend?" Olivia asks as I put my shoes back on.

She's been trying to get me to hang out longer, but she has also yawned ten times in the last half an hour, and I'm pretty certain she almost fell asleep in her carrot cake.

"I'm sure," I tell her. "The hotel is perfectly fine. You are going to be inundated with family starting tomorrow evening, and you'll be dealing with more than enough inconvenience and stress."

"You aren't an inconvenience or a stress," she tells me.

"That's very sweet, even if it is a lie. Trying to stuff me in here along with everybody else would just make everything harder for you. I would love to spend every second with you, but I will be perfectly happy at the hotel and we will see each other a ton this weekend," I tell her.

To tell the truth, I do wish I was staying at the house with her. Or that I could kidnap her and bring her to the hotel with me. It's been months since we've gotten to spend any time together, and I could use the fun. But there's no way I would jump into the family members trying to fit into the house like a game of Tetris. I'll be much more comfortable getting to spread out in my own room.

"Do you have everything?"

I pick up my bags. "Yep."

"All right," she says. "Let's go."

The sentence gets lost in a long yawn and her eyes sag even as she picks up her keys to head for the door.

"Why don't I take Bree to her hotel?" Malcolm offers.

My spine goes tense. I have already spent enough time with Malcolm tonight. I'm really not looking forward to another uncomfortable drive.

"No, that's okay," Olivia says. "You don't need to do that."

"I'm already going to be driving," he says. "There's no reason for you to go out. It's not a problem."

"Really?" Olivia asks.

She looks over at me. There's a silent question in her eyes, asking me if it's all right. As much as I want to, I don't feel like I can say no. They are all looking at me, and there's really no good reason to reject the ride. Wanting to spend any more time alone with the man who is aggravating the hell out of me and yet who I can't stop staring at just doesn't seem like a good enough excuse.

"It's fine with me," I say through slightly gritted teeth.

"Thank you, Malcolm," Olivia says. She wraps her arms around me. "I'll be at the hotel first thing in the morning and we'll put all the finishing touches on the party plans."

"I'll be ready," I tell her.

She gives me another squeeze and Malcolm and I leave. She and Brandon lean against each other, their arms wrapped around each other's waists in the doorway as they watch us leave. Her head drops to his chest as she waves and he presses a kiss to her hair. My heart squeezes painfully, and I try not to show it.

I get into the car and wave through the window. Malcolm gets in beside me and cranks the engine.

"Where are you staying?" he asks, pulling out of the driveway.

"The Azalea Inn," I tell him.

"Really?" he asks.

I give him a questioning look. "Why do you sound so surprised?"

"I was just expecting you to say one of the bigger chain hotels closer to the city," he says. "Were they all booked up for this weekend?"

"No," I tell him. "I didn't even look at them. I wanted to stay there."

"Isn't it just a tiny little mom-and-pop hotel?"

He isn't even trying to hide the judgment in his voice. I'm a little taken aback by the obvious implication that the family-owned bed-and-breakfast isn't as good as the brand name hotels.

"That's exactly what it is," I tell him. "I much prefer to stay in places like that than any of the big hotels. Any time I travel, I look for small, independent hotels. I like the personal touches and feeling like I actually matter rather than just being a faceless reservation."

He doesn't say anything, but I can see the look on his face. It's somewhere between confusion and disdain, leaving me with an even worse taste in my mouth about him. The drive to the bed-and-breakfast doesn't take long, but it's still a relief to get out of the car.

I grab my bags with a cursory thank you and walk inside. The entryway is beautifully decorated and smells like warm chocolate chip cookies. To one side is a parlor where the owners set up tea every afternoon. On the other side is the alcove where guests check in.

I walk up to the podium and glance at my phone to check the time. One big difference between this place and a big hotel is the check-in cutoff. The owners have to get to bed, so they stop checking people in at ten-thirty. Since the front door wasn't locked yet, I'm pretty sure I've made it, but there's no one standing behind the podium. Just as the thought goes through my head, Diana Kessinger, one of the owners, comes through a door to the side. She smiles warmly.

"I thought I heard someone out here. Bree Connor. I've been waiting for you," she says.

My body relaxes and I feel a smile come to my face. She steps behind the podium and starts the check-in process. I'll admit it isn't as fast or as streamlined as the hotels that let you check in online and skip the front desk all together, but I'm willing to take the time. It feels welcoming, and I appreciate the personal way she talks to me and makes sure I will have everything I need for my stay. It's only for a couple of nights, but the attentiveness makes all the difference.

When Diana is finished getting me checked in, she hands me a key and tells me my room number. The bed and breakfast takes up three of the four floors of the refurbished old house, with the top floor reserved for the owners' living quarters.

I climb the richly carpeted stairs up to the third floor and find my room at the end of the hallway. The bed has been made with crisp white sheets and a floral bedspread, and a stack of clean towels sits on the corner of the dresser next to a small basket of snacks and a bottle of water.

I set my bags down on the bed and unpack, putting my clothes away in the dresser and the small closet. When everything is in place, I text Olivia to let her know I've gotten settled in. I expect her to already be asleep but a second later, she calls me.

"Brandon passed out in front of the TV," she tells me.

"I expected you to be crashed out right beside him," I say. "You looked like you were about to fall asleep in the doorway when I was leaving."

"Well, I went to take a shower and it got me going. I put on my new lingerie to surprise Brandon and walked out into the living room to find him open-mouth snoring on the couch," she explains. "Kind of deflating."

I laugh. "Sorry your lingerie was wasted."

"I'm still wearing it. I'm thinking about giving him the Snow White treatment."

"I'm pretty sure she was dead," I say.

"You ruin everything."

"Since we're talking about Brandon and ruining things, how did he and Malcolm become friends?" I ask.

"That was an interesting segue," she says. "They've known each other since they were kids. I've talked about him before."

"Yeah, I remembered that right after assuming he was my

rideshare driver. I'm just surprised he and Brandon are so close. He just doesn't seem like the kind of guy Brandon would hang out with," I say, not trying to disguise the fact that I am not a fan.

"Why would you say that?" she asks.

Apparently she did not catch on.

"He just comes across smug and full of himself."

"He's really not that bad," she says. "Once you get to know him, you'll like him. I promise."

I have absolutely no interest in getting to know him. Malcolm rubbed me the wrong way right from the beginning. It doesn't make it any better that every time he looks at me I start thinking about him rubbing me in a completely different way.

I'm blaming Trevor for this, too.

CHAPTER SIX

Malcolm

I'm aggravated as I drive away from the bed and breakfast after dropping Bree off. How could she possibly think that staying in a little place like this could even begin to compare to a hotel like mine? The things she said about preferring the small places to chain hotels because of the personal touches and feeling like she is more than just a reservation particularly stick with me. That sounds a lot like some of the complaints I've heard about my hotels and the incessant rumors of even my most popular locations not doing as well as they used to.

It still doesn't convince me. I just don't think the two experiences can be compared. I offer a level of luxury and quality that is far beyond anything these little independent places can offer. This isn't something I am only just now thinking about. I haven't made any concrete plans yet, but I have been considering building a hotel here in Maple Valley. I haven't ventured into smaller areas like this yet, but I've been paying close attention to the tourism trends over the last couple of years and noticed that more people are visiting the little town and its surrounding area than ever before.

Spectacular foliage in the fall and nostalgic festivities throughout the holiday season in particular draw in people yearning for a bit of charm. I feel like with the right kind of accommodations and resort amenities, Maple Valley can become a year-round destination. Having more people coming through would give plenty of opportunities for local businesses to grow and expand, not to mention the appeal of a new property in my portfolio.

But now I have a little voice in the back of my mind saying it would only be as successful as I'm envisioning if people actually come. I could understand Bree staying in the bed and breakfast because it's closer to Olivia and she didn't feel like making the commute from the city. That would make sense to me and would just underscore my motivation for building something new here. But that wasn't the reason. She chose the little inn because she actually prefers it, enough that even if there was a luxury hotel here in the town, she would still be snuggling up in the Azalea Inn.

Perfect. Now I'm even more annoyed because all I can think about is what Bree would look like snuggled up in a bed.

I don't feel a whole lot better about things when I pull into the parking lot of the apartment building I've been calling home for the last couple of weeks. It's not technically in Maple Valley, but when I tasked Brandon with helping me find a place to live that suits my income for the next six months, he insisted this was my best option. I'm not convinced it's really all I would be able to afford with my new financial status. The crummy building and even crummier apartment twenty minutes away from town seems a bit extreme. I have a feeling he's playing it a bit fast and loose with his interpretation of this challenge, but I'm not going to back down. He needed to find something for me with no notice and this is where I ended up, so I'm going with it. I've never tried to get out of a challenge he laid down, and I'm not starting now.

"Skunk?" a voice calls out into the darkness as I walk toward the building.

I take a few steps back and look up at the rickety fire escape on the second floor. My neighbor is standing on it in nothing but a pair of baggy white and blue striped boxers, his skinny legs sticking out like pencils. A tattoo covers a good portion of his ribcage and around to his back, but even after seeing it a handful of times, I still don't know what it is.

"It's me, Kevin," I tell him. "Malcolm from downstairs."

"Oh. Damn. I thought you were my buddy Skunk. He was supposed to come over tonight but he hasn't shown up yet," he says.

"At least you weren't talking about an actual skunk."

"Nah. I haven't seen one of those around here in a while. Smell them sometimes though," he says.

"Why do you call your buddy Skunk?" I ask, hoping the reason isn't the obvious one.

"He used to keep them as pets when we were kids," he explains. "Loved on them just like kittens."

That was not the obvious one.

"Well, sorry to disappoint you."

"You're not disappointing me, man," Kevin says, leaning forward to rest his folded arms on the edge of the fire escape so he can look down at me. "It's good to see you. I've been meaning to ask how you're settling in."

"Good, good." I nod. "Getting the hang of the faucet in the shower."

"Yeah," he says, shaking his head in sympathy. "Those things can be a real bitch. I'm pretty sure each one of them has a personality all their own in this building. Sometimes in the winter they start making weird sounds and you can hear when everybody is taking their showers. It's actually kind of beautiful."

His voice fades as his mind drifts somewhere else.

"I'll look forward to that," I tell him.

A car door closes behind me and another man lumbers from the parking lot toward the building.

"That's Skunk," Kevin says.

"All right. I'll leave you to it."

"Want to come up for some brownies and board games?"

"It's getting kind of late," I tell him.

"Some other time then, brother."

I give him a little salute and head into the breezeway where the door to my apartment is located. I can't help but smile. The location and the apartment itself might suck, but this is the first time in my life I've had a neighbor whose name I actually know and who I've done more than wave politely at in passing. I'm surprised at how much of an upside to this whole situation it really is.

Unlocking my door, I feel along the wall beside the door for the light switch. It isn't there. After two weeks of being here, I'm still not used to not having a switch right as I walk inside. Instead, I have to go over to the lamp sitting on a side table next to the couch that used to be in Brandon's finished basement. He said he was giving me the experience of making use of whatever resources I have available to me. I think he just wanted a good excuse to get rid of the old couch he complained about all the time and replace it with the sectional he's been wanting.

Either way, it graces my minuscule living room now and points me in the direction of a TV also sourced from Brandon's discards. This one had been living tucked away in a corner after he upgraded, so now I'm giving it a new life. At least for the next six months. Kicking off my shoes, I drop down onto the couch and stretch out as I grab the remote to turn on something mindless. It's a far cry from the media room in my house, but it will get the job done helping me unwind before I go to bed.

The next morning I'm still aggravated when I get out of bed. Some of it is the sound of my neighbors coming through the thin walls and jostling me out of sleep. But some of it is also the lingering effects from last night's conversation with Bree. After doing battle with the temperamental faucet to get a shower, I get dressed and head back for the Azalea Inn.

The smell of breakfast somewhere in the recesses of the building hits me as soon as I walk inside. I follow it through the entryway down a hallway and into a bright, open dining room. French doors stand open, leading out onto a patio overlooking the grounds. There's nobody in the room, so I walk in and look around.

As I'm standing at the railing of the patio trying to figure out what the grounds have to offer guests, I notice someone out of the corner of my eye. I look back inside and see Bree coming into the room. She looks like she's considering leaving, but then sighs when she realizes I've already seen her.

The black sundress she's wearing is a stark contrast from yesterday's travel look. Her hair hangs down around her shoulders, highlighting a hint of cleavage. She completely ignores me as she walks up to the table and picks up a plate. I walk over to her.

"Are you planning on going to a funeral later?" I ask.

Bree sighs again and picks up a couple of tiny quiche from a glass stand. "What are you doing here? You're not a guest. You shouldn't be roaming around in here."

"I didn't see a sign saying non-guests aren't allowed," I point out.

"It's generally understood," she says, walking around me to get to the next display of food. "Did you just come to be more judgmental about where I'm staying?"

"Actually, no," I reply. "I came to try to understand the appeal of this place."

Bree gives me a questioning look. "The appeal of this place? Why would that matter to you?"

Shit. I've got to work on my backstories.

"Brandon is looking for somewhere for out of town guests to stay for the wedding weekend," I explain. "He was thinking about a couple of the places around town and wanted to know what's so great about this place. Why would he choose this place over another hotel?"

Her expression shifts to something that says she's not convinced, but after a second, she relents and keeps moving down the buffet line.

"Well, probably the first thing I should point out is that you can't really compare a bed and breakfast to a hotel," she begins. "They aren't the same thing. There's a totally different feeling here than at a hotel."

"All right, so this place used to be a house." I look around. "It doesn't look like a hotel. But it's still a place with rooms where you sleep. If you set aside the whole no lobby, no pool, no elevators thing, what is it about somewhere like this that you like so much?"

"I thought you worked in hospitality. Isn't this the kind of stuff you should know?" Bree asks.

I let out an exasperated huff. "Can't you just answer the damn question?"

"If it will make you leave me alone so I can enjoy my breakfast, then yes," she says. "And that's what I'll start with. Breakfast."

"Most hotels have breakfast," I point out.

"They have generic bagels, cereal, and a waffle maker, or a restaurant that's usually too busy and has the same stuff as every other place. Here, almost everything comes from local artisans, farmers, and shops. There are little note cards in the rooms describing each of the places and what they offer, along with the address so that you can go visit them. It's the same for the body products they have in the bathrooms. Everything is local and really high quality. They even offer different scents that you can request for your toiletries. It isn't just another cookie cutter hotel with the same things you can find everywhere else," she explains.

"That's not a cookie cutter. That's called consistency. Dependability."

"Boring," she says. "Predictable. I'm not saying there's nothing to be said for a nice hotel experience, but the little personalized touches here make this place feel like a true extension of Maple Valley. It's a part of immersing in the area. I know when I come here that they are anticipating my arrival, will welcome me, and will make my stay special even in some little way."

She pushes her sunglasses down over her eyes.

"You know those are for outside, right?"

"And that's exactly where I'm going. Outside to eat on the patio. Alone." She walks outside, and I head back toward the front door.

"Can I help you, sir?" a man asks from the sitting room.

"No, thanks. I was just looking around," I say.

"Well, we are fully booked for the weekend," he continues. "But if you'd like to make a reservation for another time, let me know."

"No. Thanks," I say, heading for the door. I stop before I go out and turn back to him. "Is it unusual for you to be fully booked?"

"Not especially," he replies. "We actually had a cancellation, but it was filled up immediately by a guest who arrived last night."

I nod. "Thanks."

As I walk toward my car, I see Olivia slide up to the front of the house. I wave and she gives me a curious look. I'm about to go over to her when my phone rings. My assistant's name pops up on the screen, and I start back in the direction of my car. Greg wouldn't call me while I was on vacation unless it was urgent.

"What is it?" I ask as I climb into the car.

"I'm sorry to bother you," he says. "I know you're–"

"What is it?" I ask again, my tone distinctly less patient.

"I just overheard one of the secretaries saying someone has been sniffing around trying to get information about the company," Greg explains. "She apparently offered to set up an appointment with me and they refused."

"Who was it?" I ask.

"She didn't mention her name."

I frown. "Find out. Call me when you know."

"I'll see what I can do."

I hang up and rub my hand across my mouth, staring through the windshield as anger builds up along the back of my neck. Rumors have been swirling for a while now that another company is planning to try to force me out of control of Fitzpatrick Hospitality.

Now it sounds like they are moving closer.

CHAPTER SEVEN

Olivia really meant it when she said she would be here to get me first thing in the morning. I barely have enough time to get down one of my mini quiches and a few bites of fruit before she texts that she's outside. Fortunately, Diana and her husband Rory anticipate their guests being on the run some mornings, and have paper takeout containers sitting off to the side of the dining room for breakfast on the go. I pack up the rest of what I got from the buffet and carry it with me out to her car.

She eyes me suspiciously as soon as I sit down.

"What?" I ask, hooking my seatbelt.

"Did I just see Malcolm walking out of there?" she asks.

"Probably," I say with a sigh.

Her mouth falls open. "Bree Connor, are you telling me that after all that huff about Malcolm last night, you—"

I see where this is going and I hold up a hand to halt that nonsense right in its tracks. "Nope, absolutely not. I stand by everything I said last night and even more now that I had the displeasure of talking to him while I was trying to have breakfast. He is a royal pain in the ass. He said he was here looking around to try to find out why this place is so appealing because Brandon wants him to choose a place for out-of-town guests to stay during the wedding."

For a second, Olivia's face registers the same kind of feeling of confusion I had when Malcolm gave me the strange excuse, but then she nods. "Right," she says. "That's right. He is handling that for us."

Her reaction strikes me as a little odd, but I really don't have it in me to think too deeply about it right now. Malcolm did say he works in hospitality, and there are a lot of family and friends coming in for the wedding, so it isn't completely unreasonable that they would ask for his opinion finding accommodations.

"Well," I say, opening my takeout container and plucking out a strawberry to pop in my mouth, "I gave him a rundown of why I like it here. I officially did my part." She's staring at me. "What?"

"Did you really just bring your whole breakfast along with you for the ride?" she asks.

"Not my whole breakfast. It's missing a mini quiche and some fruit," I say. "You showed up before I could finish it."

"Let me have some."

I spear another strawberry and put it in her mouth as she pulls away from the bed and breakfast. It feels good to be here with her. Even if the sight of her planning notebook on the seat behind me makes me want to scream.

I have to keep it together. I need to stuff down all the heartbreak and humiliation so I can focus on being happy for Olivia. Right about now, that feels like the emotional equivalent of jumping up and down on top of an overstuffed dumpster, but I'm going to get through it. Fake-it-till-you-make-it smile in place. Waterproof mascara on. Let's do this.

The next few hours are spent buying last-minute items for the party and stocking up on groceries and things to get Olivia and Brandon's house ready for the family arriving later in the evening.

"Tell me again why they are staying at your house." I scan a stack of towels through the self-checkout.

"It's been a while since we've all been together, and they think it's a great opportunity to spend some quality time hanging out," Olivia explains. "And Mom says she thinks it would be weird to stay in a hotel in her hometown."

"Even though your parents moved out of town to be closer to your aunt and grandmother."

"Yes," she confirms.

"But she's not staying with you for the actual wedding, is she?" I ask.

"No. She says that's different."

"How?"

"I don't know, Bree," she says, sounding exasperated. "This is my mother we're talking about. Always making sense isn't her strong suit. I'm not going to argue with her. But I also think it's getting to her a little bit that she isn't around to help me plan the wedding as much as she would want to. They're staying for a few days after the engagement party, so I'm going to do some planning stuff with them."

"That will mean a lot to them." I set the bags full of towels into the cart and reach for the stack of toiletries Olivia is insisting on stocking the bathroom with. "How is Brandon feeling about not being able to have his family at the party?"

Brandon is one of the rare transplants to Maple Valley. His family was originally from Norway and came to this country when he was young, then they moved around quite a bit as he was growing up. Once he was an adult, his parents and one sibling decided to make the move back to Norway to be with the rest of the extended family, but he stayed here.

"It's hard," she says. "But he understands they can't make that trip just for a party, especially when they are all coming over for the wedding. I know he doesn't regret deciding to stay here rather than moving back with them, but he misses them a lot, right now more than ever."

"Then I know he's excited for the two of you to go see them in a few weeks."

Olivia's face lights up with excitement. "He really is. I am, too. I'm nervous to go there for the first time and meet all the extended relatives."

"At least you already know his parents. That will make it easier."

"It's going to be amazing," she agrees. "I'm really looking forward to it. And I definitely need the vacation."

We finish shopping and haul everything back to her house. The rest of the day is spent getting the house ready for her family to arrive, packaging party favors, and talking about the wedding. She tells me Brandon has finally chosen a catering menu and the cake has been ordered. Even though I'm standing right here with her, as she flits around the kitchen laying out bagels for the next morning and chopping up fresh vegetables to keep in the refrigerator for snacks, talking about the details that are falling into place. I get a tug in my heart. I walk over and pull her into a hug.

"What's that for?" she asks.

"I just miss you," I explain. "It's hard being away from you, especially now."

"I know," she says. "I thought it would get easier the longer you weren't living in town. Like I'd get used to it. But it hasn't gotten any easier. I feel like I miss you more now than I did when you first moved."

We both start to tear up, and we're still clinging to each other when Brandon comes in from work. He pauses and looks back and forth between us.

"What's going on? Did something happen?" he asks.

We laugh and Olivia tosses a kitchen towel at him. "We're just having a moment," she says. "Go get changed."

I'm still feeling emotional the next night when I get to Olivia's house early to help her get the party set up. She invited me to stay for dinner last night so I could be there when her family arrived, but I decided to let that be just for them. As I walk into the house tonight, though, her mother, Dawn, rushes over to me with a tight hug.

"Bree! I'm so happy to see you. It's been so long," she says.

"It really has," I say, squeezing her back.

The hug makes the emotion well up even more, and I have to stuff it down when Olivia comes into the room. I don't want her to see me upset tonight. This is her night, and she deserves nothing but happiness. Despite the stress I know she's feeling, she's glowing as she sweeps into the room with a flower arrangement.

"Those are beautiful," I tell her, wrapping my arm around her waist for a quick hug.

"Olivia! You got me flowers? You really shouldn't have. This is your engagement party."

The sound of Malcolm's voice booming through the living room makes my eyes roll so far up into the back of my head that I'm afraid I'm going to tip over backward. He comes in carrying a bottle of wine and grins at Olivia. She just shakes her head at him.

"These were a gift from Brandon's family," she says. "They were just delivered."

"That was sweet of them," I say.

"And who is this lovely lady?" Malcolm asks, turning to Dawn. "You must be Olivia's sister."

He literally picks up her hand and kisses it, making me want to gag. I look over at Olivia for a moment of shared ick, but she's smiling at them.

Am I missing something here?

"Malcolm, this is my mother, Dawn. Mom, this is Brandon's best friend, Malcolm," she says.

"I've heard a lot about you," Dawn says.

Malcolm presses a hand to his chest and bows over slightly at the waist. "Well, it can't possibly all be true."

He glances over at Olivia, and I see something pass between them in the look. It's brief, but I can't help but wonder what it was.

"I need to check on the food," Olivia says. "Somebody pick some music. "She heads toward the kitchen and I follow her.

"What was that all about?" I ask when we're alone.

She leans into the refrigerator to pull out a vegetable tray and peels away the plastic over it. "What are you talking about?" she asks.

"That little moment between you and Malcolm... the way you looked at each other when he said that everything you've told your mother about him can't be true. What's going on?" I ask.

"We didn't look at each other in any particular way," she insists.

"He was probably just wondering what she's heard about him." She pauses and glances over at me. "Are you accusing me of something?"

"Of course, not."

She lets out a sigh and smiles. "Good, because I have enough on my plate getting this wedding together without having to also think about finding a new maid of honor."

I make a face at her, but the levity of the moment is ruined by Malcolm coming into the room.

"New maid of honor?" he asks. "Well, if I have to pick this one up at the airport, send me her picture first."

I grab a plate of cheese and crackers and stalk into the living room. There are several reasons why I'm looking forward to tonight being over, but Malcom Barrett is hovering right near the top of the list.

CHAPTER EIGHT

MALCOLM

Standing alone in the kitchen, I take out my phone and check to make sure I don't have any messages from Greg. He hasn't contacted me again, and I can't stop thinking about what might be going on.

"No sexting in the kitchen," Brandon says as he comes into the room.

I shake my head as I put my phone back in my pocket. "Add that to your list of things you're not allowed to say."

"Something going on?" he asks.

"Greg called me yesterday...."

"Nope," Brandon says. "You're not thinking about work. You took a vacation for the first time in years, and you're not going to spend it still working."

"It's not working," I insist, "not exactly. He told me he heard about somebody looking for information about the company. They refused to meet with him and didn't ask to meet with anyone else. They were just trying to find out stuff about the company."

Brandon looks at me in silence. "Is that it?" he finally asks. "That doesn't really seem like that big of a deal."

"There have been a lot of rumors lately about another company planning a takeover. This could have something to do with that," I explain.

"Look, you don't actually know what's going on. This is just something you heard from someone who heard it from someone else. You're working yourself up over a game of telephone. It's probably nothing. And unless you find out that it is something, there's no point in freaking out about it. Can't we just focus on my engagement party tonight?"

I feel a twinge of guilt and nod. "Yeah. I'm sorry. Tonight is all about you."

"And Olivia," Brandon adds.

"Yeah, I guess her, too," I pick up the bottle of wine I had set on the counter and hold it out to him. "I brought you this."

He eyes it and then looks at me with a lifted brow. "This seems a bit out of your price range… like, several hundred dollars out of your price range."

"Don't worry," I insist. "I bought it for you before the challenge. I didn't break the rules."

"All right, then. Thank you," he says. "I'll put it aside for just Olivia and me."

"Were you not going to accept it if you thought I'd gone over my budget to buy it for you?" I ask.

He shrugs. "I mean, I was probably still going to accept it. I was just going to give you a guilt trip over it."

"Fair enough."

The doorbell rings and he smiles. "People have arrived. This party is about to get lit."

I shake my head. "No."

We head for the living room and get there as Olivia is opening the door to the first wave of guests. I notice Dawn coming from the direction of the guest rooms with an elderly woman and walk over.

"Malcolm," Dawn says. "This is my mother, Edith Murray."

"Mrs. Murray, it is a delight and an honor," I say, taking her hand. "Can I help you get a seat?"

"This is Brandon's best friend," Dawn explains.

"Go on with that Mrs. Murray stuff," the older woman says, flapping her hand in the air like she's trying to brush away the words. "I'm Edith. And I don't need your help finding a seat. But if you know where I can find myself a stiff drink, then you're on."

I laugh and offer my arm. "Let's go."

She loops her arm through mine and we head over to the bar Brandon set up at the far end of the living room. Out of the corner of my eye, I notice Bree watching us. She rolls her eyes and turns her attention to one of the guests who has just arrived.

"They didn't spring for a bartender?" Edith asks, bringing my attention away from Bree. She's looking around the makeshift bar like she's expecting someone in a crisp skirt and arm cuffs to pop up and start polishing a glass for her. She seems to be forgetting that we're at an engagement party in Brandon and Olivia's living room, not a venue with a staff.

"Looks like it's a do-it-yourself kind of situation," I say.

"Then I would like a Manhattan," she says, looking at me matter-of-factly.

I guess I am the staff.

Fortunately, I've done my fair share of putting together a cocktail or two, so I know how to make her preferred drink. Brandon and Olivia had stocked the bar with a variety of plastic cups, and I compare the different sizes and shapes to pick the one I think would be best for Edith's Manhattan. It feels like they went for the highest end disposable barware they could, but it still takes a bit away from the effect I'm sure the opinionated lady is expecting. At least she's the kind of opinionated that makes her sassy, all full of piss and vinegar, as my grandfather would have said, rather than just being straight up unpleasant like many of the people of her generation I've encountered at work events. I'll take being set in her ways and wanting things the way she wants them if they come with her fun attitude.

"Mom, what do you have Malcolm doing for you?" Dawn asks, coming across the room toward us.

"He's making me a drink," Edith tells her. "I'm the grandmother of the bride. I deserve special attention."

"I'm more worried about how many of those you're planning on having this evening," Dawn says.

"As many as I damn well please."

I'm starting to like this lady more and more.

Dawn looks at me. "You cut her off at two. And if you see her getting anywhere near an empty chair or heading for the music, you stop her."

I nod. "I'm on it."

Edith shakes her head as Dawn heads for the kitchen. "You have one too many on Easter and dance on a chair one time, and nobody can let it go."

"Don't worry," I say. "She didn't tell me how strong I could make those two."

"That's a good boy," Edith says, taking the drink I hand out to her. She takes a sip then holds the cup back out toward me. "This is going to need another couple of splashes."

I'm starting to understand Dawn's concern at Edith hitting the bar as soon as she got to the party, but I have to admit I am kind of looking forward to seeing how this unfolds. I add some more liquor to her drink and she sips it as she makes her way over to Olivia. She wraps her arm around her granddaughter's waist and kisses her on the cheek.

It makes me hurt a little bit for Brandon. As close as he is to his future wife's family, I know he misses his own. Living in a different country from them isn't easy, and he doesn't get to see them nearly as often as he would like to. They'll be traveling for a visit, soon, though, so I know he's looking forward to spending some time with them before the wedding.

I pour myself a drink and look around at the guests filling the living room. I don't know any of them. A couple of them look vaguely familiar in that way that I think I've probably crossed paths with them before or probably seen them in pictures Brandon has shown me, but I can't rattle off any names. Just as I'm thinking this, one of them looks over at me and waves enthusiastically. Apparently, he knows who I am. I scour my brain trying to come up with any memory of this man as he walks toward me, his hand already extended when he's within a couple of strides of me.

"Malcolm," he says.

I take his hand and shake it. "Hey."

"Good to finally meet you," he says.

Oh, thank God. I don't actually know this man.

"There you are, Paul," Brandon says, walking up behind the man. "And already with Malcolm–I was going to introduce the two of you."

"I got ahead of you," Paul says. "I'm impatient like my daughter."

Brandon laughs. "I won't tell her you said that."

Olivia's father. There we go.

"Won't tell me you said what?" Olivia asks, coming up to Brandon's side and wrapping her arms around him. She looks up at him suspiciously and then over at her father.

"We were just talking about how happy we are for the two of you," I say quickly, trying to gloss over the uncomfortable moment.

"Malcolm, you are a terrible liar," Olivia says with a smirk.

I hear a sound behind me I can only describe as a bitter snort of humorless laughter, and I turn to see the only person I can possibly think of that would make that sound at me. As I do, said person steps forward to grab something from the bar table and runs directly into me. My drink flies out of my hand and in an instant, Bree is gasping in fury, her arms out to her sides, her fingers splayed, and my drink dripping down into her cleavage.

For a brief moment, all I can think about is dipping my tongue down between the swells of her breasts and licking up every drop. Then I remember Brandon, Olivia, and her father are standing directly behind me, and I should not be having those kinds of thoughts in their proximity. I force the image out of my mind and reach for the pile of napkins on the corner.

"Don't try to help me," Bree snaps angrily, taking a step back.

Olivia walks around me and picks up the napkins, going up to Bree and starting to dab at her. She takes her by the wrist and leads her out of the living room, which is probably a good thing considering it looked like she was about to spew something she wouldn't want the elderly relatives to hear, except possibly Edith.

"I promise I did not do that on purpose," I say, turning to Brandon.

He holds up his hands like he is separating himself completely from the situation. "I don't know what's going on between the two of you, but I'm not touching it with a ten foot pole. I'm just going to keep on keeping on and enjoying my engagement party."

He walks away and Paul follows, leaving me to look like the total jackass who just threw a drink on the maid of honor. Bree doesn't look like she wants anything to do with me any time soon, but I feel like I should probably apologize. Not that I meant to drench her with bourbon, despite reactions south of my belt that may say otherwise.

I can hear Bree and Olivia talking in the kitchen as I approach.

"I'm sorry. I can't believe I'm doing this."

"You don't need to apologize. It's all right."

"But this is your night," Bree insists. "This is supposed to be all about you and Brandon, and I'm in here acting like this."

"You got a drink poured down your boobs," Olivia points out. "That would probably upset just about everybody."

"No… I mean, yes, that is a particularly unpleasant addition to my evening. But I didn't realize that Cyrus McGuire was going to be here tonight. And I also didn't realize he was going to remind me of my appointment to go check out his apple orchard wedding venue."

"Oh, shit," Olivia says.

"Yep, that was about my line of thought," Bree says. "I just can't believe I forgot to call him."

Since I've been just hovering at the doorway for the last few seconds, I decide to take this opportunity to jump into the conversation so I don't seem like a total creep if they notice me.

"Hey, I didn't realize you're engaged, too. Congratulations," I say, stepping further into the kitchen.

Bree looks over at me and rolls her eyes again, tossing the towel she's been using to dab her chest onto the counter and starting out of the room.

"No," she nearly growls as she walks past me.

"Malcolm," Olivia starts, but I've already turned toward Bree.

"Why not? Is he not a bourbon guy? I could toss a different drink on you if it would help. What's his favorite?" I ask, chuckling.

She does not chuckle.

Bree stops, her back still toward me, and I notice her head lift very slightly, her hands curling at her sides. I wait for her to say something, but she doesn't. Without even looking over her shoulder at me, she rushes out of the room and back toward the living room.

"What the fuck, Malcolm?" Olivia asks. She's glaring at me with nothing short of daggers in her eyes when I turn back around.

"What? I was just joking."

"It wasn't funny," she says. "They just broke up."

"I didn't know…."

"Yeah, well, try not to be such an ass for the rest of the night. Can you manage that?"

She walks out of the kitchen, and I'm left feeling like I just ran into a brick wall and I'm not fully sure what happened.

CHAPTER NINE

BREE

Get me the hell out of here.

Explaining that no, I'm not engaged, and no, I don't have my future husband with me, and no, I'm not planning a fall wedding at the apple orchard sixteen times was enough for me. Explaining it one time was enough for me. By the time all of Olivia and Brandon's guests have finished giving their well wishes and left the party, I'm left feeling like I'm hanging on by a very narrow thread.

I really did come into this party thinking I could handle it. I had every intention in the world of being the very best maid of honor and best friend I could possibly be, keeping right up with my toothpaste commercial smile and not letting anything get to me.

I really should have expected that there was no way that was actually going to happen, not in Maple Valley, and not surrounded by my old friends and neighbors who have apparently all been eagerly anticipating my arrival and meeting the glorious man who swept me off my feet and is making an honest woman out of me. I swear to all that is holy, I actually heard those words come out of somebody's mouth. To my face. In public. Apparently Olivia mentioned the breakup in passing to a couple of people, but she was too swept up in her own engagement party haze of bliss to make sure everybody knew not to talk about my impending nuptials… that are no longer impending.

Like I said, Get me the hell out of here.

I have really enjoyed being here with Olivia. Having the opportunity to spend time with my best friend has been fun and very long overdue. But I am more than happy that the party is over, and that I'm not going to have to deal with my embarrassment over my breakup, or Malcolm, anymore. And in all honesty, I can't really decide which one of them I am more relieved to finally be done with.

I white-knuckle my way through the rest of the engagement party, but if I don't have to see his arrogant, smug face again until the wedding day, I will be delighted. And I am going to do everything in my power to make sure that's exactly how this works out.

Olivia meets me at my bed-and-breakfast the morning I'm leaving for home so that we can have breakfast together. I am all packed and have my bags with me when I go into the dining room. Part of me is expecting to walk down the steps and catch Malcolm prowling around down here again, just because that would be my damn luck. I'd send off into the universe to not have anything to do with him for the next couple of months, only to have him shoved right in my face again.

Fortunately, all that's waiting for me in the lobby is a sad-looking Olivia. She sighs when she looks at my bags.

"What was that for?" I ask.

"You're all packed and ready to leave," she explains.

"You do know you're here to have breakfast with me before you bring me to the airport, right? The whole heading back home thing is kind of part of that process."

"I know," she says. "But that doesn't mean I want you to go. There was part of me that was kind of hoping that you would change your mind. Maybe you would decide to move home."

She gives me that same kind of hopeful smile I've seen her use countless times throughout our relationship when she's trying to convince somebody that something she's saying is a good idea, even though she knows full well that it isn't.

"Maybe instead, you and Brandon should just move so that you can live closer to me," I suggest. "It would be a great fresh start for your newlywed life. Brandon could explore the exciting job opportunities of the city. You could discover all of the coffee shops and cupcake bakeries."

"We have plenty of coffee shops and cupcake bakeries right here in Maple Valley," she argues. "Well, one cupcake bakery. but I think that's plenty. And, did you just 1950s housewife me? Would that be what moving to the city would turn into?"

I laugh. "I will miss you so much. I hate being so far away from you."

She pouts a little bit more. "Me, too."

"Okay, that's enough. We are not making me cry before I can get on the plane. I am not going to be that weird sad girl who sits in the window seat and has everybody staring at her… again."

Olivia laughs away the start of tears that have formed in her eyes and we head into the dining room. I put my luggage on a rack in the corner and we fill our plates. The weather outside is humid and threatening rain, so instead of going out to eat on the patio, we take one of the tables up against the windows.

"These little lemon poppy seed muffins are so good," I say, popping a second of the miniature baked goods into my mouth. "I want to fill my carry-on with them."

"They are apparently a major claim to fame for this place," Olivia says. "I've even heard that a couple of the gift boutiques in town have asked the owners to sell them to them wholesale so they can offer them."

"That would be a great opportunity for expansion."

"They aren't interested," Olivia tells me, brushing crumbs from her hands. "Millie is in my book club."

"You're in a book club?" I ask. "Like a real book club?"

"I mean… there are books present when we get together," she confirms. "But anyway, Millie was telling us about people asking for the recipe or having her sell them boxes of these muffins. She gets a lot of stuff from bakeries and restaurants around town to try to build them up, but these little babies she makes all herself. And she's not budging giving them up to anyone else. She wants to keep them just for her guests."

"See? That's the kind of thing I was trying to explain to Malcolm, but he wouldn't listen to me."

Olivia's eyebrow raises as she reaches for a little hexagonal glass jar of jam sitting in the center of the table. "What you were trying to explain to Malcolm? I didn't realize the two of you had any kind of extensive conversations."

"Trust me, we didn't," I say. "In fact, we had as little interaction as I could possibly manage."

"I don't understand the friction between you. He's really a great guy."

Now it's my turn to lift an eyebrow at her.

"All right, so we're going to put aside the whole engagement bourbon commentary," she adds. "That wasn't his best moment. But other than that, he actually is nice."

"Generally, I would say I'll have to take your word for it." I reach for the jam when she's done. "But I'm just going to go with *nope.* Anyway, he was just asking me why I would stay at a little place like this rather than one of the big hotels, and I was trying to explain how I like the personal touches and how it seems like a real place rather than just a generic people warehouse with nice carpeting."

Her eyes slide up like she is looking into her brain and after a second, she nods and gives a slight shrug. "You know, I never would have thought about hotels like that, but I can see where you would get that in some places. Not all big hotels are like that, though. Malcolm just has very particular tastes and thoughts about that whole topic."

"He's pretty loyal to the hotel he works for then," I agree. "I guess that's commendable. But for somebody who just works in hospitality, it seems like he has a bit more invested in his opinions of other people's accommodations than he really should." I close my eyes and hold up my hands. "I don't want to talk about him anymore. I dealt with him through this weekend, and I am proclaiming a Malcolm embargo until the wedding, starting now."

"Then let's talk about my bachelorette party," she says, giving me a mischievous look. "What do you have planned?"

"You don't get to know that," I tell her. "Your bachelorette party is all about me trotting you out and putting you on full display in front of everyone we can possibly encounter. There will likely be a sash involved. Maybe a scavenger hunt."

I haven't gotten all the details about the bachelorette party nailed down yet, but I'm pretty certain it's going to involve renting a limo and heading into the nearby city. There isn't a whole lot of debauchery and revelry to be done in Maple Valley.

Olivia and I finish breakfast and head for the airport. She walks me right up to the very last step she can take before I go into security and we give each other a tight hug.

"I'll call you as soon as I get home," I tell her.

"You were home," she mutters defiantly.

"I mean the home where I actually live," I tell her.

"Fine," she says with a pout, and she steps back from me. "I'll keep you updated on everything my mom and grandma and I do this week. I really wish you would have stayed to do it all with us."

"I know. But the three of you need some time together, and it will mean the world to them to be able to help you make decisions and see things before anyone else. There are plenty of other things I'll get to be a part of before the wedding. Besides, I am up to my eyeballs in work, and I need to get back into the groove so I'm not walking down the aisle with a laptop in my hands."

"I would have to kill you," she says with a gentle, sweet smile.

If nobody has figured out how to have a company that helps people handle all of the nitty gritty, inconvenient details of life after a breakup, somebody needs to jump on that fast. Not that I am a huge proponent of capitalizing on people's pain, but if there are people who are paid to walk around behind animals in parades and clean up after them, this is a money-making opportunity just waiting to happen—somebody walking the parade route of life and cleaning up the shit.

If I had one of those people on speed dial right now, they would have done little things for me like remember to call Cyrus McGuire about my orchard appointment. Or cancel the stack of bridal magazines I eagerly ordered as I pranced around the online wonderland of wedding planning, still in my delusional phase. But because I didn't have somebody there to remember things like that and scrub them from my life, I'm greeted when I get home to a pile of grinning women in miles of white satin and lace.

Sweeping them off the floor, I stomp right outside and across the parking lot to the dumpster. The container is mostly empty, so the stack of glossy magazines makes a satisfying thud when it hits the metal bottom. I resist the urge to give the side of the dumpster a kick for good measure and go back inside.

The next morning I wake up with determination to claim my life back. I need to pull myself up by my garter belt and stop this nonsense. I built my career. I established this life for myself. I'm not going to let some guy dumping me send me spiraling any farther than he already has. I'm going to start new routines. Get myself healthy again. Start taking walks. Excel at work. Learn to bake lemon poppyseed muffins. Live my own best life like the fierce lady boss I am.

My phone signals the arrival of a new email.

"How did you like your napkin samples? Ready to order?"

Damn it all to hell.

For the next three weeks, I work hard on my whole lady boss conquering the world plan while also navigating the landmines left behind from my relationship with Trevor. Constant reminders of our years together and the anticipated proposal that most certainly didn't happen seem to pop up with my every turn. At least I have transitioned from bursting into tears when I hear a love song on a sappy commercial to just feeling a flash of blind rage. I'd say that's a step in the right direction.

Olivia's constant calls about the wedding are not helping.

The closer we get, the more calls I am getting about every little detail. She doesn't want me to feel left out of the planning process, so I am consulted about every decision, and brought along via video chat for venue visits and vendor meetings. I've even gotten a handful of calls of her threatening various versions of elopement because she just can't take a single more decision or various family members trying to shoehorn their own opinions in.

I'm pretty sure the final straw has come when her father informs her that his father's cousin, who she has only met once in her life, found out about the wedding and is planning on coming, along with her six-person family, and insists on bringing along food to make sure her picky son has something he likes–her sixty-year-old picky ass son.

Honestly, I'm on team elopement. I was hoping the next call I got would be from her at the airport telling me they were jetting off to Vegas and a sparkly Elvis and they'd meet me at the casino. That is a wedding I could get behind. Instead, she calls me back later to tell me that Paul had smoothed things over with Cousin Bertha and the wedding was forging ahead.

I love my best friend. I truly do. And I am really happy for her and Brandon. They are an absolutely adorable couple, and they're completely obsessed with each other and they are going to be deliriously, sickeningly happy. But I am going to be so relieved when all of this is over and I don't have to deal with it anymore. I can't wait to finish blowing bubbles, or waving sparklers, or tossing rose petals, or whatever rice alternative she settles on, to watch that limo door close and put all of this behind me.

I feel bad that that thought keeps rolling through my head, but I am still struggling, and that just makes me feel worse, which, in turn, makes me feel even worse. It's a vicious cycle, and I am very done with it.

At least I think I am until my phone rings as I am tossing a trash bag into a heap and grabbing a fresh one out of my waistband.

Guess who.

"Hey, Olivia," I say. "I am actually right in the middle of–"

"I don't know what I'm going to do, Bree," she says. She sounds like she's been crying and is right on the edge of losing it.

"Hold on. I'm volunteering at the park clean up right now, but let me get somewhere I can hear you better." I wave at the team leader for the group I'm working with and gesture to my phone. He flashes me a thumbs up and I walk toward a nearby bench. Her breath is coming through the line fast and frantic when I sit down.

"Olivia? What's going on? Take a deep breath. Is everything all right? Is Brandon okay? The family?"

They are in Norway visiting Brandon's family, and I immediately have a sick feeling in my stomach that something horrible has happened to one of them.

"Everyone is fine," she says. "Except for the fact that my entire wedding is ruined and I am about to have a heart attack."

"Your wedding is ruined? What do you mean?"

"The owner of the venue just called me. There was a fire. It was completely destroyed. They aren't going to be able to host any events there at all for at least eight months, probably longer," she says.

"Oh, my God," I say. "That's horrible. I'm so sorry. But there has to be somewhere else—"

"They already rebooked us with Cyrus."

"At the orchard?" I ask, my throat tightening a little bit just saying it.

"Yes," she confirms. "Only they made a mistake and booked it for six weeks before my date. He has us reserved for two weeks from now."

"Damn," I say. "But that shouldn't be a problem. Just tell Cyrus and—"

"I did. Oh, trust me, I did. But there's nothing he can do. He said he thought it was pretty serendipitous that I needed that date in the first place because it's the only one that he has available for the next year. Year, Bree—the next year. Brandon and I have been calling around all over trying to find anywhere that's available for our date, but everyone is booked. There's nothing. It means everything to us to get married in Maple Valley and I don't want to postpone it for months. I've already been waiting so long to marry him and I just want to be his wife. I just want the pretty dress and the amazing cake, and I just want to be married. I don't know what I'm going to do." She's sobbing now.

My heart is breaking for her, and the suspicious little part of me who jumped over every crack in the sidewalk until I was twenty years old and has never once walked under an open ladder is whispering in my ear that I did this shit. I put the stink-eye on her wedding, and now it's gone to hell and it's my fault, which means I have to fix it.

"You're going to get married in two weeks," I tell her. "That's what you're going to do."

What did I just say?

"How is that possible? Brandon and I are in Norway. We can't just cut the trip short to go back to Maple Valley and plan a wedding."

"No, you can't, which is why I'm going to do it for you."

No, seriously. What did I just say?

"You are?" she asks, sounding a little calmer and more hopeful.

"Of course, I am. I'm your maid of honor. That's what I do. You are going to relax and keep enjoying yourself. Don't worry about anything. I am going to handle everything, okay? When you get back, all you'll need to think about is putting on your dress and having your fairytale wedding."

"Thank you so much. I love you. I can't thank you enough," Olivia gushes.

"I love you, too. I'll talk to you soon. Don't worry about anything. In two weeks, you will be Brandon's wife."

I hang up the phone and reality hits.

I have to put together an entire wedding. In a different state. In two weeks. With an amazing cake.

Frost my life.

CHAPTER TEN

MALCOLM

"Wait, start again, what happened?" I ask, pressing a hand to my ear to try to drown out some of the sound from next door.

Apparently, my neighbor has decided that today is the ideal time to test out their array of speakers with an assortment of grating death metal while also vacuuming their floors and possibly making smoothies in a blender full of spoons and cats. At least that's what I can ascertain from the amount of noise coming through the paper thin walls.

My neighbors being particularly annoying has become a trend over the last week or so. I am very strongly considering bringing a pillow and some blankets to the office and just camping out there for a while. But I'm not sure if that fits with the rules of my challenge. So I will just keep trying to tough it out.

"A fire," Brandon says loudly through the phone. "There was a fire at the wedding venue."

"That was the wedding venue?" I ask. "I heard on the news that there was some big fire in town, but I didn't realize that was where you're getting married."

"Well, it isn't now," he says. "The entire structure was completely destroyed, and there's no way that the damage can be cleaned up and repaired in time for the wedding. With the winter coming and the schedule for the contractors and everything that has to go into rebuilding a historic structure, they are thinking it could be almost a year before they are up and running again. That means obviously, we aren't going to be able to get married there in October."

"Everything is a complete mess," Olivia says in the background. "Tell him about the orchard. Tell him."

"The orchard?" I ask. "McGuire's orchard?"

"Yeah," Brandon says. "The original venue was trying to scramble to reschedule all of the weddings and events that they had booked for the next several months and managed to get us booked at the orchard. Unfortunately, they booked us for the wrong date. They ended up switching our date for the date of a baby shower that was supposed to be held there, so now we have a wedding reserved at the orchard in two weeks."

"What happened to the baby shower?" I ask.

"Seriously?" Olivia asks in the background, her voice reaching dog-whistle levels of pitch. "That's what you took out of that? The place we chose for our wedding has burned to a crisp. It is literally a pile of debris and ashes, and now our wedding has been rebooked for six weeks before we were supposed to get married, and what you got out of it was that somebody's baby shower has been thrown off schedule?" She sounds right on the verge of snapping in two.

"I think they were booked somewhere else," he says. "The point is, there is nothing else available anywhere in Maple Valley for months and we don't want to wait, so we are going to go ahead and take the date that they have available. The thing is, we are going to be here for almost that entire time. So we're kind of panicking trying to figure out how we are going to arrange an entire wedding and get as many of our guests as we possibly can there in two weeks."

Brandon doesn't sound like he's doing a lot better than Olivia, but he's trying to suppress his freaking out as much as he can so that she can have that space to herself.

"Shit. That's a lot. Is there anything I can do to help?" I feel terrible for them. Brandon and Olivia put so much into planning their wedding already and have been looking forward to it for months. This was their dream wedding and now it literally went up in smoke. I know how important it is for the two of them to finally be married, but it's going to be a massive undertaking trying to shift a whole wedding up a month and a half.

"Actually, yes," Brandon says. "There is something you can do to help."

"Name it." In the back of my mind, I'm ready to dig my debit card out from where it's been tucked away and start slinging whatever money is needed around to make this happen for them.

"Help Bree."

What?"

"Help… Bree," I repeat.

"Yes," he confirms. "She agreed to go to Maple Valley and handle making all the arrangements for the wedding. But that's a lot for one person to do on their own. If you can pick her up at the airport and bring her to the house, then help her handle the plans, it would be absolutely amazing. I know the two of you could figure it out together."

"Ummm…." Images of the last time Bree looked at me, her eyes flashing like she was ready to rip my head off with her bare hands, flash through my head. I don't think that reuniting at all is a great idea, but doing it because of something as stressful as putting together a wedding in two weeks sounds like a disaster waiting to happen.

"Come on, buddy. I know you and Bree got off to kind of a rocky start, but it's been a few weeks now. she's probably feeling a lot better and you can work it out. She won't be in town for the whole two weeks. All you need to do is help her out with whatever plans and arrangements need to be done. This is for Olivia and me. Please say you'll do it."

"You know, there is another option," I suggest. "Rather than going through all the hassle of trying to throw together a wedding at the very last minute just by running around town looking for help, I could pull some strings for you. Money does talk, as they say."

"Money only talks when you have it," Brandon says. "And as far as you're concerned for the next few months, you don't have it."

"I think you could consider this extenuating circumstances," I argue. "My bank account could come in seriously handy right now. Imagine the vendors I would be able to hook you up with and how easily we could fix this whole thing."

"Not going to happen," Brandon says.

"Is he trying to get out of his challenge?" Olivia asks in the background.

"Yes," Brandon tells her.

"Seriously?" I ask. "We are talking about your wedding here. You're going to be so stuck on this challenge that you're not going to accept me just paying for it for you?"

"We made an agreement," he insists. "This is kind of part of the point—learning to deal with obstacles and life's challenges when they come. Other people have to deal with stuff like this all the time. Think about all the other people who had events planned at the venue. They don't have billions they can just throw around to make it all better. They have to work with what they have and figure it out, which means you're going to be working with the budget we have available to us. The venue is working with the orchard to handle the payment for that, so that's taken care of. But I don't know how the other vendors are going to handle this. That's where you and Bree come in. You'll have to try to negotiate it and then use our budget as you can. You know where I keep my spare debit card, and I'll send you all the details you need to know."

"I'm not so sure about this," I say.

"I need you," Brandon insists.

I can hear the desperation in his voice and I know I can't turn him down. This is a disaster, but Bree and I might be able to fix it for them.

"All right," I say. "I'll do it."

Brandon lets out a huge sigh of relief. "Thank you so much."

I'm still shocked that they won't let me even take a little hiatus from the challenge to scoop their wedding from the wreckage, but I guess I understand where they are coming from. This whole thing was meant to teach me a lesson, so this is just one big learning experience.

The next day, I head to the airport to pick up Bree. As soon as she walks out of the gate area and lays eyes on me, I know she is way less than thrilled to be seeing me.

"Hey, Bree," I say.

She doesn't even maintain eye contact with me as she walks right past, dragging her bag on wheels behind her, another draped over her shoulder. "Nope."

"I'm here to pick you up."

"I'll just rent a car." She takes a few more steps then pauses. "Damn it. Olivia said I can use her car while I'm in town. I'm only going to be here for a few days, so I guess it would be pretty ridiculous for me to rent a car when I have a perfectly good one sitting at the house waiting for me."

"So, yes, you will accept my ride?" I ask.

Bree takes in a long breath and forces a smile. "Yes, I will accept your ride."

"Great. Do you want some help with your bags?"

"I've got it."

"Well, clearly, since you got off the plane with them. That isn't what I asked you. Do you want help with them?"

She looks at me with an expression that is somewhere between dumbfoundment and disgust. "Can you get through one conversation without being a total ass? Is that just too much to ask from you?"

"Really? I'm offering you help."

"No, thank you," she says, starting toward the terminal door again.

"Suit yourself."

I follow her out into the parking lot and wait for her to realize she doesn't know where I'm parked. When she stops and turns to look at me with a frustrated, tight look on her face, I go ahead of her and let her follow me the rest of the way to my car.

I unlock the trunk, but don't open it. She doesn't want my help. While she juggles her bags to open the trunk and get them inside, I walk around to get in the car. She finally makes it in beside me and I look over at her. "Ready?"

Bree hooks her seatbelt and turns to stare out the window.

It's just a few days. I can make it through a few days.

But why does she have to be so sexy with her messy bun and perfect body poured into those yoga pants?

We're a few minutes down the road when she turns her attention away from the window and flips down the sun visor to look in the mirror. It seems like she's wearing the barest minimum of makeup, so I'm not sure what she's checking, but I notice her pause as she's looking into the mirror and then shift to look over her shoulder into the backseat.

"What's that?" she asks.

"What's what?"

"The bags in the backseat."

"Those are my bags," I tell her, not sure what other kind of descriptor I'm supposed to use.

"Your bags for what?" she asks.

"My stuff."

She rolls her eyes. One of these days, she's going to do that too hard and they are going to get stuck. "Why do you have bags of your stuff in your back seat?"

"Because that was a lot easier way to transport them than by just tossing them all into the car loose."

Bree lets out a huff and slams herself back to facing forward, crossing her arms over her chest. "You are impossible."

"Take it easy," I say. "It was a joke. My apartment building is being fumigated, so I needed to clear out for a bit. Brandon and Olivia said that since I'm going to be helping out with the whole Operation Insta-Wedding thing that it would work for me to just stay at their place."

CHAPTER ELEVEN

BREE

"I'M SORRY... WHAT?" I ask.

Malcolm looks over at me with a confused expression. "What?"

"I thought I just heard you say that you're going to be staying at Brandon and Olivia's place," I say.

"You did," he confirms. "Like I said, my apartment is getting fumigated, so I couldn't stay there."

"Well, you can't stay at Olivia and Brandon's house, either," I insist.

"Why not?"

"Because that's where I'm staying," she replies. "Olivia said that since I'm helping them out so much and am going to be in town for a few days without anyone in their house, it wouldn't make sense for me to have to go stay at the hotel again."

I can't believe Brandon would tell Malcolm he could stay at the house while I'm in town. There must have been some sort of misunderstanding. Malcolm probably told him that his place was getting fumigated and that he wasn't going to be able to be there, and without thinking about it because he's just such a nice guy, Brandon went ahead and offered up their place, not considering I was going to be there. Obviously that's not going to work out, and now that Malcolm knows I'm going to be the one staying at their house because I came in from out of state to do this for them, he will offer to figure something else out.

"I guess we're bunking together, then," he says.

My mouth falls open. "You can't be serious."

"Why not?"

"You were so interested in what the hotel is like. Why don't you go stay there and find out for yourself?"

"I can't afford the hotel," he tells me. "So that's not an option. But this will work out. Staying in the same place will make it easier for us to make all the wedding arrangements together. This way, we can talk about stuff and everything without having to figure out when to get together."

I hold up a hand to slow him down. "We aren't going to need to make any wedding arrangements together. I don't need your help. I can handle this on my own. That's what I told Olivia. When she called me to tell me what happened with the venue, I offered to take on getting the new wedding planned so that she wouldn't be stressed about it. She didn't say anything about you tagging on for the ride."

"Interesting turn of phrase, considering you are currently taking a ride in my car," he points out. "And Brandon is the one who asked me to help you out. He said it would make it easier if we did it together. Besides, they gave me their budget information and access to their payment card and accounts, so you actually do need me."

I hate to admit it, but Malcolm is right. I do need him. If Brandon asked him to help me and they handed over all their budget stuff to him, obviously they want him involved. I can't believe Olivia and Brandon are doing this to me.

Turning back toward the windshield, I close my eyes and take a breath. I have to remind myself that they are going through a really difficult time right now. This is a really challenging situation that they had no way of preparing for, and I am the one who offered to help them. I can't really blame them for thinking it would be easier if there were two of us tackling the mountain of tasks that are going to be necessary to get this wedding back on track and make sure it happens in two weeks.

The truth is, I probably should have thought about the fact that trying to do all of this on my own was going to be a huge undertaking that I might not actually be able to pull off, especially not living in a different state. I can't be in Maple Valley for the full two weeks, so I'm going to have to stuff as much of the planning efforts into the days I have that I possibly can, and having an extra person capable of making phone calls, doing negotiations, and running errands makes the whole thing a lot more accessible.

I just really don't want that extra person to be Malcolm. This time, I won't even have Olivia and Brandon here as a buffer. It's just going to be the two of us, staying in the same house and butting heads of every little detail. I hope he understands that I'm the one in charge of this wedding and he is just around to help me.

I glance over at Malcolm again and withhold a groan. I always say I would do anything for Olivia. This is just one big way of testing that. "I need to stop by the grocery store before we get to the house so I can grab a few things."

"Is that you asking me to take you?" he asks, his eyes sliding over to me.

I take a breath and press my lips together in the best semblance of a smile I can muster. "Will you please take me by the grocery store so I can pick up a few things?"

"Sure, no problem."

Dropping my head back against the seat, I look through the window again. This is going to be a long week.

Malcolm pulls into the parking lot and finds a spot.

"I'll be right back," I say.

"I'll come in with you," he says, taking off his seatbelt.

"That's not necessary. I know how to shop by myself."

"So do I, which is why I am going in to buy some things," he says. "I would like to be able to eat while at their house, too, you know."

"Oh."

"Do you always make everything about you?" he asks, walking around the car and heading for the sliding glass doors.

"I don't make everything about me."

"Could have fooled me." He gets inside and grabs a cart, wheeling it inside without a glance back toward me.

I get my own and head in the opposite direction. I can't concentrate while I'm in the store, and I end up filling my cart with a random assortment of stuff before deciding I'll just buy what I have and come back to the store tomorrow when I can think straight. I walk around the store looking for Malcolm, but don't find him. Finally, I go through the checkout line and return to the car. He's sitting in the driver's seat, scrolling through something on his phone.

"You just weren't going to tell me you left the store?" I ask.

"I thought you could shop on your own."

The drive to Olivia and Brandon's house seems excessively long, but we finally pull into the driveway. We both collect our groceries and bring them inside first, depositing them in the kitchen then return to the car for our luggage. We get to the door at the same moment and he steps back, doing an exaggerated bow and gesturing for me to go inside first. As soon as I step over the threshold into the house, he is right behind me. I'm already most of the way to Olivia and Brandon's bedroom when I realize Malcolm is walking right along with me.

He doesn't turn toward the guest room when we get to the back of the house. Instead, he follows along and we arrive at the door to the primary bedroom at the same time. I can't believe this. He can't honestly think that he's going to get the good room.

"The guest bedroom is that way," I say, gesturing down the hallway.

"Good thing you know that. You won't get lost on your way there."

"Why would I go there? I'm not staying in the guest bedroom," I say with an incredulous scoff. "Olivia is my best friend. I offered to help her get her wedding planned and she said I could stay at the house. That means I get this room."

"Well, Brandon is my best friend. He asked me to help you get the wedding planned and he said I could stay at the house, which means I get this room," he retorts.

He can't be serious.

"Absolutely not. You can take the guest room. Or there's a fold-out bed in the office."

He can have the sofa for all I care. I'm not letting him have this room. Our eyes narrow at each other and our hands tighten around the handles of our bags. Somewhere in the back of my mind I hear that tune that was in every Western movie when the guys squared off in the dirt road at noon.

CHAPTER TWELVE

MALCOLM

This isn't an argument I saw coming. It didn't even occur to me that I would need to argue over who got Brandon and Olivia's bedroom. When I found out that my apartment building was being fumigated and I was being kicked out unceremoniously for the next three days, I knew staying at the hotel wasn't an option. There's no way I could squeeze that into my budget. But since Brandon and Olivia were asking me to pick Bree up from the airport and be her wedding planning assistant for the week that she's going to be here, I figured I could make it work for my benefit, too, and I asked if I could just crash at their house.

They didn't bother to mention to me that Bree was going to be staying at the house, too. I just assumed she was so attached to that damn tiny hotel that she was going to be hunkering down there again. Maybe I should have thought that all the way through. It really wouldn't have made sense for her to go to the hotel when the house was empty... well, empty other than me.

But here we are, arguing over which of us is going to get the primary bedroom in the house and who is going to be relegated to one of the guest spaces. It was obvious right from the beginning that

Bree just assumed I was going to back down and do what she wanted by finding somewhere else to stay. She clearly believed she would come first, and that the moment I caught on that she really didn't want me there with her I would be happy to just bow out and let her have the whole house to herself.

Screw that.

I have just as much right to be at the house as she does. Brandon is my best friend like Olivia is hers. They gave me permission to be here. They even gave me control over their wedding budget. And she's obviously not willing to play nice, so why should I?

"Okay, this is ridiculous," I say.

" I agree," Bree says. "It's obvious who should have the room."

"Me," we both say at the same moment.

"Why should you have it?" I ask.

She pulls herself up, looking offended, but also like she is trying to look appealing. "Because I'm the girl."

I let out a burst of laughter that makes her face contort into anger. Her fists clench, and she glares at me. "Why does that matter? If anything, that should make it even more obvious that I'm the one who should have the room. I'm much bigger, so I should have the room with the bigger bed. It's just common sense."

"This room has a bathroom in it," she insists. "And I'm going to need the space to get ready and everything."

"Wow," I say. "You really are leaning hard into that whole delicate flower argument, aren't you? Isn't that offensive in some way?"

"No." She folds her arms over her chest.

"No, no, I think it is," I say. "I think you are being a misogynist. You can't ask for special treatment because you're a girl."

"That's not how that works," she insists.

"I don't really care." I shrug. "That argument doesn't work for me. I need to be able to take showers and get ready, too. And there are other bathrooms in the house that you can use. I'll be using the one in this bedroom because I'll be sleeping in it."

I reach down and pick up my bags, a gesture that Bree promptly mimics so we are standing facing each other, gripping our luggage.

"No, you won't be," she argues. "I should be the one to have this room. Olivia is my best friend. She has been for years."

"And Brandon is my best friend and has been for years," I say. "As a matter of fact, I could argue that I spend more time with the two of them than you ever do, so I am the closer friend and should have their room."

Bree gasps. "You are not going to hold the fact that I live in a different state against me. Olivia and I talk all the time. You are not closer to her or to them as a couple than I am."

"All right, this has gone back to being ridiculous," I say.

"Yes, it has. We need to settle this right here."

We both turn and try to go through at the door to the bedroom. It's a tight squeeze, but we manage to pop through and end up in the room together. I don't really care that she's in here with me. I have made it into the bedroom and I'm not going anywhere. Walking over to the bed, I drop my bags onto it and open one of them.

"What are you doing?" Bree demands.

"I'm unpacking my clothes." I reach into the bag and pull out a stack of T-shirts. I go over to the dresser and find a couple of empty drawers. Brandon must have cleared everything out to pack for his trip. That works for me. Stuffing my own clothes in the drawers feels like officially staking my claim on the room.

Bree stands in the center of the room still holding her bags, glaring at me furiously. She is fuming, but I really don't care. I'm in the room, my stuff is getting unpacked, and I'm not budging.

"You should go settle into your room," I tell her.

"I'm not going anywhere," she insists.

"Fine with me. You can stand there for the entire time you're in Maple Valley if you want to. That's probably going to make it pretty hard for you to plan the wedding like you're supposed to, but that's not my problem." I grab a pair of lounge pants and a T-shirt and head for the bathroom. "It's been a long day and I am going to take a hot shower."

I go into the bathroom and shut the door behind me. Her exasperated growl coming through the door makes me laugh. Damn it if she isn't adorable when she's angry.

Turning the water on hot enough to sting when it hits my skin, I stand in the shower luxuriating in the feeling of actually having water pressure. The shower at my apartment sucks. I barely feel like it gets me all the way clean much less relaxes my muscles and gets the tension out the way that I like my showers to do. I stay under the water for a while before I start to wonder what Bree might be doing. I did just leave her alone with all my stuff.

Getting out of the shower, I dry off and get dressed. When I walk back out into the bedroom, I find her calmly folding clothes and putting them into the drawers–drawers that no longer have my clothes in them.

"What did you do with my clothes?" I ask.

"Oh. I put them in your room," she says, "you know, the one down the hall."

I look at the door, then back at her and her smug little smile. I shrug and head for the bed. "Fortunately for me, I don't need anything."

She whips around as I climb into the bed. "What are you doing?"

"Relaxing," I tell her.

"In my room," she says angrily, obviously surprised I didn't just admit defeat and leave the room when she moved my bags.

"Still my room," I tell her. I crane my neck to look at the TV behind where she's standing. "Think you could move a bit? I can't see the TV."

She snatches clothes out of the dresser and stomps toward the bathroom as I flip on the TV.

"Thanks," I call after her.

The door slams and I hear the water running. I try not to let my mind wander, but I can't help but think about the water pouring down over her naked body.

CHAPTER THIRTEEN

Brandon is going to have to find himself a new best man because I'm going to kill Malcolm.

How could one human being be so infuriating? And so infuriatingly gorgeous?

I hate myself for even having that second thought. I shouldn't be thinking of him as gorgeous. I should be thinking of him as exactly what he is–rude, arrogant, full of himself… muscular, sexy… damn it.

I really thought he was going to be so frustrated by me moving all his stuff into the other room that he would just leave. Or at least go in there to try to get everything and I would just be able to stop him from coming back. But no. Not only did he not leave, he crawled up into the bed and is all kicked back relaxing watching Lord only knows what and cackling so loudly I can hear him over the water.

I can feel myself getting even angrier and I close my eyes to take a deep breath. I need to get myself together. Everything is going to be fine. Malcolm is going to have to leave the room to eat eventually. And when he does, I'll just lock him out. No big deal.

I finish showering and put on my pajamas, then go back out into the bedroom. He is still laughing at the top of his lungs, but pauses when I walk out. Lifting his eyebrows, he gestures at the other side of the bed like he's inviting me to get in with him. Not going to happen.

Without even saying a word of response, I stomp over to the armchair tucked in one corner of the room. Curling up in it, I pick a book out of the built-in shelves along the wall and open it up.

My plan is to get a couple of chapters in, but I'm exhausted from travel and soon find myself nodding off. But every time I doze, Malcolm lets out another of those belly laughs and scares the bejeezus out of me. It's really starting to get aggravating. And when I nearly tumble out of the chair right onto my ass, I've had enough. I go over to the chest at the foot of the bed and snatch out an extra pillow and blanket, bring them over to the chair, and try to find what constitutes a comfortable position. I pull the blanket over my head in hopes of drowning out some of the sound and try to go to sleep.

Half an hour or so passes before I realize he hasn't laughed in a while. I peek out and see that Malcolm has fallen asleep. Unfolding carefully out of the chair so I don't disturb him, I bring my pillow over to the bed and use it along with another to create a barrier down the middle of the bed. I climb into the bed and stretch out, instantly feeling my body relax and sleep take over.

I don't know what happened.

That's going to be my story no matter how many times you ask. I don't know what happened.

I was sleeping peacefully, comfortably behind the Berlin Wall of pillows, and something woke me up.

I am no longer stretched out safely on my side of the bed. Somehow the pillows are gone and I have not only crossed the dividing line of the bed, I am sprawled across Malcolm's chest. I'm not talking a little bit of hip-touching action or my hand on his belly. I wake up with my face buried in the center of his chest, my stomach on his stomach, and my leg—oh, dear Lord—draped over his hips.

There is a moment when consciousness hasn't fully come to me when I catch the clean, spicy smell of his body wash and the bleached smell of his shirt and let out a sigh, snuggling deeper against him. He lets out a sound something like a sigh and looks down at me. Our eyes meet and my breath catches. Our mouths move closer to each other until we are sharing the same breath. I can almost taste him.

And then I snap into reality.

I can't stand the sight of this man, and everything he says to me makes me want to tear my own hair out, and here I am cuddling with him without a shred of decency. And I almost kissed him–like, cue the women's network movie instrumental music and the hazy lighting almost kissed him.

Scrambling away from him as fast as I can, I toss myself onto my side with my back to him and pull the blanket up tightly over me like he won't be able to see me anymore and might think he had just imagined that whole incident. I can only hope.

I'm not sure when I fall asleep again, but I wake up a while later to the delicious smell of something cooking in the kitchen. It's like that old coffee commercial with the guy showing up to surprise his family and having his little sister make coffee with him for his parents. They don't budge when the front door opens or two people walk around the house having a full-blown conversation, but the second that drip coffee maker drips its first drop, Mom and Dad are fully conscious and heading for the kitchen. That's what I feel like now as the smell of food has my stomach rumbling.

It's been many hours since the airline snack and I am feeling seriously hungry, but I try to ignore it. This is my chance. I should lock the door and hunker down for the final standoff to claim the room. But the more I breathe in that smell, the more my stomach growls and finally I can't take it anymore. I venture into the house and let the wafting smell pull me to the kitchen.

When I get there, I find Malcolm cooking in only the light of the stove hood. It's extremely sexy, and I just stand here staring at him for a few seconds. My stomach rumbles again and whatever he's making smells incredible, but there's no way I'm asking him for any of it. Without saying anything, I head for the cabinet where I stashed my groceries.

And remember that I didn't actually buy any real food.

I was going to go back to the grocery store to get actual food tomorrow. So now I'm stuck with nothing but a bunch of junk food. That's just going to have to do. I grab out a bag of party mix and a box of cheese crackers. I contemplate for a second before going back for a bag of pita chips and heading over to the refrigerator for the one nutritious thing I managed to get into my cart earlier today–a container of roasted pine nut hummus. I'm going to go ahead and say that's a healthy choice and counteracts the rest of everything else I'm going to eat.

Dropping everything into the center of the kitchen table, I go to another cabinet and stand up on my toes to reach a glass. This puts me at the perfect angle to sneak a glance over at the stove to what Malcolm is cooking. There's a pot at the back of the stove with what looks like noodles bubbling away and a large saucepan in front of him with a thick, fragrant sauce swirling slowly with the wooden spoon in his hand.

He catches me looking and I quickly turn away. Bringing the glass over to the refrigerator, I fill it with water from the door. I plop down at the kitchen table and start digging into my pile of snacks. Malcolm peers over his shoulder at me a couple of times, and I try not to let him catch me watching him cook.

"Want a taste?" he asks.

I shake my head and hold up a pita chip with a large glob of hummus on the edge.

"I'm good."

He shrugs and turns back around, continuing to stir. Reaching into the drawer beside him, he takes out a small spoon and dips it into the sauce to taste it. He sets the spoon aside and pulls out another pan. Crossing to the refrigerator, he takes out a package of chicken chunks and brings it over to the stove. He adds a drizzle of something that smells rich and nutty to the pan and drops in the chicken.

The smell of cooking chicken adds to the sweet, garlicky amazingness of whatever is in that pot, and I have to refrain from licking my lips.

I don't need him and his sexy midnight cooking. Party mix is delicious. I can even pick out the bagel chips and eat all of them without caring what anyone thinks. And hummus is a fantastic source of protein. This is very satisfying. I'm going to enjoy my midnight snack, then scurry back to the bedroom and lock him out while he's still doing what he's doing.

I'll even bring my crackers with me for reserves.

CHAPTER FOURTEEN

MALCOLM

I'M NOT SURE IF BREE IS AWARE THAT SHE'S MURMURING TO HERSELF about the snacks she's eating or if this is some sort of private mantra moment I'm not supposed to be witnessing, so I decide not to say anything to her about it.

Instead, I stir the chicken around in the pan to make sure it's perfectly caramelized, then turn to look over my shoulder at her again. "Are you sure you don't want some of this? I made a ton."

She looks at me over the pile of party mix she is sifting through–probably in search of those bagel slices she was talking to herself about–and seems to be contemplating the question intently.

"No, I'm fine," she says.

"All right," I say again, turning back to the chicken.

She's still watching me.

If I look out of the corner of my eye, I can just barely see her sitting at the table and she hasn't turned her attention away from me since I made the offer.

"What are you making?" she asks after a few seconds.

There it is. I've got her now. "Thai peanut noodles with chicken."

"That sounds so good," she says.

"It is. You're welcome to some of it. Like I said, I made a ton."

Bree's eyes slowly lower to the snacks in front of her, then come back to me. "Okay."

"Great. It's ready. I've just got to drain the noodles. Do you want broccoli?"

I grab a large mixing bowl and reach into the microwave where there's a bag of steamed broccoli waiting for me. Tugging it out by one corner, I let it flop into the bowl to avoid the steam that will inevitably leak out of the bag while I'm moving it and burn the shit out of my hand. I know this from unfortunate experience.

"Sure," she says.

I grab a pair of kitchen shears from the knife block on the counter and snip the bag open. "Ah, the wonders of modern technology. I don't even have to pour the broccoli out and add water to microwave it anymore."

"The thrills never cease," Bree says.

Setting the mixing bowl down, I reach into the cabinet for plates and set them out on the counter. Draining the pasta, I dish out a mound of noodles onto each plate and follow it up with a couple of ladles of sauce, then top them with broccoli and chicken. Setting a fork on the edge of her plate, I offer it out to her.

Bree looks at me suspiciously for a few moments, like she's not entirely sure that this peace offering is legit. There's a bit of questioning in those entrancing, spite-filled eyes that says she thinks there's a strong possibility I pulled a vaudeville-style sleight of hand to poison just her peanut sauce.

But the potential threat of death by Thai sauce doesn't seem to be enough to dissuade her completely and she stands up, slowly coming across the room to take the plate from me.

"Thank you," she says.

"No problem. I always cook too much," I say. "You should see my refrigerator at home—top to bottom leftovers all the time."

"Too bad Tupperware isn't still a thing," she says. " Those ladies would love you."

"I think it is."

"You think what is?" she asks, dipping the tip of her finger into some wayward sauce and tasting it.

"Tupperware. I think it's still a thing," I take out my phone and run a search. "Yep. It is indeed still a thing and there are still parties."

"Hmmm," she says in acknowledgement. "You learn something new every day. Not that I really particularly needed that little tidbit of information, but I'll tuck it away in my mental trivia folder."

"Do you go to a lot of trivia nights?" I ask, envisioning her having a favorite local bar where she goes every week to knock back a few while trying to answer random questions.

Bree stares at me blankly for a few seconds. "No."

"Oh." There's an awkward pause. "Want to go into the living room and catch some late-night TV?"

"Okay," she says.

I grab a few paper towels from the dispenser hanging on the wall beside the sink and we head for the living room.

"Why do you cook so much food?" she asks as she settles onto the couch. "Did you grow up with a big family?"

"Not exactly." Not at all, actually, but I'm trying to avoid talking about my life. I don't want to wade into the dangerous waters of possibly revealing too much about myself.

"Then why?" she asks, swirling her fork around in the noodles and taking a bite.

"I wish there was some sort of good reason for it, but I guess it's just that there aren't really recipes or anything out there for just one person. Everything is to feed a bunch of people and so that's what I do."

"Well, you should keep doing it. This is delicious."

"Thanks. It's one of my favorite things," I tell her.

We both look at the remote sitting in the middle of the coffee table in front of us and at the same moment, we lunge for it. I manage to snag it first and she lets out an exasperated sound.

"We should watch a movie," she says.

I look at the remote in my hand. "That's interesting. See, it seems to me that I'm the one holding the remote, so I am the one who gets to choose what we watch."

"See, but I'm the guest in the house, so I should be allowed to choose," she insists.

"Oh, so now you're a guest? Does that mean you're acknowledging I have more of a connection to the house than you do? Because if that's the case...."

"Oh, no. You are definitely a guest, too, even more than I am."

I laugh. "So does that mean that I have more of the privileges and should get to choose?"

She opens her mouth like she's going to say something, then closes it again. Suddenly she reaches out for the remote, trying to grab it from my hand, making me laugh again. Bree is smiling now, sending another shock of attraction through me. I need to find more ways to bring that smile to her lush lips and the shimmer to her eyes.

"Fine. What is it that you want to watch?" she asks.

"How about *Top Chef*?" I ask, pulling up the menu of streaming networks. "Or are you more of a *Cutthroat Kitchen* type of person?"

"A what?" she asks.

"You don't watch cooking competitions?"

"No. I mean, I've heard of *Top Chef*, but I've never watched any of it. I'm more of a true crime watcher."

"Why doesn't that surprise me?" I open *Cutthroat Kitchen* and scan through to pick an episode. "All right. You've got to watch this. It's fucking hilarious. And really impressive at the same time. Basically chefs screw each other over with all kinds of sabotages while cooking stuff but the judge that chooses the best one doesn't know what happened to them."

"You're doing a bang-up job making this appealing," she says.

I sigh. "Just try it."

"You really like these cooking shows, huh?" she asks. "You enjoy watching people mix stuff and get all flustered over like... cans?"

"Yes. They're what I watch when I actually let myself relax," I say.

"You know, true crime has actual psychological insight and gives you tips for how to stay safe. But... floppy carrot drama is right up there, too."

"These shows are great," I insist. "It's interesting to learn about food and how to cook, and this one is funny and nobody is chopping anybody up."

"Okay," she says. "All right, I'll try it. Go ahead."

"Are you sure?"

She nods. "Yes."

"Are you just going to make fun of it the whole time?"

"No."

"Because you look like you're going to make fun of it the whole time," I say.

She lets out a dramatic sigh. "I'm not going to make fun of it. Just put the show on."

I hesitate for another second, then turn on the episode. "OK, so these are the competitors...."

Her eyes slide over to me. "Are you going to explain the whole thing while they are explaining it?"

"Sorry."

We go back to watching the show and I find myself sneaking looks over at Bree to gauge her reaction to the show. I'm oddly invested in her enjoying it. Every time her lips twitch up into a smile, my heart warms a little.

"Wait," she suddenly says. "They can't go back in there? Even if they forget to get something they need?"

"Nope," I say. "That's kind of part of it."

"But how are they supposed to make what he wants?"

"Just wait."

It's almost as funny to watch Bree try to understand the point of the show and get involved in it as it is to watch the show itself. She keeps making faces and tilting her head back and forth like that's going to give her all the answers to the universe, or at least to the ongoing question of what is wrong with this man's mind. At one point I laugh and she looks over at me.

"What?"

"The look on your face," I say.

She lets out a slight laugh and points at the screen. "I'm just... I mean, this is insanity."

"Exactly."

"Do they really not know what they are supposed to cook ahead of time?" she asks.

"They really don't,' I tell her.

"What happens if he announces what they are supposed to cook and they don't know what it is or don't know how to make it?"

"That's happened before. They just have to figure it out," I say.

"See, like that," she says, pointing at the screen as the contestants race to start cooking. "I have no idea what that is. I wouldn't even know where to start."

"Really?" I ask.

She shrugs. "There isn't a whole lot of opportunity to be adventurous with food here in Maple Valley. And my ex liked his food predictable and familiar. We always went to the same restaurants and ordered the same things, or made the same things at either of our places."

"You didn't live together?" I ask.

"No." She swirls her fork in the remaining noodles on her plate. "We did not."

I suddenly remember the look on her face when I made the crack about her relationship at the engagement party. "Look, I'm sorry for what I said at the party. I was being a jackass and I didn't mean to upset you."

Bree shakes her head. "Don't worry about it."

"What happened? I mean... it sounds like you just broke up pretty recently,"

She gives a slow nod. "We did. I'll just say that it's left me with some serious problems with people who can't be honest or upfront about themselves."

She's obviously avoiding going into much detail about what happened to her relationship, but it's the comment about honesty that gives me a bit of a twinge of guilt. I try to talk myself out of the feeling. It's not like I'm purposely lying to her or making something up about myself for my own benefit. It's just a temporary situation that doesn't have anything to do with her.

We chat our way through another couple of episodes before I can see that Bree is getting tired again.

"Why don't you go on to bed?" I suggest. "You take the primary room. I'll crash in the guest room."

"No, it's fine," she says. "You should have the bigger room."

"No. You take it. You already have your stuff put away." I wink at her and I think I see a bit of color come to her cheeks. That gives me more of a thrill than maybe it should.

"Thanks." She lets out a sigh and stands up. "We've got a lot to do. We should get an early start."

I nod. "I'll meet you first thing in the morning and we'll get going."

"Goodnight."

I watch her walk out of the room before taking our dishes and bringing them into the kitchen. I think about her crawling into bed and my mind goes to her mouth so close to mine, her body pressed against me.

This is going to be a long couple of weeks.

CHAPTER FIFTEEN

Bree

My alarm wakes me up before I want it to. As exhausted as I was when I went back into the master bedroom last night and closed the door behind me, I had trouble actually getting to sleep. I kept thinking about Malcolm and the way things have gone between us since we first met.

I know I haven't been the nicest person toward him. He met me at a really unfortunate point in my existence and I know I've taken a lot of it out on him—some of it justifiable, mind you. It isn't like this man has been a perfect angel and done everything to make my life easy but I've just shot it all down. There have been plenty of moments when he could have been a lot kinder and less difficult.

Like that jab about my breakup at the engagement party—I definitely could have lived without that one.

But last night he really was nice to me. He even glossed over waking up to me on top of him and those couple of breathless seconds when I very nearly lost every single ounce of my brain and almost kissed him. Maybe Olivia was right and I have been too hard on Malcolm. After all, she thinks he's a good guy, and I've never known her to be that far off in her judgment of people.

I decide to keep up the olive branch extending by making breakfast for us. The noodles he made last night were absolutely delicious, and I figure that a good breakfast to get us started on our first day of planning the wedding would be a good way to say thank you and smooth the waters between us. The house is still quiet when I leave the bedroom and head into the kitchen. We did agree to meet first thing in the morning, but the sun isn't even all the way up yet, so maybe it's still a bit too early for him.

There are a few things in the kitchen I can use to make breakfast, but not enough. Jotting down a note that I'm headed to the grocery store, I leave it on the kitchen counter and hop in Olivia's car to make the short drive to the local store. I stock up on food for breakfast as well as some groceries for the rest of the time I'm going to be at the house, then go back. I'm expecting Malcolm to be awake when I get inside, but the house is still dark and quiet.

I make breakfast, occasionally walking down the hallway to look at the door to the guest room. I'm expecting at some point I'm going to see the light on under the door to indicate that he has actually gotten up, but it doesn't happen. I get all the way through making breakfast and have it spread out on the kitchen table, and he is still asleep. Aggravation is starting to build in my stomach. As much as I try to keep it down and tell myself that I need to be more understanding and flexible, I'm getting more frustrated by the second.

Finally, I decided I'm not going to wait for him anymore. I went through all the effort of making this breakfast. I'm not going to let it get cold and not enjoy it for myself. I sit down and eat. I go through three cups of coffee and a heaping plate of eggs, bacon, and biscuits, and Malcolm still hasn't emerged.

Beyond annoyed and frustrated and into anger territory at this point, I go about doing the dishes as loudly as I possibly can. I can't believe he agreed to get started early this morning and is still just lying around in bed.

It seems my efforts at banging everything I can find in the kitchen as I clean up gets through to him at last, and Malcolm shuffles into the kitchen, rubbing at his hair and yawning.

He looks around the kitchen. "I thought I smelled food."

"You did. When I made breakfast. But that's over now."

I am definitely feeling less charitable toward him now.

"Sorry. I haven't been getting a lot of rest recently. I finally got some sleep last night."

I don't really care. The only thing that matters to me right now is getting this wedding planned. I only have two weeks. That's a crazy amount of time to arrange an entire wedding, and I'm not going to let him get in my way. I storm back to the bedroom and pull out my planning notebook. bringing it back into the kitchen, I sit down at the table and start making notes.

Malcolm takes a box of cereal out of the cabinet and pours himself a bowl. I notice I'm looking over his shoulder at me a couple of times, and he snickers.

"What?" I ask.

"You're seriously using a notebook and pen to make plans? Haven't you ever heard of a computer? Or a tablet?"

"Technology isn't the end-all be-all of existence," I say. "I much prefer to write out things long hand when I am trying to make plans or workout problems. Your brain works better that way. It's science."

He chuckles again and goes to the refrigerator to get the milk. "Okay."

"Look, I don't have a lot of time to get this whole wedding planned, and I'm already getting a late start because you decided not to get out of bed this morning. I'm not going to waste any more time. I'm going to call Cyrus and tell him that I'm coming by to look at the venue. That way, at least I know what I'm working with and can get a better idea of what needs to be done."

"You mean we are going to go by and look at the venue," he says. "Don't forget I'm the one with the budget."

I haven't forgotten. I'm still aggravated at Olivia and Brandon for not just giving access to the payment accounts to me so I could handle everything on my own. I'm sure she would say that she wanted to make sure I wasn't trying to do too much by myself, but that's my whole point. I want to do it by myself. It would be far better than having to rely on Malcolm.

"Fine. But I'm not waiting around for you anymore. I need to get the details about the venue from Cyrus so I can start figuring everything else out. I'm going to get ready and then I'm leaving. If you are coming, you'd better be ready."

I head back to the bedroom to fix up my makeup and do my hair so I look more presentable for my errands for the day.

"Good morning to you, too," Malcolm calls after me.

It makes my hands curl up into fists and my teeth clench. This man has to be some cruel trick of the universe. Even his bedhead is sexy, and yet I feel like he's going to push me right over the edge.

We walk out of the house ten minutes later and Malcolm starts over toward his car. I don't even entertain the thought and go to Olivia's, hitting the key fob to unlock the door perhaps a bit too emphatically.

"I can drive," he says.

"I'm aware," I reply. "I've been in the car with you while you were doing it."

"I meant I figured I would drive us today."

"I know what you meant." I open the door and climb into the driver's seat.

There's no way in hell I'm letting him drive today. He has already thrown off the schedule. I'm not going to deal with being at his mercy when it comes to where we go and when. He shows up at the passenger door and taps on the window until I unlock it.

"It would be stupid for us to take two cars," he says.

"Then I guess you should get in."

He gets the distinct look on his face like he is not accustomed to people not doing what he wants, but he's going to have to get used to it fast. After a couple of seconds of staring at me, he gets in the car and I head off toward the orchard. Cyrus is supposed to meet us in twenty minutes so he can give us a tour of the event space and go over all the details about hosting the wedding.

The drive is tense and quiet. At one point, Malcolm looks like he wants to reach for the radio to turn on music, but my eyes cutting to the side at him stops his hand and he turns to look out the window.

As soon as I see the sign for the apple orchard, my heart clenches. I've been trying not to let myself think about my own wedding that will never be, wanting to pour all of my energy and attention into Olivia's plans.

But driving down the scenic road toward the venue I had envisioned for my own day has emotion rushing over me. I remember the excitement when I first looked at the venue online. The orchard has been a mainstay of Maple Valley for generations, but Cyrus has transformed it into a beautiful venue that has obviously already proven very popular considering he was only able to wedge Olivia and Brandon into a spot after a cancellation.

I could see my wedding unfolding there when I scrolled through the website and couldn't wait to actually walk around it to see it for myself. I envisioned Trevor's arm around me, a big rock on my hand, and all the butterflies and excitement of preparing for my future filling me as we strolled through the orchard and looked at the event spaces.

Now I'm stalking up to the main building with Malcolm trailing behind me, definitely no rock on my hand, and the butterflies have been traded for something a whole lot closer to a hornet's nest. I force a big smile when Cyrus comes out of the building toward us.

"Hey there, Bree," he says. "Looks like I'm getting to give you that tour anyway."

Sigh.

"Yep. Thanks for doing this. Olivia is understandably a bit stressed about this whole situation."

"Well, don't you worry. We're going to make sure she has the perfect wedding. Come on, I'll show you around. we'll start at the ceremony site."

We walk through a lovely grove of apple trees and Cyrus describes how the ceremony will be set up, then we move on to the banquet hall that will post the reception.

"Is there a space available to have a cocktail hour?" I ask.

"Absolutely. We can set up a tent outside. If it's chilly, I have space heaters."

"Perfect."

"Great. Give me just a second, and I will get you some paperwork."

Malcolm snorts slightly under his breath, and I glare at him as Cyrus walks away.

"What?" I ask.

"Seriously? Are you seeing the same place I am? Why would they want to get married here?"

"Why wouldn't they? It's beautiful."

"It's cute for a barn dance or some family pictures or something, but why would anybody want to have their wedding here when they could have it at a nice hotel?"

"Because Olivia and Brandon want to get married in their hometown that they love. They want something with history and meaning, not just some generic hotel that could be the backdrop for any event for anyone. They don't want to travel for an hour to go to some place that doesn't mean anything and where they have no memories."

I'm surprised at how emotional I'm feeling about being home, but it really is getting to me.

Cyrus comes back with a handful of papers. "This is the contract, which Olivia has authorized you to sign for her. I also have the rules and stipulations for using the venue and my list of preferred vendors. Now, preferred is the operative word here. They're the ones I most recommend but at this point, you're going to be lucky finding just about anything, so go with God and get what you can."

Well, that's encouraging.

CHAPTER SIXTEEN

MALCOLM

I seriously don't get it. Like I said, the apple orchard is cute. It's nice to walk around the trees, especially with the fall weather. But it seems so much more suited for people roaming around in jeans and sweaters taking hayrides or sipping cider than it is a wedding. Having it in one of my hotels would be a far better option. The entire atmosphere, not to mention the service and amenities available, would be far nicer and more elevated than the orchard.

Maybe Brandon and Olivia just haven't really thought this all the way through. It isn't like they chose the orchard for their wedding. They had an entirely different vision for the event when they were doing the planning themselves. Now that I have seen this place, maybe they will listen to me when I tell them that it isn't the right call and they will let me handle everything for them.

I take my phone out of my pocket and hold it up toward Bree. "I'll be right back."

She barely nods and keeps her attention on Cyrus as he goes over the papers he's showing her. I step out of the banquet hall and call Brandon.

"Hey," he says. "What's up? Is everything going okay with the wedding planning?"

It all sounds like one continuous stream of thought. It's obvious how concerned both of them are about pulling this event off. That actually gives me some hope. They want to make sure they have the wedding of their dreams and it goes off without a hitch. I can absolutely make that happen for them.

"It's going. Bree and I are actually up at the orchard right now. Cyrus gave us a tour."

"What do you think?"

"Honestly, I don't see your wedding happening here," I say.

"Oh. Why not?"

"Because it's an apple orchard, Brandon. It's not a wedding venue."

"Actually, it is a wedding venue," he points out. "That's why they were able to book our wedding there."

"You know what I mean. The ceremony site is outside, and Cyrus said you could put up a tent to have your cocktail hour. A tent, Brandon—this isn't camping. It's your wedding. I really think you need to let me just take the reins and host the whole thing at one of my hotels."

"I really don't think he's talking about a camping tent, Malcolm. Olivia and I want to get married in Maple Valley. We want to be comfortable and home. We want to feel like we can revisit the memories of our wedding day just going about our lives, and we don't want our friends and family to have to go through a bunch of hassle traveling."

"It's only an hour. It's not like I'm talking about a destination wedding," I point out.

"I get that," he says. "But the orchard is right in our hometown, and Olivia used to pick apples there when she was a little girl. It means something to her. Besides, you technically can't host our wedding for us. The challenge is still going on. You can't offer up the use of one of your hotels to us."

"But I wouldn't be spending any money," I say. "I would just be letting you use the space. And the catering."

Brandon laughs. "It still counts."

"I think you can count this as extenuating circumstances. We didn't know this was going to be an issue when we made the challenge. Besides, the agreement was that I was going to only have access to a certain amount of money. We never said anything about not being able to use the hotels I own."

"That was kind of implied when we made the agreement to move you into the other apartment. We really appreciate you wanting to make our wedding perfect for us, but our idea of the perfect wedding is in Maple Valley. It wouldn't be the same being somewhere else."

I have officially been defeated. It's obvious Brandon and Olivia aren't going to budge. I hang up and turn to go back inside, but Bree is coming out. She eyes my phone.

"What was that all about?" she asks.

"Nothing," I say, putting my phone back in my pocket. "What's that?"

"Just stuff about the venue," she replies. "They have preferred vendors, but it's unlikely any of them are going to be available for an event two weeks from now, so we're going to have to call and visit everybody we can think of until we find someone." She flips through the papers she's holding. "And these are the rules about decorating the reception hall, which reminded me that we have to decorate the reception hall." She lets out a sigh. "So, first thing we have to figure out is flowers. We're going to need them for the ceremony and for the reception. I know Olivia had some idea of what she wanted, but we might not be able to pull that off. We're going to have to find the flowers that are going to be available and figure out the rest of the decorations and everything around that."

"The best thing to do would just be to go into the shops," I say. "Calling isn't going to be as effective as if we are actually standing there in front of them asking if they can help us."

"All right. Well, the florist on the list is Angela's Blooms. It's not far from here. I guess we should start there."

The drive to the florist is less than ten minutes, and as soon as we pull up, I already have the feeling that this isn't going to work out for us the way we want. The shop is tiny and has a boutique feel about it, the kind of place that doesn't do rush orders or have extras just sitting around. It's likely a preferred vendor for the venue because of its close proximity, but also because it offers exclusive service. Bree takes her planning binder with her and we head inside.

A chime that goes off somewhere in the back of the shop when we open the door is like the modern equivalent of the little jingle bells, and a woman in a green apron comes out. I take it this is Angela.

"Hello," she says. "Can I help you?"

"I hope so," Bree says. "I'm planning a wedding."

"Congratulations," Angela says with a bright smile, looking back and forth between us.

"Oh, no. Not my wedding. Not our wedding. We aren't…. no," Bree says, shaking her head.

That was emphatic.

"Oh. I'm sorry. I just assumed."

"It's fine. I'm actually—we are actually planning my best friend's wedding. But there was a whole situation with the venue and things got mixed up and they ended up getting rescheduled for the wrong date, and…."

"I heard about the rescheduled weddings. I didn't realize one was put on the wrong date."

"Yeah," Bree says. "And it's really important to them to not have to wait a year to get married and so we are scrambling to get this together for them by the new date."

"When is that?" Angela asks.

"Two weeks," Bree says.

The florist looks horrified. She immediately shakes her head. "I'm sorry, there's just no way I'd be able to get anything together for a wedding with that short of notice."

"Nothing?" Bree asks.

"Sorry. But there are other florists. Check with Gibson's."

Bree sighs. "Thank you."

We leave the shop and she looks up the next one. It's further into town, but it looks like a larger setup. She goes through the same explanation that she did with Angela when Neil Gibson greets us.

"What did you have in mind?" Neil asks.

That seems optimistic, and Bree looks happier. "White roses for the bridal bouquet. Orange for the bridesmaids. Then orange and burgundy centerpieces for the reception."

Neil cringes a little, and I notice Bree's face drop. "That's pretty specific," he says. "I don't know if we'd be able to source enough flowers for that kind of continuity in such a short time."

"But you have other flowers?" I ask.

Bree glares at me, but I ignore her.

"Yes," Neil says.

I look at Bree. "Why does everything have to match?"

"Because it's a wedding," she says.

"So? Is there some sort of law that says that every table has to have the exact same flowers or that they all have to be the same kind?"

"That's just the way it is," she tells me, looking at Neil for support.

But he's looking at me, a curious lift to one eyebrow. I've got him hooked. I walk over to a large black bucket containing simple bouquets designed to be easy to grab for someone just wanting to give someone flowers rather than going through the hassle of getting something custom designed.

"What if there were a bunch of different kinds of flowers? You can pick a color scheme and have them all go together that way, but they don't have to match exactly."

"I don't think that would work," Bree says. "The flowers are important. They need to be perfect."

"And they have to look like cookie cutters to be perfect? I think that's just boring and predictable. Give them something different that's just for them," I suggest.

"That could be gorgeous," Neil says.

Bree is clearly surprised that the florist is so eager to go along with what I'm saying. Her eyes narrow as he goes over to a display and starts pulling out individual stems, putting them together into an arrangement that incorporates fall colors with different types of blooms and accent greens.

"See? That's beautiful," I say. "And he put it together in ten seconds."

"This is something I could do," Neil says. "I could source the flowers that are easy to get in the next couple of weeks and create unique pieces for the tables and the bridal party."

"What do you think?" I ask.

Bree looks at the flowers again. Her head tilts to the side as she examines them. "That really does look good," she says. "I never would have thought to put those flowers together. I think that could work."

"Fantastic," Neil says. "Then just give me the specifics for how many centerpieces and bouquets you are going to need, along with anything else you'll want for the ceremony or reception, and I'll put together an invoice for you."

She opens her notebook and looks over one of her pages of notes, rattling off the different types of flower arrangements we'll need for each element of the wedding. When she's done and Neil is at his computer tallying the order, I see her looking at the arrangement again. She looks impressed, and I realize just how much I like impressing her.

Neil finishes the invoice and I pay for the order. He promises it will all be ready and perfect the morning of the wedding and assures Bree she doesn't need to worry about any of it. She doesn't look completely convinced, but at least she can make a little checkmark in her plans next to "flowers."

CHAPTER SEVENTEEN

This is not how this is supposed to be going.

I'm supposed to be the one in charge here. I'm supposed to be the one who is making these plans and getting everything in place. Malcolm is along for the ride. He is a debit card with eyes. And yet, he's the one who just figured out the flowers and I look like a raving bridezilla by proxy because I wanted the flowers to match. To say I don't love that he has already gotten a checkmark in his column for solving the flower issue would be a massive understatement. He shouldn't even have a column.

Debit card. With. Eyes.

And yet, I have to admit that his idea to mix up the flowers into the different bouquets did turn out to be much prettier than I expected it to be, and it fixes that dilemma with a minimum of drama, which I should appreciate. In all honesty, I probably never would have thought to mix up the flowers like that. In my mind, wedding flowers match. Even if it is two or three different kinds, they still all go together and look alike. But in about ten seconds flat, Malcolm proved me completely wrong.

I try to swallow my frustration so we can just get on with the planning. As I push through the door to the florist and head down the sidewalk to the nearest bakery, I glance over at Malcolm.

"Thanks for figuring out the flowers," I grumble, perhaps a bit more begrudgingly than I should.

"I think they are going to look really pretty," he says. "They'll add a more unique touch to the wedding. Olivia wouldn't want her wedding to look like some cookie cutter event right off the pages of a magazine."

I have to bite my tongue to stop myself from saying something the little old lady walking down the sidewalk in front of us would not approve of. Who does he think he is making a declaration about what Olivia would want? She is my best friend, not his. He doesn't know her anywhere near as well as I do. And I'm not just saying that because my plans for her wedding so far have come directly from the pages of a magazine. It's not like I'm unique in that. Let's be honest. How many people actually plan a wedding without a full-on vision board these days?

Maybe don't answer that.

As we're walking toward the bakery, I noticed a little boutique and recognized the name as the one from the amenities at the hotel. I point it out to Malcolm.

"That's where the hotel gets the little toiletries and other amenities I was telling you about," I say. "Maybe we should go in there and look for some things to put in the welcome bags for the out-of-town guests. I know Olivia wants them to be really nice, and the things that the boutique sells to the hotel are wonderful."

Saying that makes me stop in my tracks. Malcolm takes a couple more steps and pauses, turning to look at me. "What? I thought we were going inside."

"The out-of-town friends and family," I say. "The people coming in for the wedding."

"Yeah. I understand the concept. People are coming in from out of town and need welcome bags in their hotel rooms. What about it?"

"Are they going to have hotel rooms?" I ask, lifting up my eyebrows at him. "I didn't even ask if Olivia contacted the hotel to make sure that the room block she reserved for her out of town guests was changed to the new dates. Are they going to be able to accommodate anybody?"

Malcolm looks a bit stunned by the question. He obviously didn't think about that, either. I immediately fish my phone out of my bag and call Olivia. I have no idea what time it is for her, but I can't really care about that right now. This is a bit of an emergency.

"Hello?" she answers, sounding groggy.

"Hey," I say. "Sorry to bother you. I just had a quick question."

"Is something wrong?" she asks.

"No. Everything is going to be fine. I just wanted to make sure that you called the hotel to move the room block for your out-of-town guests to the new date."

"Oh no! I didn't even think about that! What am I going to do?" she asks.

"Don't worry about it," I say, trying to sound as calm as possible. "Everything is going to be perfectly fine, just like I said. You don't need to worry about it at all. We'll just add that to my list. Not a problem. I'm going to take care of it for you. Just relax and enjoy the rest of your trip and when you get back, it will be time for your perfect wedding."

I hang up, hoping that I managed to conceal the complete panic that I'm starting to feel. Adding anything to the list of wedding plans that I have to coordinate is challenging enough. When those things are making sure that people not only have a place to stay when they get in town for the wedding, but are actually invited to the wedding as well is a bit overwhelming. But I'm going to do it. I told Olivia that I was going to handle it for her, so I'm going to.

I put my phone away and look up only to see that Malcolm is gone. I look up and down the sidewalk and then catch sight of him through the boutique window. He has already gone inside.

I step into the boutique and am immediately hit by an absolutely heavenly smell. I pause and draw in a deep breath. The scent of all the specialty bath and body products waft to me from displays all around me, drawing me in to take extra sniffs of some. I notice there are coordinating candles to go along with the body wash, lotions, body spray, and other goodies. I could lose myself in this place for the whole day. It is absolutely perfect for putting together welcome bags for the guests.

I just hope that there are guests to give those bags to.

Putting aside the worrisome thoughts for a moment, I let myself indulge in smelling the products and trying a few of the testers. I'm not sure which of these smells would be Olivia's favorite, but I can narrow it down to a couple of different ones. I figure I can get a few different scents that would work for different guests.

"Can I help you with something?" a voice asks from behind me.

I turn around and see a woman in a polka dot blouse and meticulous makeup smiling at me.

"Actually, yes. Maybe. Are you the manager?" I ask.

"I own this shop," she says. "I'm Mandy." She reaches out to shake my hand, and I smile at her.

"Nice to meet you," I say. "I'm Bree. I am planning my best friend's wedding. There was a bit of a snafu with her original venue and date, and it ended up inadvertently being moved to two weeks from now, so we are in a bit of a crunch at the moment."

"I heard about that," she says.

I try not to cringe. I have to remember how small Maple Valley is and that just about everybody hears just about everything the second that it happens. I guess that would be especially true for businesses that might have something to do with weddings or events when there is as much of an upheaval as there has been.

"Yeah," I say. "It's a bit of a challenge. But one thing on my planning list is welcome bags for the out-of-town guests. I have stayed at the hotel a couple of times and really fell in love with the amenities there. I think they would be perfect for giving to the guests."

"That's definitely something we've done before," Mandy says. "It's so nice to give guests something to pamper themselves with before the wedding and after. Did you have specific products in mind?"

"I'm actually not sure. There are so many amazing things, and some I haven't even tried. I don't know which scent would be best."

"No problem. Why don't I put together a little basket of samples and testers for you with some of my most popular products and a few of the specialty items that I have used for weddings and events in the past? That way you can bring them to the bride and let her try them out so that she can choose which ones are best for her guests."

"Well, the bride is out of the country right now, and she's going to be until right before the wedding. That's why I'm doing the planning for her," I explain.

"Oh," she says. "Even better. That means you get to enjoy the pampering all yourself. Give me just a minute."

Mandy smiles and walks away. I sniff a few more of the candles around me and run my hands over a plush robe hanging on a display. I catch myself watching Malcom stroll through the aisles, scrutinizing everything he passes. A few minutes later Mandy comes back with a basket overflowing with products. She hands it over to me.

"This is amazing," I tell her as I take it out of her hands. "Thank you."

"So, you really do sell these products to the hotel?" Malcolm asks, suddenly appearing behind me.

He's gripping a bottle of air freshening spray in apple pumpkin scent, one of the products tucked neatly into my basket, and staring at Mandy intently.

"Yes. I've been working with them for a couple of years now. I've actually designed some specific products just for holiday seasons and other events. It's one of the little touches that the guests really seem to appreciate. And it does good things for my business as well. When people find out that those products come from a boutique right in town, they come and visit me to stock up so they can bring it home. And sometimes I'm fortunate enough to be included in special occasions."

She gives me a conspiratorial smile and I grin back. Malcolm looks at the spray in his hand.

"It's really that big of a deal to the guests?"

"Absolutely. I can't tell you how often I have people come in to say how much they love a certain scent or to find out what other things I have. There are people who stay at that hotel just because of the little touches like that. Not just because of my products, obviously, but because of that kind of detail."

I can tell Malcolm is gearing up for a rant, so I lift the basket a little bit like I'm displaying it to her.

"Thank you so much for this," I say. "I really appreciate it. I will try the things out and come back to let you know exactly what I need."

"You're welcome. I hope you enjoy it."

I start out of the boutique and Malcolm falls into step behind me. I'm glad to see he doesn't still have the spray in his hand.

"I'm going to need some coffee," I tell him. "Olivia confirmed that she didn't change the room block at the hotel and also didn't change any of the invitations, so I have to get those tackled as soon as possible."

I head straight for the coffee shop. Stepping up to the counter, I order the largest serving of their strongest coffee with hazelnut creamer. I consider getting a snack from the display cabinet, but nothing really catches my eye. Besides, if things go well at the bakery, I might be tasting a lot of samples, so I don't want to be too full.

Taking my coffee from the barista, I go over to a counter a few feet away and add sugar, then bring the cup with me to a table next to the window. Steeling myself with a large swig of the coffee, I take out my phone and dial the hotel. I try to sound upbeat and optimistic while explaining the issue to the manager, hoping that a chipper attitude will subtly convince him to go along with the change without hassle.

Not so much.

As soon as I'm done telling him what I need, the hemming and hawing starts. To his credit, he's trying to be friendly about kicking me in the ass, but he's kicking me in the ass nonetheless. Much like I was anticipating, he essentially tells me the block has already been reserved and there's no way to refund the money with this short of notice as well as reserving that many rooms so soon. I try to interject, but it doesn't do any good.

Malcolm can clearly see the look of disappointment and frustration on my face, because he reaches across the table and takes the phone from my hand. At first I'm aggravated at the move, but when he rattles off an explanation of why making the change would be advantageous to the hotel, I'm intrigued. He pauses and listens before a rapid-fire negotiation that ends with him thanking the manager and handing the phone back to me.

"Done," he says.

"Done? He did it?"

"Yep. The same block is now reserved for two weeks from now. The payment has been transferred. And they will have a special spread of snacks and drinks available the night everyone arrives so they can visit each other before the wedding."

I blink.

"Seriously?"

"Yeah. So, that's taken care of."

"How did you do that?"

"I told you. I have experience working in the hotel industry. I knew what to say." He looks up at the menu. "I think I'm going to grab a coffee after all."

He gets up from the table and walks up to the counter. I watch him as he orders. Part of me feels like I should be annoyed that he took over like that, but I can't make myself be upset by it. The power play was sexy, and I like how he took charge and made sure things got done the way I wanted them.

CHAPTER EIGHTEEN

MALCOLM

I feel dirty.

And not just in the way Bree's presence has brought up all kinds of dirty thoughts since the first time I laid eyes on her.

I just willingly talked to the manager of that rinky-dink little hotel and convinced him to shift the room block for the wedding. Not only that, but I made sure that he was going to go the extra mile in making the experience special for Olivia and Brandon.

I could tell that he wasn't going along with the change when Bree was talking to him. It was clear on her face that he was giving her trouble. Right then, I could have just decided to let the chips fall as they may. I could have just waited for her to give up on the conversation and recommended that we change the reservations to one of my hotels in the city. Maybe then it would have been a good segue into just getting the entire celebration there. If Brandon had to deal with not having a place for his guests to stay while they were in town, it might convince him to go ahead with something on a larger, more elegant scale.

But no.

I couldn't just let that happen. I couldn't just make it easier for myself.

I had to look at Bree's gorgeous eyes and see that sadness, and I was done for. I can't stand to see that look in them. Even if the alternative is usually something a lot closer to disdain. I'll take that over her looking so upset and disappointed any time if there's something I can do about it.

When I get back to the table with my coffee, she has her planning notebook open on the table and is going over the list of things we still need to do. I glance at it. The little check mark next to the flowers and venue are looking pretty sad compared to the rest of the items just waiting for us to handle them.

"We should go check out the caterer," I say.

Bree looks up at me. The worry and sadness are gone from her eyes, and I wouldn't quite say that the disdain has taken its place, but the expression in them is far from enthusiastic and friendly. It is very obvious she was not anticipating that I'd get as involved with the planning as I have been. But I'm not about to let my best friend's wedding not be everything it could be, even if my definition of that isn't quite an alignment with theirs. I know Bree is capable and she can handle a lot, but taking on an entire wedding in two weeks is ridiculous, and I'm not going to let her stubbornness mean problems for Brandon and Olivia.

"We need to go to the bakery," she says. "The cake is the centerpiece for the entire reception. It is a top priority for Olivia. We have to find a baker who will make the perfect cake for her."

"The cake is just a cake," I point out. "Dessert. And most of the time wedding cake sucks. Everybody knows that."

"And that's exactly why I need to find a baker who is going to make a cake that is beautiful and delicious. She doesn't want her cake to suck, as you put it. She wants it to be amazing. She wants a dessert display and then the cake as the focal point."

"So, you're telling me that the cake isn't even the only dessert, and you think that it's so important we need to go there before anything else?"

I'm incredulous at this point. I know people fawn overelaborate cakes at weddings, and the whole cutting the first piece and feeding it to each other thing is a picture moment, but I can't honestly put myself in the place of thinking it's so important that it should take top billing in our priority list.

"That's exactly what I'm telling you."

"But the cake is just cake," I repeat. "The caterer handles the actual food."

"The actual food is nowhere near as important as the wedding cake."

"That's ridiculous," I say. "Nobody gets invited to a wedding and gets all excited thinking about having a slice of cake at the end of the night. They do think about what they're going to eat, and if people show up at a wedding and they don't get good food, they're going to riot."

"Riot? And I'm the one being ridiculous?"

"You know what I mean," I say. "Having good food is non-negotiable. We should make sure that we have the caterer on lock before we try to find a bakery."

"No," she insists flatly. "The cake is more important. It is the first thing that anybody notices when they walk into the reception. People look at it all night long. It gets in every picture. Them cutting it and feeding it to each other is a pinnacle part of the celebration. Then everybody eating it is considered good luck and a lot of cultures."

"Are you in one of those cultures?" I ask.

"Maybe I am."

"Is Olivia?"

"She specifically asked me to make sure that the cake is perfect, and that's what I'm going to do."

Bree is adamant, and I know I'm not going to get anywhere just sitting here arguing with her over coffee.

"The cake will be perfect. The caterer and the bakery are right next door to each other. We can do them one right after the other.

"Fine," she says.

She grabs her cup and her planning notebook and heads out of the coffee shop. I follow behind her and we go down the sidewalk. I've caught up with her by the time we get a couple of doors down and I point out the caterer.

"Look at that. The caterer is first. Guess we should go now," I say.

Bree rolls her eyes and lets out an exasperated sigh, but she follows me into the catering shop. I walk up to the counter and explain our predicament to the smiling man who introduces himself as Leonard, one of the owners of the catering business.

"Well, it just so happens that I have that day available. As long as you don't want anything over the top that would take too long to source the ingredients, I should be able to accommodate you just fine," Leonard says.

"That's fantastic," I say.

"Yes, that's amazing," Bree says beside me, visibly relaxing and actually smiling.

"Great. If you can give me just a little while, I can put together a simple tasting menu for you. It won't have everything on it that I would be able to offer, but it can give you an idea of what I will be able to do for you."

"We can do that," I say.

"Perfect. Come back in a couple of hours and I will have the tasting set up for you.

"That gives us time to go to the bakery and see about the cake," Bree says with a smile as she sweeps out of the door and heads for the bakery.

The smile that had finally made its way onto her face when she heard that the caterer would probably be able to accommodate the wedding was not long for this world. It only took about forty-five seconds of us being in the bakery for it to totally disappear and get replaced with that same despondent look from when she was on the phone with the manager of the hotel.

"Nothing?" she asks the baker. "There's no room in your schedule at all?"

"For a wedding cake in two weeks?" the woman in a mint green apron asks with a note of disbelief that Bree is even standing there asking. "No. I don't have any room in my schedule at all for that. I might not even have room in my schedule for an elementary school bake sale at this point. I am extremely busy, and a wedding cake takes days. it's just not something I can do. I'm sorry."

Ever the persistent optimist, Bree takes a sticky note out of her planning notebook and jots down her name and phone number. "Here's my contact information. Just in case somebody cancels or you're able to move things around and can accommodate us. Just give me a call."

The look on the baker's face when she takes the sticky note from Bree says that there is a snowball's chance in hell she is actually going to be making that call, but she'll take the note just so Bree doesn't break down right here in front of the cupcake display.

We go back outside and Bree walks over to a bench where she drops down and pulls out her planning notebook. I sit down beside her and glance over at the intricate lists and diagrams she's flipping through. it might not be my thing, but it is impressive just how organized and detailed she is about this.

"For just finding out that you are putting together this wedding, you sure have it under control. It certainly looks like you know what you're doing."

Without looking up, she lets out a little bit of a sigh. "Well, it's not the first wedding I've planned."

"Oh. Have you been married before?"

As soon as the question comes out of my mouth, I regret it. I notice her jaw clench just slightly.

"No. No, I haven't."

She doesn't seem like she has any interest in talking about it, so I don't push any further. She spends another few seconds looking over her lists and flips the book shut.

"Well, we have some time before the caterer is going to be ready with the tasting. I thought I could run by the bridal boutique and check on Olivia's dress. They were doing a couple of last minute fixes, and I want to make sure that it's going to be ready in time for the new date."

"Fine with me," I say. "I'll go along with you. Where is it?"

"We're going to need to drive," she says. "It's a few streets down from here."

We go to the shop, and I'm surprised not to see any dresses.

"Where are the dresses? Shouldn't there be dresses in a bridal boutique?" I ask Bree under my breath.

"They're in the back," she explains. "They bring them out for people to try on. Haven't you ever seen a bridal shop?"

"I have never personally been a bride," I tell her.

A woman in a short pink dress comes out of the back of the shop, and a bright smile crosses her face when she sees Bree.

"Bree! It's so good to see you. I didn't realize you were in town."

"Hey, Jessica." Bree gives the woman a quick hug. "I'm here trying to get Olivia's wedding all sorted out. Did you hear that the date had to be changed?"

"I did," Jessica says, her eyes opening widely like she's trying to demonstrate just how shocked she is by the entire situation. "I can't even believe that would happen. I would be a total mess."

"Honestly, I think Olivia would be, too, if she was here. But she is out of the country, so I get to be here being the honorary mess for her. But, I have everything under control. I'm just here to make sure her dress is going to be ready for the new date."

I'm impressed by Bree's ability to just throw out there that she has everything under control and sound like she actually believes it.

"Absolutely it will be," Jessica assures Bree. "It was already just about done when I heard about the change in the date, and I changed around some things on schedule to make sure that it will be perfect. don't worry at all."

"Amazing. Thank you so much," Bree says.

"While you're here, you should try on your dress. You haven't had a chance to have a fitting since you picked it out. Not that it needed much alteration or anything, but it's a good idea to take a look at it to make sure we don't need to do anything before the big day."

"I don't know," Bree says, sounding unsure. "I have a ton to get done."

"You don't want to get to the wedding day and find out that your dress isn't perfect, do you?" Jessica asks. "The maid of honor can't walk down the aisle in something that doesn't look amazing. It will take just a second. Go on in the dressing room and I will meet you there."

She obviously isn't going to give Bree a choice. She sweeps back into the back of the shop and Bree gives me a look, then goes through a mirrored door in a curved bank of more mirrors. Jessica comes back carrying a garment bag on a hanger and goes into the same small room.

A few moments later, the door opens again and Bree comes out in a deep purple gown. It takes everything in me to keep my jaw from dropping. She looks stunning. The gown hugs every curve and makes her skin look even creamier.

Her eyes meet mine through the mirror, and I feel my gut tighten.

CHAPTER NINETEEN

BREE

I see the way Malcolm is looking at me in my dress. The obvious heat in his eyes makes me feel strangely flustered and I turn away as quickly as I can. Why was I even looking at him? I don't care what he thinks about my maid of honor dress or how I look in it.

Right? I don't, do I?

Of course, I don't. I chastise myself for even entertaining the idea of having a crush on that man. Aside from being sexy as hell with no shirt on, a good cook, and able to negotiate with a hotel manager, he's been nothing but an infuriating hassle. And flowers. Shit. I don't want to acknowledge any of this.

Doing a couple of quick cursory glances in the mirror at different angles, I nod at Jessica. "Looks good."

"I was about to say it looks like it fits like a glove. I don't think anything needs to get changed before the big day."

"Perfect."

I get down off the platform in front of the mirror and hurry back into the changing room. Taking off the dress, I put it back on the hanger and into the garment bag and put my regular clothes back on. I hand the dress back to Jessica when I step out of the room so she can keep it with Olivia's dress until we come to pick it up before the wedding.

"Anything else?" Jessica asks. "Are you good on shoes? Do you need to talk about undergarments?"

Heat flashes across my cheeks, and I can't even bring myself to look at Malcolm out of the corner of my eye. "Nope. I've got that all nailed down. Thank you."

"Okay, then I guess I'll see you in a couple of weeks. Let me know if you think of anything."

"I will, thank you," I say, hurrying out of the shop.

"I should probably check on the suits, too," Malcolm says.

I'm about to protest, but then realize that's actually a good idea. Damn it.

I check the name of the shop where they ordered the suits in the information that Olivia gave me. I recognize it as the place where all the guys used to rent their suits for prom when I was in high school. It isn't far from here.

Once we get there, it seems Frank, the owner of the shop who is the same man who used to rent all those suits all those years ago, isn't in the same loop as all the other vendors and didn't hear about the wedding kerfuffle. We fill him in and he takes a disturbingly long pause before reassuring us that these suits will be ready in time for the new date. For a second there I felt like I couldn't breathe, but now I feel like I could just kiss Frank right on the top of his little old head.

"Let me go ahead and try my suit on because I'm here," Malcolm says.

"Sure thing," Frank agrees.

A few minutes later, I am on the other side of the long, admiring gaze. Malcolm looks incredible in his suit. It fits him perfectly, accenting his broad shoulders and nipping in slightly at his waist. He glances at me in the mirror, and his little smirk makes me feel like I was caught with my hand in the cookie jar. I look down at my phone and dash off a text to absolutely no one. It gives me enough time to get the thoughts about Malcolm out of my head.

It feels good to check the dress and the suits off of my planning list. As we're leaving the shop, I get a call from the caterer saying that he has the tasting all set up for us. I'm pleasantly surprised that he was able to get it together so quickly. It feels like a good omen. If he is this on top of things and able to put something together for us at the last minute like this, then maybe it will be smooth sailing.

We get back to the catering shop and Leonard shows us into a side room. A table is set up in the middle with a cream colored tablecloth and a chair at either end with one set up on the side. There's a menu sitting at each of the seats at the ends and Malcolm and I sit down.

I look over the menu and start to feel my optimism wane. It's just a single sheet of paper that looks like it was printed out right in his office. I can handle that. This was a last-minute kind of thing, so he might not have been ready to have a formal menu printed up for us.

But what's on the menu is my main cause for concern.

"Looks like this is right up your alley," Malcolm mutters, glancing at me from over the top of his own menu.

Pigs in a blanket.

Chips and salsa.

Chips and onion dip.

Pita chips and hummus.

Crudité platter.

Fruit with yogurt dip.

Mini quiche.

Mini crab cakes.

I flip the paper over, hoping maybe that was just the list for the cocktail hour or an appetizer service prior to the actual meal. No such luck. That is all the food that's listed.

Leonard comes into the room from what I'm assuming is the kitchen carrying two platters. Another man that comes behind him with a third. They set them down on the table, and the second man slinks back into the kitchen like he doesn't even want to be there to witness the tasting. Malcolm and I look at the food, then at each other. The caterer sits down in the third chair and opens his hands out over the platters to welcome us to taste the food.

"These are some of our most popular options," he says. "They are a lot of fun for people and easy to feed a crowd."

I pick up one of the mini quiches and take a bite. It tastes a little bit like glue. Malcolm's expression after biting into one of the pigs in a blanket isn't much more complimentary.

"Some of your most popular options?" I ask. "So this is just a few of the appetizers? You could do a full meal?"

Leonard's face drops. "Well, actually, this is the majority of what I would be able to offer for an event in two weeks. I could probably add in some spaghetti and meatballs and corn on the cob, maybe some pulled pork sandwiches if that sounds good. That's really all I can promise. We have other events that weekend and aren't going to be able to pull up anything else."

It does not sound good, but I don't say that. I taste one of the crab cakes. It's better than the quiche, but still not very good. All hope I had built up thinking that this was going to be a huge weight off my shoulders is gone. Malcolm and I get through the rest of the tasting and I shake Leonard's hand.

"I'll give you a call to let you know what we decide," I tell him.

"I look forward to hearing from you," he says.

That makes me feel guilty as I walk out of the shop and look at Malcolm. "That's not going to work out."

"Definitely not," he says. "I didn't want to say anything, but there's no way we could have that be their catering."

I let out a heavy sigh. "We're just going to have to figure something else out. I don't know what, but something."

We start back down the sidewalk toward the car and have only gone a few steps when a tiny black and white puppy runs in between us and darts away. Malcolm immediately takes off after him. I chase after Malcolm and when I glance over my shoulder, I can see a woman waving a leash chasing close behind me. We weave through the people on the sidewalk trying to get to the puppy, which Malcolm is calling after, making kissy noises and patting his thighs as he runs.

I'm worried the little dog is going to get out into traffic and run as fast as I can to get to them. We run for a couple of blocks before the puppy notices Malcolm chasing him and swoops around, going between his feet and coming back toward me. Malcolm and I try to keep him between us, and as I dive forward to try to catch him, my planning notebook falls out of my arms and drops to the ground, papers going everywhere.

"Oh, no!" the woman behind me says.

Malcolm gets the puppy and holds the squiggly little dog against his chest as he walks toward us.

"Here you go," he says.

"Thank you so much," she says, taking the puppy and clipping him to his leash, but still keeping him snuggled against her as she crouches down. "I'm so sorry."

She starts picking up papers and handing them to me.

"It's all right. I'm just glad you got the baby," I reply.

"He's a little gremlin." She kisses the puppy's head. "But I adore him." She looks down at the papers and seems to notice they are wedding plans. "Are you two engaged?"

She has a grin of pure delight as she asks the question, but it drops away when I shake my head.

"No. This isn't for our wedding. Actually it's for both of our best friends. They are marrying each other. Unfortunately, their original plans got shot all to hell, and now we're trying to piece together a wedding for them in two weeks. We have managed to get a couple of things in place, but don't have a caterer or a wedding cake."

I realize the entire explanation has tumbled out of my mouth in an uncontrollable spew of words, and I expect the woman to scurry away as quickly as possible. Instead, the smile comes back to her face as she hands me the last of the papers and stands up.

"You need a wedding cake?" she asks.

"Yeah," I say. "We haven't found anybody who can do it."

"My sister makes cakes. Bitsy Cleaver. You should look her up. I'm sure she has availability. My name is Sarah, by the way."

She extends her hand, and I shake it with uncertainty. "Hi, Sarah. I'm Bree. I'm not sure. I mean, this is a big deal. It's not like a birthday cake or a graduation cake. This is a wedding cake. I want it to be perfect."

I don't mean to sound rude or dismissive. It was really kind of her to think of her sister and want to try to give us a solution, but I don't know if I could trust something like this to just a casual home baker. If I was going to have somebody make the wedding cake in their own kitchen, I would probably just try to tackle it myself.

"She makes really incredible stuff," Sarah insists. "She's done it for a long time. She makes cakes for everybody we know. Here. Let me show you."

Taking out her cell phone, she pulls up her sister's social media profile and turns the gallery of pictures toward me. I'm all prepared to find something nice to say about some sheet cakes and possibly a Pinterest unicorn. Instead, I see a series of legitimately beautiful cakes. They are well-decorated and in the few that show the cakes cut, I can see that she does a wide variety of flavors.

"Those are pretty good. She just does this as a hobby?"

"I mean, that's what she calls it, but I think that's crazy. She's really talented. She started doing it because she wanted to be able to make birthday cakes for her children, and it just kind of took off. Do you want me to get in touch with her?"

I nod. "Yeah. That would be great."

Sarah lets out a delighted squeal. "I'll let her know to get some samples ready." She reaches in her pocket and pulls out a card with an address under a stylized pink cake logo. "Just stop by tomorrow and pick them up. Thank you again for catching Mochi."

She waves and rushes back down the sidewalk. I watch her, then notice Malcolm glaring at me.

CHAPTER TWENTY

MALCOLM

That did not just happen. I did not just witness Miss "The Wedding Cake is the Most Important Thing at the Reception" agree to pick up samples from the sister of some woman we ran into on the sidewalk.

Bree narrows her eyes at me slightly. "What?"

"Are we seriously going to consider that woman's sister for baking Brandon and Olivia's wedding cake?"

"Her name is Bitsy."

I roll my eyes. "Because that just makes it so much better."

"It's not like we have an abundance of other options we're working with here," she says, continuing toward the car. "The bakery that already turned us down is the only one in town that does big cakes. Unless we want a bunch of little cakes stacked up together, this is what we have to go with."

"Isn't a big cake just a bunch of little cakes stacked together?" I ask.

"You know what I mean. The pictures Sarah showed me looked good. This woman has done weddings before, and they were pretty. We have to at least give her a chance. We can taste the samples and hope."

"Just because that bakery is the only one in Maple Valley that does big cakes doesn't mean that our only option is to depend on a woman making us something in her kitchen. There are plenty of bakeries in the city, ones that have a lot of professional experience."

"It would be absurd to get a cake delivered from an hour away. Do you know how many things could go so very wrong doing that? It could be a complete disaster in buttercream. Do you want to be the one to explain to Olivia why her cake is smeared all over the windows and carpet of a delivery van halfway down the highway?"

"People get wedding cakes delivered all the time. That's why the delivery vans exist."

"Look, the least we can do is give this woman a shot. It would be easier to have someone close to the venue and besides, all that professional experience makes me highly doubt that any of the bakeries in the city would be available to whip up a wedding cake for an event in two weeks. We're going to taste the samples and hope for the best."

"And if it's another Leonard situation?" I ask.

"If it's another Leonard situation, then we figure something out from there. And speaking of which, we need to find a different caterer."

"Let me see what I can do."

I take out my phone and start searching for other caterers in the area. It feels like a bit of a long shot. Apparently, the next few months are the hot season for weddings and other events throughout Maple Valley, and everybody needs food. I can only hope there is a new caterer out there looking for some business for that weekend. I call two and get nowhere before I notice a far-off, sad look in Bree's eyes as she looks at her phone.

"It's going to be all right. We're going to find something. Every caterer in the entire area can't be fully booked. And even if they are, we can look into restaurants. We will find someone. I promise."

She shakes her head, sweeping one hand back to smooth a strand of hair off her forehead. "It isn't just the catering."

"What is it, then?" I ask.

"Nothing, just a photo I saw. Don't worry about it."

"Tell me. There's obviously something bothering you. If it isn't the catering, what's wrong?"

Bree looks at me like she's trying to decide if she's going to answer me. I remember the way she closed off when she was talking about her ex and I don't want to push, but I hate how sad she looks. Finally, her shoulders drop.

"Olivia and I have been best friends basically our entire lives," she begins. "I don't even remember a time without her. We've done everything together and planned out our whole lives. Something we talked about all the time when we were little was our weddings. We would dream about what our dresses would look like and what kind of flowers we would have. We even went to the library and looked up old romance poets to try to find readings to include in our ceremonies. We used to go to the park and pretend we were having our weddings in the azalea garden. It was our favorite place in the world, and we always thought it would be the absolute perfect place to get married."

"What azalea garden?" I ask.

Bree looks surprised. "You don't know the azalea garden?"

"No."

"Have you ever been to the park in town?"

"I haven't."

She gives a little shrug. "It isn't what it used to be, and I just saw a photo online that reminded me of it. Back when I was younger, it was really well maintained. People were there all the time. There were little events there and everybody would go for picnics or just to walk the paths. It's not quite like that anymore, which is kind of sad."

"Would you show it to me?"

One eyebrow lifts. "You want to see the park?"

"Yeah. It sounds really nice."

"Okay. I'll take you."

We drive through town and pull down a narrow road leading into a parking area that looks somewhat weathered. The lines delineating the parking spots are faded and worn in places. There are some plants growing up through the pavement. But there are several cars scattered around the lot, and the sign marking the entrance to the walkway leading into the woods looks fairly new.

Bree leads me on to the wooded path, and we walk along in silence for several minutes. I can see where this used to be a beautiful and well-loved part, but it is looking a bit shabby. We pass by a playground that looks like it's from another era and a picnic pavilion with leaves and dried pine needles piled up on the roof. We continue on and eventually she turns off the main path into an area that almost reminds me of a hedge maze. The narrower paths are marked off by wooden beds filled with tangled bushes and vines.

She takes a shuddering breath as we get to the middle and she sees an open area cluttered with dead plants and a few pieces of discarded trash.

"This was the azalea garden," she explains. "It used to be so beautiful. All of these beds were full of azalea bushes in all sorts of different colors—pinks and white, purple. It was amazing when it bloomed every year. And right here in the middle was the gazebo. It was white and had benches all around the inside. This is where Olivia and I used to have our pretend wedding ceremonies. We would also visit with our families and have picnics. It was such a special place. I can't believe how neglected it's become."

"What happened to it?"

"I guess it isn't easy funding a place like this. and keeping up with it requires a lot of work. It just fell off people's radar, I suppose."

I can see how emotional Bree is getting, looking around at her old childhood spot and seeing how much the years have affected it. It's obvious how much the whole park, and this area especially, means to her. I understand what she means about publicly funded areas falling off the radar. It seems like a lot of places that are supported by local governments or organizations are suffering from not getting as much funding as they used to. Use of places like this might not seem as trendy and popular as it used to be, but there's something to be said for making sure that they are preserved and kept available. The better these places are, the more they will appeal to people and be enjoyed.

"What else was around here?" I ask.

"There are a couple of other playgrounds, some soccer fields, a lot of walking trails. There's another picnic pavilion. I'm not sure if it's still there or not, but there used to be a little circuit of exercise stations like a bench to do setups on and uneven bars."

"That sounds cool. Do you want to show me?"

"We should probably just get back to the wedding plans. There is still a lot to do. We should really get on those invitations. People don't have a lot of time to make their plans to get here."

"Yeah," I say. "If that's what you want to do. We can go back to the house and do that."

Bree takes a lingering glance over her shoulder as we get back into the parking lot, and I pretend not to notice it as we get in the car. As we drive back to Brandon and Olivia's house, I find myself stealing glances at her.

CHAPTER TWENTY-ONE

BREE

As soon as we get back to Brandon and Olivia's house, I go straight to the kitchen cabinet and pull out a bottle of wine. I feel like I am going to need a glass or two to get me through the evening.

It already feels like the day was a couple of days long and I still have more to do, including trying to figure out the invitations for the wedding. I can't believe Olivia didn't do anything about them, and even more than that, I can't believe it didn't occur to me that she wouldn't have. I'm the one who is supposed to be handling all of the arrangements and making sure that it goes off without any problems, and yet somehow I managed to totally miss the little detail of telling people where and when the rescheduled event is going to be.

Of course, Olivia isn't going to be able to do it. She isn't even in the country. She's not going to have all the contact information for her guests conveniently accessible or the time to sort through re-inviting everyone. You know who does have all the contact information for her guests conveniently accessible? Me. Because she left it for me. The invitations should have been in my planning notebook to begin with.

I'm right on top of stuff over here.

I sit down at the kitchen table and spread everything out in front of me. I look at all the names and remind myself of the daunting reality that the wedding is in two weeks. This brings me to a conclusion I really didn't want to have to come to. I swig down the rest of my wine and refill the glass.

"We're going to have to do e-vites," I declare.

"E-vites?" Malcolm asks.

"Yep. I really hate the idea, and I know it is far and away not something Olivia would want. She would have some pretty choice words to say about it, as a matter of fact. But we really don't have the luxury of being choosy right now. We don't have the time to come up with new invitations, address all the envelopes, get them in the mail, and actually expect them to get to anybody in time enough for them to make the decision to get to the wedding. It's already going to be difficult enough for them to change their plans with this little notice. Sending invitations through email is going to be the fastest way to get the information to everybody and collect the RSVPs. I already have everybody's names and email addresses. All we have to do is find an invitation template, plug in the details for the new date, and send them through."

"Is this something you prepared as a backup plan in your previous wedding planning?" Malcolm asks.

"Absolutely not," I say. "I would never have considered that I would be sending out digital wedding invitations–save the dates, possibly, but not actual invitations. I am a stationery and wax seal on the envelope kind of girl."

"Wax seal on the envelope? Wow. Full medieval vibes. That's next level."

I glare at him. "It's classic and traditional."

"All right." Malcolm takes out his phone and starts scrolling. A few moments later, he turns the screen toward me. "This one has a digital wax seal. How do you feel about that?"

"Somehow worse," I say. "But we'll go with it. I'll pull it up on my computer. It will be easier to type in all the information that way."

It doesn't take long to get the invitations filled out, then it's just a matter of getting all of the names and addresses put in and they are off into cyberspace. I send a little hopeful prayer along with them that people will be able to adjust their schedules and make it to the wedding.

I know chances are they aren't going to have anywhere near as many as they would have on the original date, but every loved one they can have there will mean the world to them.

With the invitations done, I look at my to-do list again and start trying to strategize how I'm going to handle everything else, which feels like just about everything. I look at the few little check marks along the side of the list to remind myself that I have actually made some progress.

But I'm having some trouble concentrating. As much as I'm trying not to think about it, I am having a lot of feelings about Trevor... well, not Trevor specifically. More about the absolute absurdity of me getting so wrapped up in him and the future I conjured up in my own head that I nearly planned my entire damn wedding without us even being engaged. And the breakup. That's causing some unpleasant twinges all its own.

"Bree?"

Malcolm saying my name sounds like it isn't the first time he said it in the last few seconds, and I realize I totally zoned out, drifting off into my own post-breakup hell.

"Hmm?"

"There are a couple of things that I need to do, so I'm going to head out for a little while. Is there anything that you need?"

"No. I'm good. I'm just going to be here trying to figure this stuff out."

"I won't be gone long." He gets his keys and leaves.

I spend another few minutes going over the list and planning tomorrow's efforts, but my brain keeps wandering back to Trevor. A third glass of wine doesn't help matters. Soon I find myself going against my best judgment, and all the best judgment in the entire world, by opening up social media and finding Trevor.

I should not be looking at his page. I should not be trying to find pictures of him or reading his posts, half hoping that I will find some sort of veiled message of regret and longing. Maybe three-quarters hoping. And I definitely shouldn't be scrolling back to see what he was up to while I was wallowing in misery. I should have blocked him and wiped all thought of him out of my computer, my phone, and my brain long ago.

And yet, here we are.

It doesn't take me long to confirm that there aren't going to be any angsty posts, coded or not. From the looks of things, he doesn't have much time to be coming up with anything like that. He is far too busy draping himself all over our friend Desiree. They are looking mighty cozy together, and I can't help but notice her showing up on his page a lot more frequently right around the time of our breakup.

It looks like she has been right there by his side to hold his hand through the breakup. In fact, she's been doing a lot of hand holding. At the movies. At a baseball game. At what used to be our favorite lunch restaurant… with some other friends at a party.

There isn't a single shred of evidence that he mourned our relationship for a second after walking away from my apartment. He seems to be out there living his best life, and that makes me inordinately angry. I manage to stop myself from leaving any comments on his page, but I do pick up my phone and call Olivia. I still don't know what time it is where she is and I still don't care. Time zones be damned. This is a situation that necessitates talking to my best friend.

"What's wrong?" she answers.

"Damn. That's chipper."

"Sorry. I just thought I'd save time."

"I could just be calling to say hi and check in with you."

"Shit," she said. "What's wrong? Did the orchard cancel, too? I'm going to kill Cyrus…."

"I am cyberstalking Trevor."

She goes silent right in the middle of her threat to the orchard owner. "You're what?" she asks, her voice flat.

"I got to thinking about all my wedding plans and that made me, of course, think about Trevor–"

"Stop. Nope. I can't even." She makes a gagging sound and I can almost see the look on her face. "Nope. You can't be serious right now." Another gag.

"All right," I say. "I got the point."

"Did you, though? Because I would have thought that you got the point when the jackass broke up with you on your anniversary when you thought he was going to propose."

"You aren't making me feel better."

"I'm sorry. Tell me what's going on."

"I went on his page just to check in." Another gag, but I continued. "And I don't know what I was expecting. I mean, okay, I guess I do. I was hoping…."

"That you'd see a bunch of pictures of the two of you together and mopey song lyrics and vague memes against unrelated watercolor or black and white landscape backgrounds expressing his longing for you?"

Damn, she knows me. "Sort of."

"Bree, be honest. Is that what you want?"

"No. That's the thing. I don't want him back. But I… want him to want me back? Oh, God, what is wrong with me? How did I become this?"

"You're fine," Olivia says. "It gets to the best of us. What did you see on his page?"

"That's the other thing," I say. "Desiree."

"Desiree?"

"You remember the girl I was telling you about a few months ago. She works as a bartender. Anyway, she was one of our friends. And now it seems they are very good friends, possibly for a suspicious length of time."

"Oh, Babe, I'm sorry. But honestly, you don't need to be thinking about that. It's not your problem anymore. You need to just close it out and stop looking him up. It's not going to do you any good."

I know she's right. I click out of the profile and close the computer. "All right. It's gone."

"Good. So casting him out of our thoughts and changing the subject. How is wedding planning going?"

"It's going great," I tell her, not wanting to worry her with a more accurate assessment. "Getting things done."

"Awesome. How is Malcolm?"

There's a teasing hint in her voice and I know exactly what she's thinking.

"Sorry to dash your dreams, but it's not really much different. He's nice to look at and that's about it."

"That's it?" Olivia asks.

"That's it. He's good at carrying your debit card around. There's something."

Olivia sighs. "All right. I've got to go. Don't look Trevor up again. Promise?"

"I won't."

"I'm going to need to hear you say it, Bree."

"I promise I will not look Trevor up again," I say, holding up a hand like I'm swearing even though she can't see me.

Ending the call, I get up and grab the basket from the boutique earlier, taking it with me into the bedroom. I really need to unwind at the end of the frustrating day, and since I'm all alone in the house right now, it's the perfect opportunity to try out some of these products.

I close the bedroom door and start the tub filling. My phone's battery is dying, so I plug it into the charger next to the bed and leave the bathroom door open a few inches so I can hear if the phone rings.

Sorting through all the goodies in the basket feels like a luxury all its own. I eventually select a bubble bath called "Champagne and Roses" and pour some into the running water. The tub immediately fills with rich, lofty bubbles and a sweet, heady smell. I twist my hair on top of my head and drop my clothes to the floor.

Stepping into the tub, I sink down into the bubbles and feel my entire body relax. It's nothing short of indulgent. The scent of the bubble bath is perfectly sweet and floral without being overwhelming. It has a velvety note to it that I wouldn't have expected. It soothes and relaxes me until I find myself falling asleep. The sound of Malcolm's voice snaps me awake a few minutes later.

"Bree?"

My head pops up as the door to the bathroom opens further. I scramble to cover myself with my hands, the bubbles, anything I possibly can.

"What are you doing? I'm in the bath!"

"I'm sorry," he says, turning his head sharply. "I'm sorry. I didn't see anything!"

CHAPTER TWENTY-TWO

MALCOLM

I definitely saw something.

I saw a lot.

But I get out of the bathroom as quickly as I possibly can and head for the kitchen. I have to do something to stop myself from thinking about how incredible Bree looked in that bath and just how intensely my body reacted to seeing her. I wanted to climb right into the tub along with her, but the way she seemed to panic when she realized I was standing there, and how frantically she covered up every bit of skin she possibly could, tells me that I wouldn't have been a welcome companion to her bath.

In the kitchen, I start taking ingredients and tools out so I can make dinner. She seemed to really enjoy the peanut noodles I made the other night, so I figured I would end our fairly stressful day of planning together with another home-cooked meal.

I have pork with my own mix of seasonings cooking on the stove and am chopping up vegetables for fresh guacamole when Bree comes down the hallway into the kitchen. She's wearing pajamas and has a robe tied tightly around her. The expression on her face is embarrassed and unsure whether she should even come into the room or just stay locked up in the bedroom and pretend that nothing ever happened.

Part of me thinks I should just gloss over the whole thing and go along with the pretending that nothing ever happened, but I can't bring myself to do it, not with the embarrassed look on her face. I just feel so bad, I need to say something.

"I'm really sorry for coming in like that," I say. "I didn't mean to intrude."

"You could have knocked," she says. "That's what people do when they get to a closed door."

"Well, technically the bathroom door wasn't all the way closed."

"The bedroom door was," she says.

"It was," I say. "And I knocked on it. And I called your name. And then I went in and I knocked on the bathroom door, too. But then you didn't answer and I was worried that something was wrong. People do drown in bathtubs, you know, or you could have fallen and hit your head. I didn't know. So I went in. Again, I'm sorry."

Bree shifts her weight back and forth on her feet and looks like she's debating how she wants to feel in this moment.

"Well, thanks for checking to make sure I wasn't dead."

"No problem. I had just gotten back and didn't see you still in the kitchen going over the plans, so I thought that you might be in the bedroom and was worried when I didn't see you or hear anything from you. And again, I didn't see anything."

Bree closes her eyes and holds up a hand like she's trying to stop me from saying anything else. "Can we just change the subject?"

"Sure. I am making dinner, pork and pineapple tacos. It's nothing fancy or anything, but they are really good. I'm making fresh guacamole to go with them. It should be ready in just a few minutes."

"Oh. I was just going to grab something quick out of the freezer." Her eyes travel over to the freezer and then to the stove where the pork is cooking. She draws in a breath and I know she is smelling the food.

"You really don't need to do that. I've already made a ton of stuff for tacos. There's no point in dirtying up more dishes or going through the hassle of making another meal, especially because that just means that I would have to pack up the leftovers and put them away, anyway. Just eat with me. I have pork, pineapple, rice, roasted corn, and fresh guacamole."

"Cheese?"

A hint of a smile comes to my lips. "I could grate up some cheese."

"All right," she says.

I don't really understand her apparent reluctance to eat with me. Maybe this is a Beauty and the Beast situation and she thinks if she eats with me, she is making too much of a connection and might actually get to know me a little bit, which, admittedly, could have its pluses and minuses.

"Good," I say. "Go ahead and start getting the plates out. If you want to find the cheese grater and grade up the cheese that's in the refrigerator, that would help, too. And there is a head of iceberg lettuce that you could tear up."

She goes to the refrigerator and opens the crisper to get the lettuce, then takes out a block of cheese and puts some on the counter. She already knows where the cheese grater is and takes it out, along with a bowl to grate the cheese into. She goes about her tasks in silence for a few seconds, then I notice a smile come to her face.

"When I was younger, my father used to make tacos all the time," she begins. "It was one of his favorite things, and he always liked to make as much of it as he possibly could. He even used to make tortillas some of the time. They were never really thin like the ones that you buy from the store because he didn't have a tortilla press, but he made them as thin as he could and they were so delicious. Sometimes I would sneak so many of the warm tortillas fresh out of the pan that I wasn't even hungry when it came time to actually sit down and eat. But one of my favorite things that my mother did on taco nights was take corn tortilla shells, just the regular hard ones, and bake them, then coat them with melted butter and roll them in cinnamon and sugar. She would serve them with vanilla ice cream, and it was kind of like fried ice cream that you can get in a Mexican restaurant. It was so delicious. Every time I eat tacos, it makes me think of them."

"It's nice that you have those memories," I say. "I don't really have any of that. I didn't have a mother, or a father, who did any real cooking. I actually can't come up with a single concrete memory of either one of them in the kitchen making a meal."

"Not even on Thanksgiving or Christmas?"

"Nope. They just weren't the cooking type. I'm sure that at some point in my life, one of them made something, but it just wasn't part of our daily lives. I started cooking a lot when I was younger because of that. I wanted to be able to choose what I wanted to eat and make it for myself rather than having to go out and find it or find somebody else who was willing to make it for me. Then as I got older, I got into the cooking shows and it just became a thing. It's really relaxing."

I artfully skim around the fact that the reason that my parents didn't do much cooking, or really any at all, is because we had a full kitchen staff and they were always responsible for preparing all of the meals and snacks that my family consumed, especially on the holidays. If it wasn't the staff cooking for us on Thanksgiving or Christmas, it was because we were having the meal catered by a restaurant or we were traveling for the holidays.

I remember thinking about it when I was younger and wondering what it would be like to have a mother who did things like make chocolate chip cookies or have special snacks waiting when I got home from school.

I never said anything to my parents about it. I don't know why. It just wasn't something that I thought needed to be mentioned. It seemed like I would sound ungrateful or like I was complaining about something frivolous. Looking back on it now, I wonder if I had said something if they would have changed. I want to believe that my mother would have made an effort to make something for me if I had wanted her to.

But I'm glad that I took that opportunity to develop the skills that I have come to enjoy so much. Even though I do my fair share of eating out and have private chefs come to my house on a fairly regular basis, it's still nice to be able to just go to the grocery store and get whatever I want and make it for myself without having to deal with anybody else.

Even though I don't share all of this with Bree, it still feels oddly good to tell her a little bit more about myself and have her look like she is genuinely interested in hearing about it. We finish preparing dinner and sit down at the kitchen table to eat.

"So, tell me about the body products from the boutique," I say.

Bree immediately looks embarrassed again and I wish I hadn't said anything, but she finishes her bite of taco and nods a little.

"They really are fantastic," she says. "The bubble bath that I used smelled absolutely amazing, and I tried a different lotion and it was really good, too. She gave me samples for a couple of different products that I had never tried before, and they are all so nice. When I was in the boutique smelling everything, I was thinking that it might be a good idea to get a couple of different scents of the products because different people like different things. Like we don't want to give the same smells to the men that we give to the women. And we might want to try mixing things up for the older guests and the younger guests."

"That sounds great," I tell her. "You just pick the ones that you think would be best for everybody, and we'll go back to the boutique tomorrow to get everything. Maybe we should give her a call first thing in the morning and let her know what we need. She could tell us what she has available and when we would be able to get everything else. That way, we have a better idea of what will actually go into the welcome bags."

"Good idea. Once we have those products on hand, we can choose some other things to put into the bags as well. I was thinking maybe some nice chocolates and a couple of just convenience things like little first aid kits, some pain relief pills, sewing kits, maybe?"

"I'm sure we can fill in with everything that we need. We'll tackle that tomorrow."

Bree looks like she is going to say something, but a notification chirps on her phone. She reaches over and flips it over so she can see the screen. Immediately a disgusted look comes over her face and she flips it back forcefully. Standing up sharply, she stomps over to the liquor cabinet and pulls out a bottle to pour a drink. She throws it back and pours herself another.

"Want one?" she asks, holding up the bottle.

"No, I'm okay. Is everything all right?"

"Everything is just peachy." She storms out of the kitchen toward the living room.

Obviously, she's upset. I give her a few minutes to herself while I clean up and then go into the living room to check on her. She is standing at a shelf looking over stacks of board games. There is nothing relaxed and at ease about her posture. In fact, it looks like any second she could start grabbing the boxes off of the shelves and flinging them around. Her hand grips the glass tightly and she's leaned close to the boxes, her jaw set as she reads the names of the games.

"Are you sure you're okay? You seem upset."

"Nope. Not upset. Doing great. Want to play a game?"

"Sure. What do you feel like playing?" I'm not exactly the board game type. The closest I ever really get to them is giving Brandon a good ribbing over him and Olivia devotedly collecting games from different generations and even from around the world. They are very proud of their collection, and I am happy to playfully make fun of them over it any opportunity I get.

But now does not seem like the right moment to tell Bree I don't really enjoy playing the games. She looks like she needs something to distract her and if a game will help, then I will go along with it. She snatches a box off the shelf and turns to show it to me.

"How about *Scrabble*?"

"Set it up," I say.

She sets the game up on the coffee table and we start playing. It doesn't take long for me to notice a fairly distinctive pattern in the words she is choosing to spell out.

Betrayed

Angry

Alone

Bitch

When we get to that last one, I figure there's a story behind this whole situation. She was fine when we were eating. She seemed fine right up until she got that notification on her phone. Whatever she saw when she looked at that screen sent her into what my nanny would have described as a tizzy. I figured out as a teenager that was just her really nice way of saying shit fit. However you want to put it, she's clearly worked up and I'm concerned.

"Do you want to talk about it?" I ask.

Her eyes sear into mine when she looks up from the score sheet, but then she lets out a heavy sigh.

"The notification was from my social media page. Somebody posted a memory that had my ex and me tagged in it. It just wasn't something that I felt like seeing right now."

"He really did a number on you, didn't he?" I ask.

"I think that is a pretty good assessment." She takes the final sip of her drink and looks into the glass with an expression that says she is contemplating whether she wants to get more, but has decided that it's probably in her best interest to cut herself off. At least for now. "All right, do you want to hear the story?"

"If you don't mind sharing it," I say.

"Here it goes," she begins. "I dated Trevor for years. I thought we had a really good relationship. As you know, we didn't live together, but I didn't put a whole lot of emphasis on that. I thought it was kind of sweet and romantic that we have this old-fashioned arrangement. We still had to actually date each other. It let us miss each other... all of those justifications and attitudes that I could tell myself that would make me feel better about the fact that I really should have been questioning why we never discussed living with each other after years of being together. Honestly, though, I really did think that we had something good going. We had a good rhythm. We got along well. I even thought we had fun together. and looking back at it, I can say that in the very beginning of our relationship, we did. And that's why I got it in my mind that he was the one. I figured that I had spent all this time dating him and that it was that time in my life when I needed to start thinking about settling down and figuring out what my future was going to be.

"He and I talked about our future together. At least, I thought we did. I thought that when we had those conversations, that it was both of us talking about it. Stick with me until the end of the story, and you will find out that is not actually the case. But, I don't want to get ahead of myself. Then you would miss the fun of reliving my humiliation at getting it into my mind that we were going to get engaged imminently."

"Which is why you were planning your wedding," I say.

She points at me. "You catch on quick. So, I decided this not just completely out of the blue. As I said, I thought we had been talking about our future. We had been together for a long time, and I will be willing to bet that Olivia getting engaged did get me fired up to plan my own wedding. When we were younger, we always liked to talk about having a double wedding and of course, that wasn't going to work out once we were actually adults, but it sounded like so much fun to be able to plan our wedding together and go through all of it at the same time. And then there was the little detail about it being Trevor and my anniversary."

"Oh, no," I say.

"Oh, yes," she continues. "He said he wanted us to get together and I figured that was the night. It was finally going to happen. We were going to get engaged and I was going to get my happily ever after. I could come back to Maple Valley and show everybody that I had made such a fantastic life for myself. I got all these plans already put into place, including having called Cyrus and made arrangements to tour the orchard venue while I was here for Olivia's engagement party. I was actually on the phone with her that day going over some of the plans that I had made and telling her about the samples of napkins I had ordered. I was completely wrapped up in this idea.

"And then Trevor showed up. I immediately noticed that he wasn't as dressed up as I thought he would be for a special anniversary dinner at which he was going to propose to me. But even that didn't tell me right off the bat that something was wrong. I thought maybe he was just being casual or he had planned something different than I had thought for the proposal. But, pretty quickly the conversation turned into me realizing that he didn't even know that it was our anniversary and that he had made plans with me and not to propose, but to break up with me. Remember what I told you to remember?"

"That you were the only one talking about your future?"

"There it is," she says. "He told me that the two of us had not been talking about our future together, but I had been the one that was talking about our future together and just didn't listen to him. He essentially told me that he was bored and wasn't happy with me, he felt like we hadn't been good in a long time and that we needed to not be together anymore. He left me standing there in my apartment all dressed up and knowing that Olivia was just waiting here at home for me to call and send her a picture of my engagement ring. And recently I discovered that he has been seeing a whole lot of a woman I used to consider a good friend and who we spent quite a lot of time with as a couple. I have a strong feeling that it isn't a new thing. So, there you go. The entire gory escapade."

I blink a few times. "Wow. you aren't kidding."

"No, I was not."

CHAPTER TWENTY-THREE

AS MUCH AS I DID NOT WANT TO POUR MY HEART OUT TO THIS GUY, IT IS a relief to tell Malcolm the whole story and finally get it off my chest. I realized there really isn't any reason why I should have kept it so locked up, anyway. It isn't like I have any reason to be embarrassed telling him about the breakup. I mean, any more embarrassed than I am just because of the basic facts of the whole situation.

"Well, if it makes you feel any better, I have a couple of breakup horror stories of my own," he says.

I give him a doubting lift of my eyebrow.

"Oh really? What have you got?"

"In high school, I asked a girl I liked to the homecoming dance," he explains. "I barely even knew her. I think we had exchanged maybe four or five words in the two years we had been in school together, and I just strolled right up to her and essentially said that we were going together and that I would pick her up at her house at seven."

"Oh, I'm sure that went spectacularly. Nothing that a girl likes more than a man demanding her be somewhere at a certain time when she gave no indication that she wanted to do something with him."

"Yeah, I thought I was being cool," he says. "You know, the whole bad boy, edgy thing. And I was just kind of an entitled jackass. I figured that there was no reason why any girl I wanted to go out with wouldn't immediately jump on the opportunity. So I told her and she said that was fine. Over a couple of days, I heard other people talking about us going together, so I figured that the plans were in place. I got all dressed up and I headed over to her place to pick her up, but she wasn't there. Her parents acted like they had absolutely no idea why I was there, and then I got a message from her with a picture of herself at dinner with another guy."

"That sucks, but it's not really a breakup nightmare story," Bree points out. "The two of you weren't dating, so it wasn't a break up. And, you asked for that."

"Okay, then how about the time I got a call from an art museum in the city telling me that there had been a cancellation and asking if my fiancé and I would be interested in moving our wedding date up? Problem was, I was not engaged."

"Cutting a little bit close to home," I say. "Also, that's an episode of *Friends*."

"Which means you would think that this woman would have realized it wasn't going to work. And yet, that's how it happened. Also, I should point out that not only was I not actually engaged, but I hadn't even actually met the woman who was planning our wedding. Turns out she was on the cleaning staff at my hotel and had come up with this entire relationship in her head."

"Okay, that's pretty bad, but it is still not a breakup story. Again, you weren't dating this woman, so it wasn't to break up." I get up and go into the kitchen, coming back with two glasses and a bottle of wine.

"Fine." Malcolm holds up his hands like he's surrendering. "Here it goes. I had been seeing this woman for just a few weeks. It wasn't anything serious. We had just been seeing each other kind of casually and had gone to one event together. I didn't think much of it and I decided that the two of us just really weren't compatible. I thought she was nice and had been attracted to her, but we just didn't click. There really wasn't anything to talk about when we were together, and I couldn't see spending any more time with her, so I decided that I would just tell her that it wasn't working out and it would be fine."

"It wasn't fine?"

"It was decidedly not fine," he says. "I didn't act like I was making any sort of special plans. I didn't tell her that we needed to get together, nothing like that. I literally started the conversation with the classic phrase that tells everybody what is about to happen."

"We need to talk," we say in unison.

"Exactly." He takes the glass of wine I'm handing out to him. "I figured that would be enough to let her know that we weren't going to be moving ahead. Again, I didn't think it was going to be a big deal. It wasn't like we had been together for a long time or had ever had any sort of conversation about being in a serious relationship. It was just not working. So I told her simply that. Thanks for the time together. Hope you have a great life. Done."

"Where did you tell her this?" I ask.

"You see, that's where my decision making probably wasn't the best. I didn't want to have her at either one of our houses and have it feel awkward at all. It was supposed to just be a quick thing and over with. So I met up with her at a coffee shop."

"I thought you said you didn't say you should get together."

"I didn't. I told her that we needed to talk and asked her to meet me there. When I told her, she completely went off the rails. She suddenly jumped up from the table and started screaming at me. She knocked my coffee all over me. She picked up a handful of napkins and threw them up in the air so that they fell around her like snow. She ran up and down the restaurant knocking over other people's drinks and screaming at them trying to get them to be on her side. I didn't even realize that this was a situation that was going to warrant sides at all. Then she started shouting about how heartless and irresponsible I was because she was five months pregnant."

"Wait...."

"Yep. Do the math on that one."

"She was expecting you to take care of somebody else's baby? How did you not notice she was pregnant?"

"Because she wasn't," he explains. "She made it up. I don't know if she had just lost track of how long we had been seeing each other. Or she thought that five months sounded good. I have no idea what was going through her head, but she started ranting and telling everybody who would listen and who hadn't already called the police about her that I was this horrible person who had taken advantage of her and needed to step up and be a man. Then the police came and she came back over to the table, sat down, and started drinking her coffee like nothing happened. When I asked her what was going on, she said we had just been having a conversation. Just a conversation. She ended up getting arrested, and I haven't spoken with her since."

I hold out my glass to toast him. "Now that is a breakup nightmare story."

He clinks the edge of his glass against mine and looks at the Scrabble board. "Are we going to keep going with this?"

"No. I think I'm done. How about some popcorn and TV?"

"Sounds good. You make the popcorn. I'll find a show."

He chooses an old sitcom rather than one of his cooking shows and as we're sitting there watching, I find my eyes sliding over to him. I like the way his laugh sounds and the way his head tilts when he thinks something is funny. Something is brewing between us, but I am not ready to acknowledge it. I'm not even ready to think about acknowledging it.

At the same moment, I lean forward to put the popcorn bowl on the coffee table and he leans to grab a handful. It brings our faces within a couple of inches of each other, and my breath catches in my chest. Our eyes meet, and then his move slowly down to my lips. His breath slides out of his lungs slowly, and I can feel it lingering between us.

My body moves closer to his. His hand slides across the cushion of the couch until his fingertips just brush my hip. His head tilts to the side, but this time it isn't because he thinks anything is funny. We move closer to each other, but just before our lips touch, I move away.

"It's getting late," I say. "I think I'm going to go ahead and get to bed."

"Oh, yeah," he says. "Right. Me, too. I'll see you in the morning."

We go our separate ways and I make sure the bedroom door is tightly shut before flopping down on the bed. I try to fall asleep flushed and flustered, not sure what to think about what's going on.

The next morning, I get up as early as possible and head into the kitchen to make breakfast. It feels like we have gotten ourselves into a bit of a pattern. Malcolm makes dinner and then I make an awkward breakfast, not knowing how the rest of the day is going to go. That is especially true this morning as I replay our near kiss in my mind. I can still feel his breath tracing along the front of my neck and see his eyelashes fluttering down as he looks at my lips.

I make myself stop and crack a few eggs into a bowl to make omelets. I'm not really expecting Malcolm to actually get out of bed on time considering how well that went yesterday, so I am pleasantly surprised when the door opens and he comes out fully dressed and seemingly ready to tackle the day.

Neither one of us seems to know exactly what we are supposed to do when he comes into the kitchen. He crosses right to the coffee maker and pours himself a cup. Leaning back against the counter, he takes a few steps and looks at the vegetables I am chopping to put into the omelet.

"Do you like mushrooms and onions in your omelette?" I ask.

"Yeah," he says. "That sounds good."

"Cheese?"

"Cheese is good."

"Peppers?"

"Also good."

The tension between us is palpable, and I am desperately hoping it will dissipate. There's no way I'm going to be able to focus on getting all of this planning done if it feels like I'm having to wade through thickened air just being around him. I finish making breakfast and we sit down to eat.

A few bites in, I reach over for my planning notebook and flip it open so that I can look over what I want to get done for the day. I am making a checklist when Malcolm's phone chirps. He pulls it out of his pocket as he takes a big bite of his breakfast. I notice his eyes widen and he makes an exclamatory sound.

"What?" I ask.

He swallows and washes the bite down with a gulp of orange juice, then turns his phone screen toward me. I can't see what it says on it, but he still points enthusiastically.

"We're saved!"

"What do you mean?" I ask.

"I heard about another caterer last night and I called them. They weren't open, but I left a voicemail explaining our situation and asking if they had any sort of availability. I just got a text from them saying that they do have availability for that weekend, and that we can come in and do a tasting with them."

"Then it sounds like we are up for a pretty busy and exciting day," I tell him. "I got a message this morning from Cyrus telling me there's an event at the venue this evening, and he asked if the DJ would mind coming in early so that we could check him out. He agreed to let us come this afternoon, and he'll play some stuff for us and answer any questions so we can decide if we want to hire him. He has availability for the wedding night."

Malcolm toasts me with his orange juice. "We're on a roll."

"I was also thinking we could do another walkthrough of the venue now that we have an idea of the flowers so we can make final plans for the decorations and stuff."

He takes the last bite of his omelet. "I'm up for it."

We get ready and head directly to the caterer. The first thing I notice when I walk through the door is three very small children running around. A flustered looking woman is trying to calm them down, attempting to entice them over into a corner with coloring books and Play-Doh. She looks up when she notices us come inside.

"Hi," she says. "I'm Aspen."

"Malcolm," he says, extending his hand to her.

"I'm Bree." I shake her hand.

A little girl runs up, encircling Aspen's legs with her arms and running around in a circle before dashing off again. Aspen lets out a sigh and gives us a weary smile.

"I'm sorry. I had to bring my children in with me today. Our usual babysitter came down with the flu, and I couldn't get any last-minute childcare. I hope that doesn't bother you."

She looks genuinely worried, like we are just going to turn around and leave because the little ones are there. I shake my head, trying to give her a reassuring smile.

"Of course not," I say. "Childcare is a problem for a lot of working parents. I would rather see you have them with you and be able to be here than not. And not just because you could be really saving our skin right now."

She laughs. "I did hear about the issue with the wedding. But, like you said, hopefully I can help you out. Did you have anything specific in mind?"

Malcolm and I exchange glances. He looks back at her.

"Something that tastes good?"

She laughs and gestures for us to follow her to the other side of the room where she has a table set up. There are a few platters of food laid out on the table with little labels in front of them describing what they are.

"I didn't have the time to put together a full menu for you, so there is a pretty limited tasting available. but I can do several other things and there are some options that you can choose from as well. Go ahead and try anything you want and let me know if you have any questions."

I'm a little bit cautious as I pick up my first bite, but I am relieved and thrilled that it is absolutely delicious. I immediately try something else and it is just as good. I have scarfed down several stuffed mushrooms, various canapés, and a piece of unbelievable beef by the time I come up for air.

"This is amazing."

Aspen smiles. "Thank you."

"I'm sold. Malcolm?"

He nods and flashes a thumbs up as he chews.

"You're hired."

"Great. I'll go get the paperwork." She pauses and looks back and forth between Malcolm and me. "The two of you look really cute together. I think you're going to be really happy."

CHAPTER TWENTY-FOUR

"I thought you said you explained the situation to her," Bree says as we leave the catering shop and head back to the car.

"I did," I say.

"Then why did she obviously assume that we are the ones getting married?"

"She didn't say that. She just said that we look cute together."

She gives me a look and stays silent for the rest of the walk to the car. We drive over to the boutique and pick up all of the items that we chose to go into the welcome bags. After putting them into the car, we stop by a gourmet food shop to get some chocolates and snacks that will last the two weeks until the wedding. That done, we finish our welcome bag shopping with a stop by the general store. By the time we're finished, we need to head to the venue.

I look up at the sky as we're getting back in the car. "Those clouds are looking angry."

"The weather didn't call for a storm today," Bree says.

My eyes drop to her across the top of the car. "Do you think they told the sky that? Because it really looks like it missed the memo."

"I hope it's okay. I hate storms."

We get in the car and head for the orchard. "I'm sure it will be fine."

The DJ has already gotten set up by the time we get to the reception hall at the menu. He has colored lights flashing on the dance floor and a light featuring a monogram I'm assuming belongs to a couple shining in the middle.

"Look at that." Bree points to the monogram. "Olivia would love that."

"It's something I like to do for couples for their weddings," the DJ says, coming down from the platform where he set up his equipment and offering his hand to shake. "Shane Nelson. Good to meet you."

"You, too. I'm Bree. You made that light?"

"Yeah. It's one of the little extras that I like to do. Most DJs just do music and hosting, but I like to put a personal touch on events when I can. I made one of those lights for my sister's wedding a couple of years back and people loved it. They kept asking where she got it, and then were coming to me asking if I'd make one for them, too. Eventually I just added it as an option. Now, I hear you're trying to get a wedding together in a couple weeks."

"Yes, we are."

"Then you're going to need some music. Let me spin a couple of tunes for you and see what you think."

He goes back behind the table and a song starts playing. The speakers are high quality and the music sounds crisp and immersive. Bree starts rocking back and forth a little to the tune as she looks around like she's trying to imagine the place set up for Olivia and Brandon's wedding.

It's easier with everything in place for tonight's event. When I look around, I can visualize the flowers we picked out and the food set up, making it all seem more real.

"Why don't you go ahead and test out the dance floor?"

Bree looks up at the DJ. "Oh. No, we don't need to do that."

"You should get the experience of dancing if you really want to be sure."

It's vaguely cryptic. I'm sure he's talking about us wanting to be sure about hiring him, but it sounds like he could be talking about something else.

"It isn't our wedding," Bree tells him. "We don't need to practice anything."

"I didn't say you needed to practice," he says. "I just said experience it, and you plan on dancing at the wedding, don't you? So give it a spin."

I walk over to Bree and extend my hand to her. "Come on. Let's try it out."

She looks hesitant, but I give her a light tug and pull her with me onto the floor. She lets me guide her into my arms and I feel her body fit perfectly against me. The music switches to something slower and Bree's breath glides out of her lungs with a slight tremble. We dance close together in the middle of the floor, surrounded by the colored lights. At first, she looks over my shoulder, but then her head tilts slightly back so she looks up at me.

With just that simple gesture, I'm done for. I can't resist the way she looks gazing up at me or the feeling of her body pressed against mine. I pull her closer, pressing my hand to the middle of her back and lower my mouth to hers. After a second, I deepen the kiss. It feels like she is kissing me back, then she moves and pulls out of my grasp.

"We've got to get going," she says quickly. "We need to go pick up the samples for the wedding cake." She turns attention to the DJ. "Thank you. If you're available, I think you'd be great for the reception. Cyrus has my contact information. You can just email the contract and invoice if that works for you."

She hurries out of the venue and I rush to catch up with her.

"Bree, I'm sorry. I shouldn't have done that. I just got caught up...."

She waves her hand to dismiss the words and make me stop talking. "It's fine. Let's just move on."

She obviously wants to pretend like the kiss never happened, but I can't do that. With that one little taste of her, I know I want so much more.

It's just starting to rain when we get to Bitsy's house. She has the same kind of bright smile and bubbly personality as her sister. She welcomes us into the house and brings us into the dining room, where there are several binders sitting on the table.

"These are some pictures of cakes that I've done before. If you want to flip through them and give me an idea of what you're thinking for the cake, we could get some ideas down."

Bree and I sit down and start looking through the books. We point out a couple of the pictures that have details we especially like and Bitsy starts sketching a basic idea onto a pad. She jots down ideas for decorative elements that Bree mentions. When we're done, she goes into her kitchen and comes back with an armful of little boxes.

"These are samples of my flavors. There are also a couple of different combinations that are really popular. Take them home and taste them. See what you think. If you have any other flavors that you might like or different combinations that you would want to try, give me a call and I can put something else together for you."

"Thank you." Bree takes some of the boxes and I take the rest before leaving the house.

As soon as we get back to Olivia and Brandon's house, we drop the cake samples off in the kitchen and Bree heads toward the bedroom. The rain had gotten pretty heavy by the time we got here, so I imagine she wants to take a shower and change into something dry and warm. I'm surprised when she comes out just a few minutes later in a different outfit with her hair swept up into a ponytail.

"I need some time away from all the wedding planning," she says. "I'm going to go meet up with some old friends for dinner. I'll be back later."

I'm disappointed we won't be continuing our routine of dinner and watching TV together, but I don't show that I'm upset. I go to the kitchen to find something simple to make for myself.

"Have a good time. Be careful. The weather isn't great out there."

She leaves without saying anything and I tell myself it's ridiculous to be upset that she is going out. This is her hometown, and there are plenty of people who are still here who she doesn't get to see very often. Of course she would want to see them when she is in town. It isn't like she has any sort of obligation to me or we have any sort of actual standing plans to keep up with. And after that kiss, it seems she doesn't just want time away from the planning. She wants time away from me.

Shit.

Since I'm alone, I throw together a couple of turkey sandwiches and a pile of potato chips and carry it into the living room with me. I don't need to cover anything up, so I decide to check in on work. I've been reading through a mountain of emails and leaving voice messages to remind myself of things I need to take care of when my phone rings. For a brief moment I think that it might be Bree, but then I tell myself that it's ridiculous. Why would she call me? Looking at the screen, I see that it is Brandon.

"Hey," I answer.

"Hey," he says. "You don't sound great. What's going on?"

"Nothing, I'm just checking in on work."

"Work? Where is Bree?"

"She decided to go out with some friends tonight," I say.

"What's with the tone?"

"What do you mean? What tone?"

"The tone in your voice when you say that. You sound like you're upset that she went out without you."

"Why would I be upset that she went out without me?" I ask. "I told you, I'm just doing some work. and it's raining outside."

"What does that have to do with anything?" He pauses. "You're worried about her."

"I'm not worried about her."

"Yes, you are. You're worried about her because she's out driving in the rain. Malcolm, do you have feelings for Bree? Is that what's going on?"

I could deny it, but there really wouldn't be much point. Brandon knows me better than anybody else, and he would be able to tell right off the bat that I was lying to him.

"It's not a big deal," I say. "I might be a little bit attracted to her. That's all. We're spending a lot of time together. It's only natural that we would start to develop something. It's a proximity thing, I'm sure."

"We? Does she have feelings for you, too?"

"No *we*," I say. "There is no *we*. We haven't talked about anything. We haven't done anything. It's not a big deal."

"All right," Brandon says. "If you say so. I won't bother you about it anymore. I just wanted to see how everything is going. Did you find a caterer?"

"We did. And we got some samples from a bakery for the cake. We hired a DJ today. Everything's coming together."

"I knew you two could pull it off. Olivia is right on the edge. I keep thinking I'm going to wake up, and she will have flown back in a panic."

"She's not going to do that," I say. "She wants to be there with you. And she knows that we have this handled. Everything's going to be perfect when you get back. And then you get to get married and have your happily ever after."

There's a long pause. "Our happily ever after? Holy shit. You've got it bad."

"No, I don't. I told you. It's not a big deal." I pop the last potato chip in my mouth and bring my dishes into the kitchen.

"Right."

"Don't you have something Norwegian you should be doing?"

"I think I could find that offensive if I wanted to."

"I'm hanging up now."

Even with my protesting, as I hang up, I feel in my gut that this might be bigger than I am willing to let on. I go back to my work and the rain outside gets heavier. Thunder crashes overhead and I start to really worry about Bree.

I don't like her being out in the storm like this. It can be dangerous to drive in heavy rain, especially on the dark back roads surrounding the town. Depending on where she was going to meet up with her friends, she could find herself without visibility on a dangerous, narrow road. I want to call her, but that could be even more dangerous if it startled or distracted her. I go take a shower and hope that she's back when I get out, but she's still not here when I come out with my laundry.

Throwing a load of clothes into the wash helps distract me for another few minutes, but I have to worry for another half an hour before the door finally opens. I'm relieved when she comes in and slams the door behind her. She's soaked to the bone and looks less than pleased, but at least she's here.

She stomps right past me toward the bedroom and almost like the sound causes it, as soon as she slams the door behind her, the power goes out.

CHAPTER TWENTY-FIVE

BREE

Damn. Damn, damn, damn.

I hate power outages. It might sound ridiculous, and maybe I am some kind of baby being afraid of the dark, but power outages are one of my least favorite things. just the idea of not having any electricity terrifies me. Especially when it is storming and at night.

"Bree? Are you okay?" Malcolm's voice is right on the other side of the door. At least he isn't just coming in this time.

"I'm all right. I'm just trying to change out of these wet clothes."

"Do you have a flashlight or anything in there with you?"

"No," I say. "My phone died. I was going to put it on the charger."

"Okay. Are you still going to try to change?"

"Yeah, I can't be in these wet clothes. I'll try to figure it out. There's a little bit of light coming in from the window." I put my hands out in front of me to feel around so I can get to the dresser. "Feels like a haunted house at Halloween."

"It's kind of fun."

"I hate haunted houses at Halloween."

"Okay. Maybe not so much fun. Just get changed and then I'll come in there with a light and get you out."

I finally find the dresser and use the meager bit of light coming in through the window to find some sweats. I was really hoping to take a shower, but that's not happening. I get out of my clothes and into the warm pajamas. "I'm ready."

The door opens and the glow from the flashlight feature on Malcolm's cell phone greets me.

"You okay?"

"Yeah. I just really hate when the power goes out. It's so quiet."

"Quiet?"

"Yeah." I rub my arms to take away the chill. "You don't really think about the fact that you can hear electricity, all the time. But as soon as the electricity goes out, it is so quiet. I really hate that."

"Well, it's going to be fine. I'm sure the power isn't going to be out for a very long. And in the meantime, if I know Brandon, there are going to be lanterns all around the house. He likes to be prepared for storms."

"Then why isn't there one in the bedroom?"

"There might be. Let's look around." Malcolm holds up his light to eliminate more of the room and we look in the side table and then in the closet. Right there on the top shelf is a pair of camping lanterns.

We take the lanterns down and turn them on. He puts his phone away and we use our lights to navigate around the house collecting more of the emergency light sources Brandon has hidden around.

"What do we do now?" I ask.

"Let's grab some pillows and blankets and bring them into the living room. We can make a little cozy place to hang out until the lights come back on. I'm sure there are some snacks and things in the kitchen that we can munch on."

We detour through the kitchen to collect some snacks, then go into the living room and set up all of the lanterns.

"This kind of reminds me of the sleepovers Olivia and I used to have when we were younger," I say, wrapping a blanket around myself. "We used to set up little forts in her living room with all the pillows and blankets and cushions we could find."

"Do you want to play another board game to pass the time?"

I shake my head. "No."

"Okay. Well, what did you do at these sleepovers in your forts if you were too cool for board games?"

"We played cards."

"Like the hip, happening girls you are. All right. I think I saw a deck over on the shelf. I'll get it." He takes one of the lanterns with him and comes back with a deck of cards.

"What's your game?" I ask, taking the deck and shuffling the cards.

"War."

I scoff. "Predictable."

"What's yours?"

I keep shuffling, my eyes downcast. "Old Maid."

A burst of laughter explodes from Malcolm, but he covers his mouth with his hand and when he lowers it, his lips are pressed tightly together. His shoulders are still shaking as he tries to get himself together.

"Sorry," he manages.

I grab a pillow and toss it at him. "Stop it." I hand him the cards. "Just deal."

A few rounds of War and Old Maid take the edge off my anxiety and I start to forget that the power is even out. Then a massive bolt of lightning makes the whole room glow and my heart leaps into my throat. With the huge crash of thunder that follows, I throw myself into Malcolm's lap. He wraps his arms around me and pulls me close.

The heat is instant. I want to pull away. I should pull away. But I can't. And maybe I don't really want to.

"I'm sorry," I whisper.

He tucks his finger under my chin and tilts my mouth up to his.

The kiss is soft and gentle. He pulls back and looks into my eyes. An instant later, his mouth crushes down on mine again and he kisses me hungrily.

He lifts me as his tongue slips between my lips and I straddle him as he sets me back down. I can't help but let out a whimper as his strong arms move me into place, and the sound seems to drive him to be even more assertive. Both hands squeeze my ass and pull me down over him. His thick, hard cock presses against his pants and into my center, separated only by the thin fabric of the pajama pants.

My breath catches in my throat and I pull back from the kiss.

His lips eagerly go to my throat, kissing, then licking me, running the tip down my collarbone to the button of the silky pajama top. I lean back, giving him permission to do as he wants.

One hand leaves my backside and swipes down quickly and decisively over my chest, unbuttoning my shirt effortlessly. As it folds away from my body, the cool air of the room hardens my nipples and he takes one into his mouth instantly. I groan in pleasure as my hips begin to grind onto him, my body desperate for his.

Breath hitching, I reach below and find his zipper. As I pull down, he shifts and turns me, gently laying me back on the couch. My hands reach for him but he stands, and they fall on his crotch, perhaps purposefully. I can't tell anymore. It's as if my body has taken over, grasping at what it needs, my mind not part of the equation at all.

His pants fall, and he kicks them off, but I am focused on the bulge pressing against his boxer-briefs. I snatch at the waistband and pull them down, and his throbbing member springs out at me. I want to take him into my mouth, to pleasure him with my tongue and taste him, but before I can do more than wrap my hand around his base, he is reaching down to yank off my pants.

I guide him to me as I kick off the loose remaining leg of pajama pants and settle back as he slips between my thighs. Our eyes connect as I let go of him, and the head of his cock brushes against my lower lips, wetting it with the lather gathering there. Another crushing kiss, sinking my head back into the cushions, is accompanied by an initial thrust, and stars fill my vision.

My body shakes as he enters me, driving deep into my core, impossibly filling and bringing me to the messy grey area between pleasure and pain, where the two mix and swirl and bring a sensation I'd never really felt before. It isn't just that he was girthy and long, but curved just so, so that it's as if his body was made to be inside mine. Like puzzle pieces, we fit, and my legs wrapped around his waist as if I were trying to keep him there forever.

Slowly, he rocks back and then forward again, and a gasping yelp escapes my lips. Momentarily, he pauses, a slight worried look crossing his face, and I pull him back in for another kiss, then brushes my lips across his cheek to his ear, my nails clenching down into his back.

"Don't stop," I whisper. "Please, don't stop."

The rocking begins again, but this time more forcefully, and picking up speed as it goes. My legs begin to go numb as my body is overwhelmed with pleasure. I feel like I can't breathe, but in the most exotic of ways. As he begins to pound into me, I let myself go, acquiescing all control to him, giving him my body to use as he wished, knowing the pleasure I would most certainly feel.

One of his hands slides up my body, filling with my breast, while the other presses into the cushions above my head. I use the opportunity to pull at his shirt, yanking it open so I can run my fingers over his chest and abdomen. Fingertips dip in and out of the hardened ridges of his stomach muscles as they clench each time he slides deeper into me.

Giddily, I reach up and lick his chest, rising up his neck and bite not so gently into his shoulder. This seems to embolden him and he increases his speed even faster. Dizzyingly, I clench onto him, the wave of a climax building with such intensity and speed that I know I am unable to control it.

I try to hold it off, to time it with his own, but it's no use. The pleasure is too much.

My toes curl and my legs shake as I come, wave after wave of an intense orgasm riddling my body with twitches and clenches. Grunting above me, Malcolm seems to notice and pulls my legs up, folding me in half below him, dominating me.

We slide back onto the floor together, but he doesn't miss the rhythm at all. The orgasm only intensifies as our eyes burn into one another and I can see the exertion etched in his face.

"Come for me," I beg him. "I want to feel it!"

It starts as a dull grumble, but soon, a heavenly growling roar builds in his chest. His eyes clench and he thrusts deeply inside me, one hand squeezing tightly over my breast and the other folded by my head resting his body weight on his elbow. The throbbing of his cock inside me sends me into an even higher climax that leaves me completely breathless as he collapses on top of me.

Jerking as he continues to come, his body clenches above me and I smile contentedly. I'd never climaxed that hard before in my life, and my body feels like jelly. I could lay here, with his weight crushing down on me, happily forever. But he slowly slides to the side, still inside me, and I turn so we can lie face to face on the floor.

Then, I bury my head into his chest and exhale slowly, as his arms wrap around my shoulders and pull me deep into his scent.

CHAPTER TWENTY-SIX

MALCOLM

The power suddenly coming back on blasts me out of sleep. We turned off all of the lanterns as we were drifting off last night, and the sudden bright lights in my eyes startle me out of my peaceful slumber. Bree and I are still sprawled naked across the living room floor, partially covered with some of the blankets we brought in from the other rooms. Me waking up jostles her and she groans a little, wriggling so her warm body presses against mine even more.

I run my hand down her back and she opens her eyes. Her hair is falling over them and the disheveled look somehow makes her even sexier.

"Good morning." I move to give her a kiss, but she sits up and grabs a blanket to wrap around herself as she stands.

"I'm going to go take a shower."

She rushes off, leaving me sitting in the middle of the floor not knowing what just happened. I have no idea what I'm supposed to think right now. The sex was amazing—not just good, really incredible. It felt like we had a real connection and when we fell asleep in each other's arms, it was comfortable and natural. But now she's avoiding even looking at me and trying to get out of the room as fast as she can.

Maybe last night was just an impulsive moment. Maybe she thinks of it as a mistake. and maybe she is still wrapped up thinking about her ex too much. From the story she told me the other night, it sounds like he really broke her heart, and maybe she hasn't fully gotten over him. It's possible she wasn't ready to try anything with somebody else.

I decide not to push it. I definitely don't think it was a mistake and I don't regret it, but I'm also not going to try to make anything out of it. Grabbing one of the lanterns to bring into the guest room with me, I drop it off and then go into the hall bathroom for a shower.

Her bedroom door is still closed when I come out, and I go into the guest room to go to bed. It takes a long time to fall back to sleep. I can't stop thinking about Bree and how much I wish I was curled up in bed with her right now.

The next morning, we are back to our routine. Bree is in the kitchen when I get up. The house smells like apples and cinnamon and she is pulling a tray of freshly baked muffins out of the oven when I step into the room. I love the way she looks bent over at the oven like that and my reaction to the sight of her with those muffins is something close to primal.

But I keep myself from saying anything about it. I grab the juice out of the refrigerator and pour coffee. Bree puts the muffins on a plate and gets butter. We sit down and eat in silence. It isn't as tense and uncomfortable as it was yesterday morning, but we are both obviously lost in our thoughts.

I wonder if I should say something, but before I do, she opens that ever-present planning notebook and runs her finger down the list of things that we are still left to do.

"I think we should go ahead and finish the welcome bags today," she says. "We already got all that stuff. I think there might be a couple of extra things that I want to add right before the wedding, but we can get a bunch of them packed so that Olivia and Brandon don't have to worry about it when they get back here. There isn't going to be a lot of time before the wedding and I want to take as much stress off of them as I possibly can."

"Sounds like a plan. Have we gotten very many RSVPs?"

"I checked the e-vite site earlier this morning and we actually have gotten quite a few," she says. "It seems like most people are changing their plans to be able to get to the wedding. There are still some we haven't heard anything from and a couple of people had to say they aren't able to make it, but it looks like we're going to have a pretty good crowd. I'm really happy for Olivia. But that also means that we need to get these bags ready for all those people who are coming in from out of town. With all the hassle they are going through to change their arrangements and make it here early, I want to make sure that everything is extra special for them."

"Absolutely. Let's go ahead and get going and see if there's anything else that we can find to put in the bags and then we can start filling them."

We don't have to spend a lot of time in town. We already got most of what we will be putting into the welcome bags yesterday, so it's just a few little extras that we decide to pick up along with a pack of tags that we can use to put the names of the guests and a little note on each. We figure that will also make it easier for the hotel to get them to their proper rooms.

Once we have everything, we go back to Brandon and Olivia's house and set up in the living room. A couple of the pillows and blankets are still pushed off to the side of the floor, and I am very aware of our last use of this space and that couch.

My heart rate picks up a little when she sits down and leans over to spread out some of the items, causing the neckline of her shirt to dip low and reveal the swell of her cleavage. I can still feel my mouth on her, still taste her skin and the beads of sweat that rolled down it in response to my touch.

I force myself to look away and concentrate on opening the small paper bags we'll be filling. Bree opens her laptop on the coffee table and pulls up the list of RSVPs.

"All right, I have everything organized so we can just grab things from each pile and put them in. I'll handle adding the body products and candles so I can choose the scents according to the recipient. Ready?"

"Take it away." I make a rolling gesture with my hand.

As I start filling the bags, she goes to work writing the names of the guests on the tags. As we fall into a comfortable conversation about nothing in particular, I find myself pausing just to watch her. I know that what I'm starting to feel for her is far more than just physical.

There's something special about Bree, and I want more of it.

But even as I'm feeling that, I get a twinge of guilt. I feel bad for not being totally upfront with her about who I am. When I first met her, I had no intention of spending any real time with her. I didn't think we would see each other beyond the wedding events. and even if we did run into each other when she was coming to town to visit Olivia, it really didn't have that much of an impact on me.

All I knew was that I was playing along with this challenge with Brandon, and that included not telling Bree about my businesses or my money. at some point, we would probably end up telling her, but it wouldn't matter. I didn't care what she thought of me.

Now that has changed. I feel guilty about everything that I have been hiding from her and who she thinks I am. For a brief second I think about going ahead and telling her, but then she looks at me with a cute little smile and I change my mind. I can't do it right now. I can't just blurt that out and expect everything to be okay. I will have to choose a much better time and place. I'll come up with the right way to finally be fully honest with her.

Getting the bags put together takes a lot longer than I was expecting it to and I'm feeling cramped and stiff when I'm finally able to put the last completed bag to the side and stand up. Bree does the same and stretches her back, letting out a little sigh.

"I'm starving," she says after a while. "I'm going to make lunch. Does anything sound good to you?"

"I was actually thinking about ordering a pizza. I've been craving one for the last couple of days."

"Sounds good to me," she agreed. "But I'm not going to make it until something is delivered. I'll just grab a quick snack. Order whatever."

She goes off to the kitchen and I call up to the best pizzeria in Maple Valley. I order a couple of pizzas and a side of garlic bread for delivery, then pull up a text thread with my assistant. I quickly jot out a note telling him I have a few ideas I want to talk about when I get back to work. There are some things that have been going through my mind, and I want to talk them over with him to see how we can get them rolling.

I'm closing the thread when Bree comes back into the room with a plate of cheese and crackers.

"What are you doing?"

"Nothing important." I snag a cracker and a chunk of cheese from the plate. "The pizza should be here in about twenty minutes."

She drops down on the couch and starts scrolling through her phone. She makes a surprised sound. "The Glowing Garden event starts tonight. I used to go to that all the time. It was one of my favorite things to do when I still lived in Maple Valley. Have you ever been?"

I shake my head. "No."

"It's gorgeous. You know where it is, right?"

"Not really. I've heard of it, but I've never really looked into it."

"The Draper Estate at the far end of town. It was one of the original houses way back when the town was settled. It has all these expansive gardens and incredible grounds. They never had any children and when they died, they left the estate to the town with the caveat that it be used for public enjoyment. Essentially nobody could sell it or anything. Anyway, every year, the historic preservation society that runs the estate sets up this glow experience. There are thousands of lights and displays. People get glow necklaces and glow sticks and go walk around. They even have food trucks and live music. It's really fun."

"Do you want to go?"

Bree looks at me with a slightly unsure expression. "Really?"

"Why not? We've worked really hard. We deserve some fun. And if it's something that you used to do all the time when you lived here, you should do it again."

"All right." she grins. "I'm excited."

"Me, too."

CHAPTER TWENTY-SEVEN

Bree

I'm really looking forward to going to the Glowing Garden event. It's been a few years since I've been in town during it. The historical preservation society only puts the event on for a couple of nights each year, and I was never able to convince Trevor to take the trip to see it. I tried to explain to him just how beautiful and romantic it was, but he didn't care.

I actually think me telling him that I thought it was romantic is a big part of why he refused to go. Every time I said it, he reminded me that I used to go with my family and with Olivia, so obviously it couldn't have been but so romantic. He just didn't understand how something could change depending on who you were with.

I should have seen the signs sooner. I really should have recognized what was going on before I did... well, before he made it abundantly crystal clear.

The doorbell rings and I watch Malcolm go over to get the pizzas. I'm surprised by a little flutter that goes through my heart.

We eat and spend a couple of hours prowling the internet for some of the simpler details of the wedding like remaking their programs for the printer and ordering napkins.

"Check this out." Malcolm shows me a handheld embosser. "It's like a library stamp. We can have it made in their monogram and then emboss the programs and even the napkins."

"That would be such a nice detail. Can they get it made in time?"

He checks the delivery estimate. "It would be tight, but it could get done."

"Let's do it." I glance at the time and see how late it's getting. "We should get ready to go if you still want to."

"Of course, I want to."

I can't help the smile that spreads across my face.

We get dressed and head out. This time, I walk over to his car. Malcolm looks at me with raised eyebrows.

"I actually get to drive?"

I give a one-shoulder shrug. "Mixing it up."

The lights are visible even from a distance as we approach the parking area for the estate. Brightly colored tube lights are coiled around the spindles of the old iron gate leading into the parking area and a sign arches over the entrance road. There are already a ton of cars parked when we pull in, and we have to go up and down a few rows before we find a spot.

"Wow. This place is packed."

I nod, looking out the window at the people streaming onto the grounds. "I told you. It's one of the most popular events in town. I can't believe you've never gone."

"This isn't something that my parents would have been interested in visiting," he says. "They weren't particularly fond of the outdoors if it didn't involve sailing or visiting the beach. I'm glad I'm here now."

I look across the car at him and smile. "Me, too."

We find a spot and park. Right outside the main gate to the grounds, a kiosk is set up selling glowing novelties. Children swarm around it, but I step right up to it with them. I grab a handful of glow-sticks and glow necklaces and hand the cashier some cash, then walk back over to Malcolm. He takes the sticks and necklace I hold out to him.

"Get into the spirit," I tell him.

"Okay."

He puts on the necklace and I giggle at the sight of the bright blue glow illuminating his face. Decked out and ready, we head inside.

The event is even more spectacular than I remember. It looks like it has undergone some improvements and growth in the years since I've visited and it is amazing. Everywhere we look there are glowing displays and shimmering lights. We walk down the main path toward a large field at the center of the estate and I see the little shopping village they set up each year. There are craft vendors and specialty artisans that I know a lot of people flock to as an early start to their holiday shopping.

Nearby, columns constructed of glowing acrylic blocks mark the entrance to a tent lined with fairy lights. I point it out.

"That's the bar. Want to get a drink?"

Malcolm nods and we head that way. Inside there are more of the illuminated blocks forming tall tables where people are standing with their drinks. We stand in line until a bartender is available and then walk up to the counter. She smiles at us.

"What can I get you?" she asks.

"What's the Moonlight Magic?" I ask, looking at the menu.

"That's my favorite," she says. "It's perfect if you like sweet drinks and a little bit of magic."

I glance up at Malcolm, who shrugs and gives a nod.

I look back at the bartender. "Go for it."

She takes out two glasses and sets them on the counter in front of us. Dropping a plastic ice cube into each one, she leans down again and pulls out a plastic stand that looks like it should be in a science lab. It's holding several glass tubes with corks. Each is partially filled with different colors of popping boba pearls.

"Which flavor?" she asks, displaying the tubes. "There's peach, watermelon, apple, strawberry, grape, or lychee."

"Watermelon," Malcolm says.

"I think I'll go with lychee."

She takes the tubes and returns the stand under the counter, then hands us the tubes. "Pour these in the glasses."

As we empty the tubes, she takes out a bag and reaches inside. She comes out with a puff of cotton candy. Breaking into two, she waits until we have emptied our tubes completely and then puts a piece of the candy on the top of each glass. She takes out two bottles and holds them over the glasses.

"Are you ready for the magic?"

We nod and she pours the drink from the bottles. It melts the cotton candy and when it hits the plastic ice cubes, they light up. I laugh, delighted by the simple little trick. It even earns a chuckle and some applause from Malcolm.

We pay the bartender and thank her, then take our drinks and leave the tent. The band has started playing and the music surrounds us as we continue deeper into the grounds. Malcolm takes a sip of the swirling blue drink.

"It's definitely sweet, but I like it."

"Does it taste like moonlight?"

He laughs and takes another sip. "There's some sort of angsty teenage poetry in there somewhere."

"I am very deep." I smile at him over the rim of my glass.

Most of the activity is centered around the village and the displays at the front of the estate, but there is much more along the walking trails leading down into the grounds. It gets quieter as we walk along until it feels almost like we are the only people here. A staff member meets us on the trail and offers to take our empty glasses when we're finished with our drinks. We hand them over and keep going, enjoying the tranquility of the crisp night and the beautiful glow of the lights around us.

I suddenly feel Malcolm's hand at my side. At first it just brushes against mine. Then his fingers grasp mine. Finally, they link and we continue walking holding hands.

We stroll through the grounds for a couple of hours before going back to the parking lot and heading to the house.

When we walk inside, Malcolm looks like something suddenly popped into his head.

"What is it?" I ask.

"The cake samples. We completely forgot that we went and picked up those cake samples. We haven't even tasted them yet."

"Oh. We should definitely do that. I'll grab them."

I go over to the counter where the little boxes are stacked and carry them over to the island. I spread them out and Malcolm opens one of them, revealing tiny sample squares in a variety of colors. A card inside tells us what each one is.

He looks at the card, then takes out one of the squares. "This is classic vanilla with vanilla buttercream."

He bites the square in half.

"So?"

He nods. "It's delicious. Try it."

He holds the rest of the square out to me. Rather than taking it from him, I lean forward and sweep it from his fingers with my tongue. It is delicious, but all I'm thinking about right now is his melting gaze and the heat between my thighs.

Malcolm reaches forward and takes my wrist, pulling me toward him. Our lips meet and I sink into the kiss as he wraps an arm around my waist. Much like last time, he lifts me, only this time, he carries me effortlessly to the island and sits me down so our heads are level with each other. As I reach for his shirt to unbutton it, he is already working on my pants. Gleefully, I lift myself up as he pulls them off me and tosses them away.

I expect he is going to rip off my shirt next, and I lean back but he dips below me, going to his knees and forcing my legs to part. I gasp as his tongue slides across my thigh, and my breath hitches as he reaches my hip. Biting my lower lip, I watch as he runs the tip of his tongue along my pussy lip, then slides inside, brushing across my clit and sending a wave of intense pleasure through my body.

My legs involuntarily twitch as he slides his tongue through my folds, lapping me up and seeming to know just how much pressure and where to touch me that it drives me absolutely mad. I close my eyes and rest my head backward, focusing on the sensation as he slowly slips a finger inside me. The combination of his tongue brushing across my pearl along with the thickness of his finger teasing me and the pad running against my upper walls is almost enough to send me into a climax right there.

I reach down and fill my hand with his hair, wanting to both pull him away to give me a moment to breathe and simultaneously pull him deeper so he presses harder, deeper inside me. He groans with delight and my thighs clench around his neck.

There's no holding back now. I am powerless to stop the rushing orgasm that overloads my system and doesn't give me a chance to stop it. I cry out as his tongue speeds up and his finger dives deeper, and my toes curl on his back. I collapse onto my back as the sensation riddles through my body, and he stands, unzipping his pants and dropping them. But I'm not ready yet. My body is far too sensitive. I need a moment.

And I know just what to do.

I sit up quickly and slide off the island. Malcolm looks surprised, but that look quickly melts into that devilish grin as he sees me lower to my knees in front of him. I was denied before, but this time, I push him back so he rests against the island, and I yank down his boxers to his knees.

Just like before, his gorgeous, thick cock springs toward me, and I waste no time grasping it by the base and wrapping my lips around him, tasting him and taking him as deeply into my throat as I can stand before I choke.

CHAPTER TWENTY-EIGHT

MALCOLM

I grasp onto the island with both hands as I watch her take me into her lips. Her warm, wet mouth feels like paradise as she looks up at me with her big eyes and eager expression. She takes me deeply into her throat, until I feel the back of it on the tip of my cock, and she chokes a little before letting it slide back out. Her spittle drips from it as she strokes it toward her and she breathes deeply, a smile crossing her lips that lets me know she enjoys bringing me this pleasure, just as I had done for her.

Slowly, she strokes me back into her mouth and moans, the vibration of her voice sending a sensation up my body that I can barely handle. I want to take over right then, but I hold myself back. She's having too much fun to interrupt her, and so am I.

One hand slides underneath to cup and then massage by balls as rhythmically takes me deep over her tongue. Occasionally, she slides me out and lets me brush against her lips, her tongue slipping out to lick underneath my shaft.

"Do you want to come?" she asks, a playful smile on her lips.

"Not yet," I grumble. "I'm not through with you yet."

"Oh?" she asks, slowly standing, but never stopping stroking me. "What are you going to do that you haven't done?"

I grin, wrapping her around the waist again, and this time she jumps up, clenching her thighs around my waist and crossing her ankles at my back. I reach underneath her from behind and guide my cock up and into her and she sinks down onto me, her warmth enveloping me and causing her to moan deeply.

Walking with her on me, I carry her to the bedroom. She kisses my neck and playfully bites my shoulder again, only this time on the opposite side. I bring her to the bed and lay her down, pulling back from her just for a moment. As I do, she yanks off her shirt, exposing her incredible breasts, and I pull my shirt off as well.

Finally completely naked, I climb onto the bed, but she scoots back, laughing as she pretends to try to get away from me. I reach for her but she spins onto her stomach. Grasping at one of her ankles I stand on my knees and approach from behind her. One hand grasps her hips and she submits to me as I pull her toward me.

I sink into her again, this time from behind, and it causes her to cry out. I hold myself there, letting her get used to me as my cock throbs inside. I want to pound her, to dominate her, to fill her with my essence. But I hold off, letting her adjust. More than anything else, I want her to feel the same level of pleasure as I do.

So I go slow.

Rocking gently, I slide my cock deeper and deeper into her, curling over her back and letting one hand slide up her stomach to fill with her breast. Her hand clasps over mine and her other hand reaches back and pulls at her own skin, spreading herself for me.

I revel in the sight of my shaft, gripped by her pussy lips, sliding in and out of her, glistening with her cream as she whimpers and moans. Her toes curl and her body writhes as I increase my speed and I know she is either climaxing again or close to it. I grip her hips with both hands and go faster now, sweat beginning to roll down my chest and the small of my back. As she arches her own back, I go deeper until my hips are slamming into hers and a heavy groan is coming from my chest with every thrust.

"Harder!" she cries out, and I reach for her shoulder, pulling her entire body back into me as I thrust. Her cries are getting louder and faster, and my breathing becomes labored.

It's carnal and brutal, the passion overwhelming us both as I drive into her. She arches down again and I mount her higher, my feet under me as I fuck her from behind. Suddenly, she screams out in pleasure and pulls me tight to her and I feel the waves of her shuddering breath roll with her climax.

I exit her and lay down beside her, caressing her cheek as she whimpers and wipes sweat from her eyebrow. Then, her hand slides over to my chest and down, until it finds my cock. Her eyes open and I can see the desperation in them. She wants me to come too.

She lifts up and our lips meet again as she strokes me. Slowly, she straddles me and guides me back into her. With my back now against the headboard, her chest presses against my face. My mouth reaches out hungrily for her breasts as she rides me, slowly at first and then gaining in speed. One hand reaches behind her and cups by balls, squeezing gently as her hips rock over me.

The pleasure is so intense that I am overwhelmed. I grasp her and pull her faster, until she releases control and I toss her down onto her back. She smiles up at me as I wrap my arms around her, getting my knees under me and pounding into her again.

"I'm going to come," I groan as the electricity continues to prickle throughout my body.

"Yes, yes," she cries, her head resting back and her chest pushing up so her nipple brushes against my lips.

I explode into her, my body shaking as I empty myself. Her body vibrates and twitches as she comes with me, and her cry of delight mixes with the sound of my own. As we collapse into each other, spent and empty, the sweat rolls off our bodies and is wicked away by the sheets below us.

Again I find myself tangled up naked with Bree, only this time I don't have blinding light in my eyes and she is awake, her fingers trailing up and down the center of my stomach. I mimic the motion along her spine and lean down to kiss her hair. She snuggles closer and I feel like I could just stay here forever.

But there is work to do.

"You know...."

"What?"

"We didn't finish tasting the cake."

Bree buries her head in my stomach and laughs. "That's what's on your mind right now?"

"I mean… among other things. But I figure it's probably best if we take a break and get something useful done before we spend the rest of our time here and don't finish the plans."

She sighs and plants her chin on her hands folded across my chest. "Why do you have to be so logical?"

"It's a curse."

I give her a playful slap on her butt and we crawl out of bed. She pulls on her panties, then drops my shirt down over her head. I could drag her back into bed right this second. But I manage to contain myself and tug on my jeans before going back into the kitchen. I pick up the card describing the flavors of the cake samples again and select a new one.

"What's this one?" Bree asks.

"Lemon with strawberry frosting."

I taste it and then give her the second half of the cube. She doesn't look convinced.

"It's really good, but it just doesn't taste like a fall wedding. It is much more like spring."

"I agree." I take out another of the samples. "This one is also strawberry, so we're probably going to feel the same way about it, but I'm going to taste it anyway."

Bree giggles and jumps up on the counter, kicking her bare feet slightly. She seems so much more relaxed, less guarded. She points into the box.

"What about that one?

"That one is," I consult the card, "chocolate with mocha frosting."

"That one is really good," she says after tasting the cake. "But it doesn't feel bridal. Maybe we can talk to Bitsy about making a groom's cake, too."

We open the next box and find another card. The first flavor in this assortment is vanilla cake with cinnamon icing.

"I think this one should be a strong contender." I lick a bit of frosting off my finger.

Bree finishes her half and nods. "It's seasonal without being over-powering. That is definitely an option."

The next is a maple cake with cream cheese frosting. It goes into the contenders as well. A third option with pecan cake and salted caramel makes my mouth water and further increases our list of flavors we're considering.

"Are you still questioning whether we should let a home baker handle the wedding cake?" Bree asks.

I shake my head. "Nope. She can make every cake I eat for the rest of my life. Unless...."

My voice trails off and free it gives me a questioning look. "Unless what?"

"Nothing. What do you think about the salted caramel filling in vanilla cake?"

I'm really just babbling trying to fill space here and distance myself from the fact that I just almost said, "unless you want to make one for me." I can't believe thoughts like that are even coming into my mind.

We get through the rest of the samples and narrow our options down to our favorite three flavor combinations.

"What if we just use all of them?" Bree taps the tip of her pen against the list we've made. "There's no hard and fast law that a wedding cake has to be all one flavor. In fact, it's become more popular than ever to have different tiers with different flavors."

"I absolutely endorse that. We can ask Bitsy which one she thinks would be the most popular and have that be the biggest tier. Then the other ones can be the smaller cakes and people can just decide which ones they want."

"Maybe we could even do a small top tier and classic vanilla so that they can have it for their first anniversary," she suggests.

"Sounds like we have made a decision about the cake."

"Now all I have to do is find out if Bitsy will make me a couple more of these sample boxes so I can smuggle them onto the plane with me." Bree obviously means that as a joke, but as soon as the words come out of her mouth, her face falls.

Our eyes meet and I can see sadness reflecting what I'm feeling. It wasn't until this moment that either one of us acknowledged that it is almost time for Bree to go home. Her flight is the day after tomorrow. It's a sobering thought and I step up to her, wrapping my arms around her. Her head rests against my chest and her arms encircle my waist.

We don't say anything else, but stand here for a few minutes, then clasp hands and walk together to the bedroom.

CHAPTER TWENTY-NINE

Why did I have to say that?

I didn't even think about the impact of the words before they came out of my mouth, which is maybe something I should learn about myself and work on. It seems I've just been letting my mouth run wild recently, and I need to rein that in, especially since I just managed to pop a hole right in the happy little balloon we'd been floating around on.

I can practically hear it deflating.

Malcolm's eyes look heavy and sad when they meet mine. It hurts even more to see that expression there. But we shouldn't act like this is so much of a shock. This is the way it was going to be from the very beginning. When I came back to town to plan this wedding for Olivia, it was always the plan that I would be here for several days and then go back home. I never thought there would be any difficulty when it came time to go. I also never anticipated Malcolm.

Without saying anything, he reaches out and takes my hand, squeezing it before leading me through the house into the bedroom. We crawl under the covers and Malcolm curls around me, his arm wrapping protectively around my waist and pulling me back against him. I can feel the warmth of his body surrounding mine and the soothing flow of his breath against the back of my neck and my shoulder. His heart beats against my back and I feel myself relaxing into the rhythm.

Maybe there could be something here. Maybe this could be more than just a frivolous fling to deal with the stress of wedding planning. Maybe this could be something real.

When I wake up, I don't open my eyes immediately. I want to just lay here and feel Malcolm with me. I know he's awake too when he kisses my cheek and hugs me closer. I turn my head to kiss him. Neither of us say anything about the realization we came to last night. It's like we've both came to the decision to just ignore it for now. We don't have a lot of time to run away from reality, but we're going to do it for as long as we can.

Finally, he tucks his head against mine. "I'm going to go start breakfast," he says.

"All right. I'll be out in just a minute."

He presses another kiss to the side of my head and gets out of bed. I stretch out across the warm sheets and take a few moments to stare out the window and think about the day ahead. The smell of coffee and bacon lure me out of the bedroom and to the kitchen. I wish I could say I wasn't the kind of person who could be drawn out of hiding by the smell of bacon, but what can I say? I am basic like that.

"So, how long do you think you'll be in town for the wedding?" Malcolm asks me a few minutes later as we are sitting across the table from one another eating breakfast.

"I hadn't really made any firm plans about that yet. I'm guessing that I'll have to come into town a couple of days early just to make sure that all of the final details are in place and help Olivia get ready."

"Maybe you can stay for a day or two after," he suggests. "Brandon hasn't told me if they have any specific plans for a honeymoon or anything, but I'm sure there will be things that will need to be taken care of after the wedding that they aren't going to be able to do. Right?"

He doesn't actually care about dealing with the aftermath of a wedding. He's doing the exact same thing I'm doing in my brain—dancing around the fact that we want to see each other again but don't know how to say it.

The wedding is a built-in opportunity for us to be in the same space. But what does that mean? Is this, whatever this is, just for now? Does it only exist in this hazy stretch of time while we try to get this wedding together? Maybe when I leave, that will break the spell. It won't be the same anymore when I get back.

I don't see that happening. I already hate the idea of being away from him and want to count down the minutes until I can be back in town. And yet, I can't fully bring myself to tell him that. It feels like if I was to tell him I want to see him again it would put too much pressure and significance on this.

We haven't talked about what's going on between us. There hasn't been a single second of really acknowledging what we're feeling or what we're doing. I don't want to be that girl. You know that girl—the one who has their tenth wedding anniversary trip planned by the time the guy picks them up for their second date. I don't want to be her.

At the same time, I can't imagine just walking away from this. I don't know what this is. I can't be completely sure that there's anything tangible and sustainable here. But it feels like it's something. It feels like there's a possibility and I don't want to just turn my back on that because it was unexpected or because I don't know how exactly to move forward with it.

We keep talking, keep dancing around how we are going to see each other again. It's all wrapped up in the context of our responsibilities for the wedding. That just feels safer. When we finish eating, Malcolm loads the dishes into the dishwasher.

"I'm going to go grab a shower," he says.

"All right. I'm going to check my work."

He goes to the back of the house and I get my computer. Checking my messages doesn't take long, so I decide to take a few minutes to browse through the news. It's not something I love to do all that often considering the general state of the world, but Olivia hounds me to stay connected, so I do a cursory read through of the greatest hits every now and then.

There isn't anything terribly groundbreaking, and I'm about to navigate away from the current event articles when something catches my attention. The headline of the article promises the stunning revelation of the identity of a secretive billionaire running a hospitality empire, and the picture is of Malcolm!

My heart starts pounding heavily in my chest. Maybe it's just somebody who looks like him. I'm going to justify and deny right up until I have to face the absolute truth, which is seconds after I click on the article. It describes the powerful businessman who has been running the expansive collection of hotels and resorts in secrecy for many years.

Then there it is. In black and white, as they say. The article identifies him by name. Malcolm isn't some humble hotel worker who has been friends with Brandon almost their whole lives. He is a billionaire who owns properties throughout the world, including the hotel in the city he tried so hard to pressure me into choosing for the wedding. At least now that makes more sense.

The further I read, the worse it gets. Not only am I seeing that this man isn't who I thought he was, isn't who I was told he was, but he also isn't unattached. Further down in the article another picture shows him leaving a building with a glamorous blonde. They look very chummy and the article points to a link between him and the apparent heiress, hinting that those in the know are anticipating an engagement announcement soon.

My ears buzz, and my face feels hot. The skin down the back of my neck stings, and my fingertips are numb. I don't even know how to describe the emotion that I'm feeling right now. I'm angry, but also devastated, furious, and embarrassed.

I pull up another window and search Malcolm and his company. My computer screen immediately fills with articles detailing complaints about the mysterious owner of the company and the conditions of working for him. In a matter of moments, my perception of this man goes from a hard worker living in the trenches like the rest of us to a disconnected elitist without any concept of what it is to live a normal life, and no real desire to care.

I hear footsteps coming into the kitchen and lift my eyes to Malcolm. he smiles at me, but a second later, the expression falls.

"What's wrong? Did something happen?"

I don't even know how to respond. He takes another step into the kitchen and I stand up from the table defensively.

"Shouldn't you call Melanie?" I ask. "She's probably wondering what you're up to."

His face twists into a confused look. "Melanie? What are you talking about?"

"Melanie Jarvis, your girlfriend. Or should I say your soon-to-be fiancée."

I spin the computer around to face him so that he can see the article and the picture of the two of them together. His eyes widen and color streaks across his cheekbones.

"Bree," he says, taking another step closer.

I hold up a hand to stop him. "Don't."

"You need to listen to me."

"I don't need to do anything. I just found out everything I need to know, mainly that you have been lying to me from the very second I met you."

"That isn't all you need to know. That woman, Melanie, is nothing to me. I know her through a business associate, that's all. Us being a couple is just a rumor. There's no truth to it."

I let out a bitter burst of laughter. "Oh, is that all? Just knowing her through a business associate? Right, because you are a fucking billionaire who owns who knows how many properties around the world? Is that what you meant by you have worked in a hotel? And why you were stalking me at my hotel?"

"I wasn't stalking you," he says.

"No, you just showed up at my hotel to look around and ask a bunch of weird questions about it."

"I was doing research," he says with a defeated sigh. "I was trying to figure out what was so appealing about that place. Bree, please.

Listen to me. I didn't mean to hurt you. I didn't even mean to lie to you."

I scoff incredulously, shaking my head as I start for the bedroom. "You didn't mean to lie to me? You just thought it was no big deal to pretend to be something completely different than you are, not tell me who you actually are, and convince me to sleep with you?"

"Don't make it sound like I tricked you into bed," he says. "I didn't know anything was going to happen between us. It's not like we got along. That's why we didn't think it would be that big of a deal."

I stop and whip around to face him. "We?"

"Yeah," he says. "It was Brandon's idea, and Olivia went along with it. They challenged me to live like one of my lowest-paid employees for six months. We decided to keep it going with you, too."

I feel like someone has just punched me in the gut. My mouth opens, but no words come out. Not only did this man who I thought could be something special in my life lie to me, but my best friend betrayed me, too. I stomp toward the bedroom. "I'm leaving."

"What?" he asks, coming after me.

"Don't follow me," I growl. "I don't want you anywhere near me. I'm changing my flight and going home."

"Bree, please. Just stop for a second and talk to me."

"I don't need to stop for a second and I sure as hell don't need to talk to you. This is bullshit. I don't want anything to do with you or with any of this."

"I didn't lie to you about everything," he insists. "I am the same person."

"If you actually believe that, you have far bigger problems than being a liar. I told you before that I have trust issues. Now I just feel like an idiot."

I get to the bedroom and slam the door behind me, turning the lock for good measure. Any second now, the tears are going to start to fall. I can feel them burning at the back of my eyes. But for right now, there's enough fury and urgency to get the hell out of here that it's holding them back.

I yank my bag out of the closet and hastily fill it with everything I brought. I might have forgotten something, but I genuinely do not care. There's nothing I brought with me that is so important that I couldn't live without it if I leave it behind.

When I'm packed, I storm out to Olivia's car and head for the airport. Hopefully I will be able to talk to the airline and get my flight moved up to today. If not, I'll just wait it out. At this point, spending a day waiting at the airport is far preferable to being anywhere near Malcolm.

I get to the airport and park in the extended stay lot. I jot off a text to Olivia telling her where to pick up her car and start inside. My phone rings moments after the message is sent. I don't want to answer it. I don't want to talk to her. But I know Olivia and I know she will just keep calling me if I don't, so I might as well get it over with before I get to the airline desk.

"Yes?"

"Bree?" she asks. "What's going on? I thought you were leaving tomorrow."

"I'm getting an earlier flight. Everything is planned."

"Is everything okay?" she asks.

I don't even know how to put into words just how not ok everything is. "Why don't you give Malcolm a call and ask him?"

That's all I need to say. "Oh," she says.

"Yeah. Oh," I say. "What the literal fuck, Olivia? How could you do something like this to me?"

"I didn't mean to do it to you," she says. "That wasn't the point."

"That wasn't the point? What does that even mean? You intentionally lied to me. You made me look like a complete imbecile and you humiliated me."

"No. That wasn't what we meant to do."

"So what is it that you meant to do, Olivia? What did you think was going to happen?" I ask. "You lied to me. All three of you lied to me. You told me a bullshit story and let me go along with it. Even when…." I stop myself. I'm not getting into this with her right now.

"Even when what?" she asks.

"Nothing. I need to go. I'm at the airport."

"Bree, please. Just...."

"No. You have no idea how much you've hurt me. There's nothing else for me to say to you."

I hang up and stuff my phone away. Now the tears are starting to fall. I brush them away fiercely. I don't want to walk into the terminal and go up to the information desk sobbing. Forcing myself to keep it together, I go to the desk and tell them that I need to change my flight.

After three hours sitting at the gate, I'm able to board a new flight and head home, my heart aching the entire way.

CHAPTER THIRTY

Malcolm

WHAT THE HELL JUST HAPPENED?

I feel like I've been hit by a truck. Everything happened so fast. It was going so well with Bree. It wasn't something I anticipated. I never saw it coming, even if I thought about it every time I looked at her. But it happened and it was amazing, so amazing I was starting to think about something much more than just sharing a bed with her while she was here planning the wedding.

Then suddenly, it was over. Literally in the time it took for me to take a shower, everything came crashing down and now I'm reeling. I barely even had the chance to process what Bree was saying before she locked herself in the bedroom and then drove away.

I thought about following her. I could have just run out, jumped in my car, and followed her to the airport. I could have chased her down and demanded she listen to me.

Only, I don't think that would have worked out like the rom-com scene that it sounds like. In a movie, I would have shown up at the airport right after her and run across the parking lot, likely in a rainstorm that came out of nowhere, and caught up with her right before she got inside. I'd pour out my heart to her and she'd forgive me, letting me sweep her into my arms and kiss her as I inexplicably spun her around.

In reality, I feel like it's much more likely that I would get to the airport, we'd end up in a screaming match in the middle of the parking lot, and I'd end up with my ass tackled by some well-meaning passerby.

So instead I'm sitting at the kitchen table with my computer in front of me, reading through the articles that popped up this morning. I knew something was going on. As soon as my assistant told me that someone was sniffing around, I knew it was more than just curiosity.

I squeeze my eyes closed, pressing my fingertips over them. I shouldn't have let it get this far. I should have told her the truth. As soon as I started to think that something was going to happen between us, I should have told her everything. Now everything is a massive mess and I don't know how I'm going to crawl my way out of it.

My phone rings and for a second, I'm hopeful that it might be Bree. Maybe she changed her mind and is calling to hear me out. But when I look at the screen I see that it's Brandon.

"Hey," I answer.

"What the hell happened?"

"That was my thought exactly," I say, letting out a heavy sigh and dropping back in the chair. I stare up at the ceiling, trying to wrap my brain around how I got to this place.

"Olivia just got off the phone with Bree. She's crying and freaking out. She says that Bree found out about you and that she left and went home. I can barely understand her. I don't know what she's talking about. What happened this morning? I thought everything was going well between the two of you. Did you decide to tell her or something?"

"No, but I should have," I say. "I should have told her a while ago. As a matter of fact, I shouldn't have ever done this stupid challenge to begin with, and then I wouldn't have anything to tell her. I didn't get a chance to come clean because she found out for herself. At least she found out that I was lying to her."

"How?" he asks.

"You should check out the news," I explain. "Remember when I was saying that someone was trying to find out stuff about the company and about me? Now it's splashed all over everywhere—articles exposing my identity, talking about my employees hating working for me, and a really delightful series about how I'm going to be getting engaged to Melanie Jarvis soon."

"Who is Melanie Jarvis?" he asks.

"Does that really matter?" I ask. "Of everything I just said, is who the woman is really all that important?"

"I guess not." He lets out a breath. "Shit."

"Yeah, that about sums it up. Bree is so mad she wouldn't even listen to me. She said she was going to change her flight and go home, then she left."

"It's going to be all right. We're going to figure this out."

"No," I say, shaking my head even though he can't see me. "This whole thing has been a disaster. It was stupid to begin with and I shouldn't have ever agreed to it. I'm done. I'm not doing this anymore. The challenge is off. I need to get back to my normal life."

"I know. I'm sorry. I'll see you in a few days when we get home."

"See you."

I hang up and stare at the computer screen for another few moments. How could this have happened? I've tried so hard to stay out of the public eye. I've gone to great lengths to keep people from knowing who I am. Having the public know that I own my company and have the wealth I do would do nothing but cause trouble. It means constant scrutiny and people coming up with stories about you to fit their own agenda and interests, much like the story about Melanie Jarvis.

I've never wanted to be in the spotlight and have people wonder what I'm doing or questioning my decisions. It's why so few people have ever been allowed to know the truth about who I am and those who do are either my closest friends or employees under strict NDA.

Now that has all gone to hell.

It's even worse than it would have been if I had just come forward myself. Now there is all the speculation about why I've been "in the shadows" and elaborate stories about how I run my company.

But the worst part is the look in Bree's eyes when she stared me down. Having to go public with my identity isn't something I wanted to do, but it is what it is. That's not how I feel about Bree. I can't stand that I hurt her. I can't stand that she thinks that I betrayed her. She opened up to me, and I just sat there and let her tell me everything knowing I was doing the exact thing she said she couldn't handle—lying to her.

After a while, I get up and go to the bedroom to pack everything I brought with me. There's no point in me staying here anymore. I leave Olivia and Brandon's house and return to the tiny apartment. I don't have any intention of staying here for another night. Like I told Brandon, I'm done. This challenge is over. I'm going to take what I need and go back to my regular home and my regular life.

As I go through the apartment gathering the things I want to bring home with me, I think about what this all represents. This challenge definitely didn't turn out the way I thought it was going to. To be honest, I don't even know what I thought was going to happen when I first agreed to it. It was stubbornness and hubris that made me agree to it. I wasn't going to let Brandon give me a challenge and not take it on. I didn't think I was actually going to learn anything or that any of my thoughts and opinions were going to change. If anything, I thought I would just prove my point. I would finish the challenge and Brandon would see I was right all along.

Now I know that's far from what actually happened. I didn't finish the challenge. But even in the amount of time I did it, I learned so much. It was an eye-opening experience I wasn't expecting. And the most surprising part of it was just how fast and hard I fell for Bree.

I finish gathering the things that I want to hang onto and leave the rest behind. I'll let the landlord know that everything still in the apartment is up for grabs for anyone who might need or want it. He can do whatever he sees fit with it.

My neighbor comes out of his apartment as I'm carrying the last armful of things out to my car.

"Hey, Malcolm," he says. "Looks like you've got your hands full. Can I help you?"

"No, I've got it. Thanks, though," I say. "I'm actually moving out. I'm glad I got a chance to say goodbye."

"Moving out?" he asks. "Found something better?"

"Something like that. Thanks for being a good neighbor. It was nice knowing you."

"You're making it sound like you're heading off to die. You know where to find me. You can come see me any time."

I smile. "Thanks. I will." I glance over my shoulder at the door I left unlocked. "I left some stuff in there that I'm not going to need. You're welcome to any of it."

He gives me a wave and I head for my car, feeling surprisingly emotional. This was my first real experience having a neighbor. I've always had people living in the general vicinity of me, obviously, but there's never been anyone I could just stop and chat with. I have the unexpected feeling that I'm going to miss the little interactions.

I drive up to my house and sit in the car looking at the front door. It's good to be back here, but at the same time, there's a sense of loneliness around the house I've never noticed before. Finally I get out of the car and go inside. In the greater scheme of things, it hasn't been all that long since I've been here. I've been on vacations nearly as long as I've lived in the apartment.

But it feels different coming home this time. In spite of all my efforts to keep her out of my mind, I immediately imagine Bree coming to the door to greet me. I can see her here. But now that's never going to happen.

I unpack everything and go to the kitchen to make something to eat, opening the refrigerator and peering in before I remember that I emptied the kitchen out before going to the apartment. I don't have anything to cook. Instead I order from my favorite restaurant and go to the living room to stare at the TV until the food is delivered.

My phone keeps ringing beside me, but I ignore it. I don't want to talk to my assistant. I don't feel like getting into any of this right now. I just want to ignore it for a little while longer.

The next morning, I make myself get out of bed and go back to my regular life. I put on a suit and get in my usual car rather than the old one I've been driving. Bracing myself for chaos, I go to the office.

It's an even longer, more difficult few days than I expect it to be, and by the time Brandon and Olivia get home, I feel like I've been put through a grinder. I go to their house for lunch the day after they get back in town. I get to the house and go to the living room. I drop down onto the couch, covering my face with my arms, but as soon as I'm lying there, I wish I hadn't come in here. All I can think about is Bree and the night the electricity went out.

"You okay, buddy?" Brandon asks as he comes into the room.

"On top of the world. Don't I look like it?"

Olivia carries a large tray of sandwiches and chips into the room and sets it on the coffee table. She grabs one of the plates and sits down. "How are you dealing with everything?"

"I don't really want to talk about work right now," I say. "I just need a break from it."

"Have you heard from Bree?" Olivia asks.

Brandon's eyes cut to her. "I don't think that's the best topic change."

"It's fine," I say. "No. I haven't heard from her. I tried to call her, but it went right to voicemail and she never called me back."

"I haven't heard from her, either," Olivia admits. "This is the longest we've ever gone without talking. Even when we've had arguments before, it's never been like this. We've always figured things out and made up within a day, maybe two."

"She's really having a hard time with this," I say. "I know that she's mad, but I would have thought she would have cooled off and at least been willing to talk to you by now."

"I hoped she would, but I'm not really surprised. Bree has a really hard time trusting people."

"Yeah, I got that from her talking about her ex," I say.

"It's more than that. Trevor hurt her, but it started a long time before that. Her parents divorced when she was really young and she found out that her father was living a double life. She never got over the feeling that he had betrayed both her and her mother and that the struggles they had as she was growing up was because of his lies."

The explanation hits me hard. I didn't realize that Bree's standoffishness and reactivity were from pain that runs so deep. It only makes me feel worse. I know that Olivia feels terrible. Bree has been her best friend for so many years. She knew the pain she'd suffered, and she still contributed. That needs to be settled for both of their sakes.

"You need to talk to her," I say. "She needs you."

"She won't talk to me. I told you, we haven't talked since we had our argument. She won't answer the phone for me, either."

"Then you need to go see her. You two are too close to just let this go."

"I agree," Brandon says. "You have to figure this out."

CHAPTER THIRTY-ONE

I don't know why I thought that getting home was going to fix everything.

Somehow I deluded myself into believing that the heavy sadness was only going to be with me while I was traveling. Surely when I landed and got off the plane, I'd leave it all behind. I was going to get back to my place and dive right back into my life without a problem.

Ask me how that worked out for me.

Shitty. That's how it worked out for me.

If anything, I felt worse when I got home. Getting to my empty apartment only seemed to underscore the empty feeling in my chest and the sick feeling lingering in my gut. It was just so quiet. And I quickly learned that turning on the TV in the living room and my bedroom only does so much to make it feel like I'm not completely alone.

But I've been pushing through. I haven't really had a choice. Life is still here, and I've got to try to navigate it the best I can even while I'm missing Olivia and longing for Malcolm. I hate to even admit that. I wish those words didn't even go through my head. I shouldn't be longing for him. He lied to me and let me carry on believing he was someone he isn't even after I told him how important honesty is to me.

I've spent the last several days doing everything I can to just keep my mind distracted. I've rearranged my apartment a couple times. I organized my wardrobe and then reorganized it. I considered painting and then decided it would be too much of a hassle to try to get approval from my landlord before the feeling passed. I'm sitting in the living room getting through the last bit of a big project for work when someone knocks on my door.

I'm not expecting anybody, so I'm guessing it's one of my neighbors. We've reached the time of year when fundraisers abound. As my grandmother would have said, you can't swing a broom without smacking into a kid holding an order form—nuts, magazines, wrapping paper—it never ends. I have gotten adept at dodging the wide-eyed PTA moms who swoop in on the neighbors trying to hawk their wares. Ready with my uninterested eyes, I peek through the peephole. But I don't see any of the mothers or even children I was expecting to see. I don't see anyone.

Suddenly, a hand holding a white paper bag shoots out from just beyond the view of the peephole. I jump back slightly, then look through the peephole again. The hand and the bag are still there. And I recognize both of them.

I open the door, and Olivia sheepishly steps up to me.

"Angelo's," she says.

"You flew all the way from Maple Valley to bring me cheesy garlic bread?" I ask.

"Yes," she says. "I hoped it might make you talk to me. Did it work?"

I stare at the bag. She knows it's my favorite restaurant, and I have a weakness for the appetizer I have frequently been known to turn into a whole meal. I take it from her.

"Yes."

She smiles and follows me into the apartment. I go to the kitchen to get plates and drinks and bring them back into the living room, where I find her looking around at the oddly arranged furniture.

"Yeah, I was trying something new," I say.

"It's... I like it."

"No, you don't. It makes no sense. I just haven't had the energy to move it back yet." I set the plates down and open the bag to pull out the large box of bread inside. "I can't believe you flew all the way out here just to do this."

"I would do anything for you," she says. "I'm so sorry. I know that's not enough, but I can't think of any other way to say it. I'm not as good with words as you are. I just... I'm sorry."

I stop pulling apart one of the chunks of bread and look at her. There are tears sparkling in her eyes and my throat tightens. I have hated being separated from her. No matter what, she is my best friend. She's the person I've spent more time with in my life than anyone else. The person who knows me better than anyone has. But I can't just pretend like she didn't do what she did.

"How could you do that to me?" I ask.

Olivia hangs her head for a second. "It's stupid. It's so incredibly stupid. He told you about the challenge, right?"

"Yeah," I say. "And it makes no damn sense."

"No, it doesn't. It was supposed to just be something really silly. It wasn't supposed to hurt anybody, especially not you. We were just trying to make Malcolm see how much of a bubble he lives in. That's all. I thought it would be funny to see him try to live that way for six months. I didn't think he could do it, and I wanted to see him struggle and then have to admit that he didn't actually know what he was talking about."

"Do you realize how insane that sounds?" I ask. "But honestly, whatever, I don't even care that it sounds completely bat shit crazy. The point is you let me think that. You didn't even tell me the truth. You let me believe something about him that was completely untrue. You let me be totally humiliated."

"I know. And I'm so sorry."

"No, but you don't know." I take a breath. "I slept with him."

Olivia's eyes widen. "He didn't tell us that."

"Well, at least he has that going for him," I say.

"What does this mean? Or was it…. what does this mean?"

"I don't know," I say. "I thought it might mean something. But now I realize I didn't even know the man I crawled into bed with. So that's a fantastic feeling."

"You do know him, though. All he lied about is his job."

"And how much money he has and where he lives and the type of car he drives…."

"Okay, yes. But do those really matter?"

"Are you serious right now?" I ask.

"Yes. Think about it. In the big picture, the things he lied about are really minor. If anything, you got to know him as a person without being swayed by his money," she says.

I take a bite of the bread. "You are really reaching."

"He's a good guy, Bree."

"No. A good guy wouldn't do that to me. I forgive you. What you did sucks, but I am willing to move past it because I know you didn't mean to hurt me. But I'm not going to give him another chance."

"He didn't mean to hurt you, either," Olivia argues.

"But he didn't think enough to not hurt me, either. I just can't even think about having anything to do with him again. I'm far too hurt and embarrassed. I don't even want to look at him."

"But… you will, right? At the wedding?"

I can see the worry in her eyes. I nod. "Of course."

"You're still my maid of honor?"

"Of course, I'm still your maid of honor."

Relief washes over her expression and she launches herself across the couch to throw her arms around me in a tight hug. I laugh and hug her back. "I'm crushing the garlic bread, aren't I?"

"A little bit."

She pulls back from the hug, wiping away tears running down her face. "Okay. Let's get down to business, then. Tell me about everything for my wedding."

"You mean you don't know about the plans I made?" I ask. "I

figured Malcolm would have told you everything and probably take credit for the majority of it."

To Olivia's immense credit, she ignores the snarky comment and moves right along with the conversation. She knows no good is going to come of talking about Malcolm. As much as she obviously wants me to not harbor negative feelings toward him and give him a chance to start fresh, I'm so far beyond not in that place I would need a GPS and a backup map to navigate to it.

"I literally only know what you told me when you called me with updates. I am totally in the dark about everything else. Which kind of has a fun reality TV show vibe to it, but is also stressful as all living hell. I want to know everything that you picked and all the plans that you have in place. You have no idea how excited I am, frazzled and way more riddled with anxiety than perhaps I should be, but very excited."

I laugh. "I think that being riddled with anxiety just comes with the territory of being a bride. I don't trust those women who say that they are calm and breezy brides. I just think that means that they are building up all of their aggression and will explode in the very near future. All it's going to take is one person sitting on the wrong side of the ceremony or not signing the guest book and it's going to be all over."

"Either that, or they have already made plans to become a black widow on their honeymoon so they don't need to worry about making perfect wedding memories. It's not like they're going to be looking back on them and reminiscing fondly."

I blink at Olivia a couple of times. "Well, that went to the dark place quickly."

"I know. I ended up watching a lot of true crime on the plane. Anyway, tell me everything."

Doing my best to skim any mention of Malcolm out of the story, I fill her in on all the plans I made and everything I put into place for her. It turns out she was already thinking about the boutique for welcome gifts and is thrilled I already have that done. I'm a little bit anxious when I mention the cake, but Olivia seems surprisingly welcoming to the idea of giving a budding baker an opportunity.

She doesn't say it, but I think there might be a bit of lingering bridal competition going on there. If the cake turns out as phenomenal as I expect it to be based on the instructions I sent while traveling back from Maple Valley, she's going to be the talk of the wedding season.

And she's going to have the feather in her cap of using a completely different bakery than all the other brides in town immediately think about.

"Pretty much everything is taken care of," I continue. "There are a couple of things that I needed your input for and some last minute finishing details that need to be put in place, but they aren't really things I could have done ahead of time."

"So, you're going to come back to town with me, right? I can stay here for the next couple of days and then we will fly back together so we can get everything finished up."

"I think that sounds perfect," I say.

It's good to have Olivia at my apartment for the next two nights. It's like an extended slumber party, and I know that we aren't going to have very many opportunities in the future to have time like this together without it needing to be a whole planned thing. I've already told her that I expect us to have girl's trips at least once a year, but that's not the same thing as just being able to hunker down at my place or hers and just spend time together.

I manage to snag a seat on the same flight back to Maple Valley, and we cajole other passengers until they move and we are able to sit together. Usually I would not want to be that person. I have no interest in ending up in a pulpy tabloid article that is ranting about my entitlement. But the kickoff to my best friend's wedding weekend feels like extenuating circumstances and I was very friendly to everyone. I'm not sure if that fully excuses me, but I'm comfortable with it.

We land and walk through the terminal toward the baggage claim. I find myself looking around half expecting to see Malcolm. I know he's not here. The only reason he would be here is to pick me up, and obviously there's no need for that. But it does feel strange arriving and not seeing him.

I push the thoughts of him out of my mind and throw myself head on into focusing completely on Olivia and making sure her wedding is everything she could possibly dream of.

It all goes by so quickly, and suddenly it is the morning of the wedding. While Olivia has her pre-wedding pampering session, I go to the orchard to make sure everything is going well with the venue. I'm making a few minor adjustments to the floral arrangement on the guest book table when I hear someone walk in.

Out of the corner of my eye, I see Malcolm.

CHAPTER THIRTY-TWO

MY BREATH CATCHES IN MY THROAT WHEN I SEE BREE IN THE reception hall. I wasn't expecting her to be here. I probably should have. Of course, she would be making sure that everything is going right and is in place for Olivia.

I know she has been in town for two days. Brandon mentioned it as a throw away comment when we were on the phone the other day, just throwing it out there that Olivia was out at lunch with Bree.

He said it like it wasn't going to have any kind of impact on me, but it's all I've been able to think about. It has taken everything in me not to try to reach out to her. Part of me has wanted to just drive around town hoping to spontaneously run into her. But even I know she wouldn't buy that. She'd know in an instant I had been looking for her, and I have my very strong doubts she would have reacted well to it. So I've kept my distance and told myself I was going to see her at the wedding. She couldn't avoid it.

But I didn't expect it to be this way. I didn't think I would walk into the room and have her standing right there. If I was the kind of man to look for signs in things, maybe that's what I would see. Instead, it's just a shock to my system and an almost overwhelming need to be close to her.

She glances over her shoulder at me and I know that she sees me, but she doesn't say anything. She turns her attention right back to the flowers on the guest book table.

"They turned out really good, didn't they?" I ask, taking a cautious step toward her.

Bree doesn't even try to conceal her sigh. It's obvious she doesn't want to talk to me. Without even looking at me, she moves on to another table and starts to adjust the position of the place settings. "Yes. The florist did a good job."

"I talked to a couple of the out-of-town guests, and they really liked the welcome bags. They were asking about the body products you picked out. It seems like you made the right choices."

She doesn't even acknowledge that she heard me, much less respond. She goes back over to the guest book table and picks up what I recognize as her planner. She checks something off and scans over a page, obviously making sure she has everything handled. It looks like she's just about done in the space, and I feel a sense of urgency to get her to talk to me. Pretty soon she's going to leave to get ready for the ceremony, and I don't want the wedding to go on without us clearing the air between us.

"Bree, please listen to me. I need to talk to you."

She continues to ignore me but doesn't leave the room. She moves on to tables set up to the side of the space where I assume there will be food soon.

"Please, just a couple of minutes. I want the chance to apologize."

"I don't need you to apologize," she says.

I decide to resort back to our original mode of communication, saltiness and sarcasm. "Apparently you do, or you wouldn't be acting like this."

That does it. Bree whips around to face me, one hand planting on her hip. "Excuse me?"

I shrug, giving her a casually dismissive look. "It just seems like you are more worked up about this than you want to admit. I'm just trying to do the right thing here."

"Fine. Go ahead."

I step up closer to her. "I'm sorry. I know that's not enough, but I need to say it. I'm sorry. I'm sorry I didn't tell you the truth from the very beginning and I'm sorry that when I was given other opportunities, I didn't own up to it. I'm sorry I hurt you and disappointed you. And I'm sorry that you feel like I betrayed you and broke your trust. That's not something I ever would have wanted to do. I really do want you to know that I didn't make everything up. I wasn't playing some sort of character when we were together. The things we talked about and the person you got to know are real. That really is me, and I am willing to tell you everything else. Anything you want to know about me, I am an open book."

"I appreciate your apology," she says, "but that's really all I have to say to you, Malcolm. Like you said, you broke my trust. I can't just pretend like that didn't happen because you're telling me you're willing to tell me the truth now. I think we just need to get through this wedding and put all of this behind us. We can be cordial to each other and do what we need to do for Olivia and Brandon, then just leave it at that."

"Bree...."

"I need to get ready. You should, too."

She walks out of the room without giving me a second look. I stand in the middle of the dance floor feeling like I just got hit with a bag of bricks. I want her to come back. I want her to get a few feet away from the reception hall, decide that she can't just leave things that way between us, and come back.

But she doesn't. Finally, I know there's no point in me just continuing to stand here. I need to get ready and make sure Brandon has everything he needs.

I head for the room where we are getting dressed, doing my best not to let my face show how I'm feeling. I don't want to stress out Brandon right before his wedding. Today is about him, and I'm not going to distract him from thinking about anything other than the future ahead of him, the life he's so excited about. So, I fake a smile. I let out big belly laughs and pat him on the back. I toast him out of the engraved flasks I got for us with the money I'm allowed to use now.

Finally, it's time to go to the ceremony, and we walk together down to the orchard grove where chairs have been set up and a long aisle runner leads to the altar. The guests have already filled both sides and the energy is buzzing and fidgety with anticipation.

Brandon looks back and forth between the two sides of chairs to smile at the friends and family who have gathered to witness the ceremony. It isn't lost on him how special it is that these people have come to be with him on such short notice. He's one of those people who doesn't really internalize just how important he is to the people around him. It's good to see him get a chance to have that importance acknowledged.

We take our places at the altar next to the officiant. A few moments later, music rises up and I see Bree walk up the aisle. She is nothing short of breathtaking. She looks even more beautiful in her dress than I remember from when she tried it on. Her hair falls in soft tendrils around her face and she carries herself with exceptional poise and grace, all but floating down the aisle to take her spot across from me.

I can't take my eyes off her. Even as all the attention goes back up the aisle to Olivia, my gaze keeps sliding over to Bree.

I try to concentrate on the ceremony, but I can't stop looking at Bree. She's so beautiful, and everything inside me is reacting to being close to her again. I want to wrap my arms around her, to scoop her up and not let her go. But as the newly married couple rushes down the aisle together and Bree takes my arm for my compulsory escort, she doesn't even glance in my direction.

Her eyes stay locked directly ahead, the smile plastered on her face a carefully constructed and rehearsed part of her outfit. It is just as much a part of her maid of honor wardrobe as her dress or the delicate drop pendant around her neck.

Bree releases my arm and steps away from me as soon as she possibly can once we are down at the aisle. She walks away without saying anything, making a beeline for Olivia so she can be the first to hug her and wish her congratulations.

The photographer hurries us along, shooing us like a flock of chickens to the spot where he wants to take pictures. I know this means another opportunity to be close to Bree. He's going to want shots of the best man and maid of honor together.

But nothing changes. We pose for the pictures like we are instructed, but we don't talk. Even with my arm wrapped around her waist, she stays stiff. There isn't even a glimpse of the heat and connection that was between us. All I want is for her to be willing to give me another chance, but it seems like all she wants is to get away from me as fast as she can.

As soon as we're done taking pictures, she makes her way toward the venue without a single second of hesitation. The reception begins and we go through the motions of being introduced to the guests. I have my arm linked through hers again as we walk into the room and smile, her waving her bouquet and doing a little dance. Something about the playful moment makes it even more painful to be walking along beside her. It's like she's just underscoring that I am inconsequential, like she can just go about her life without even acknowledging that I exist.

Just like we planned, the introduction of the new couple leads right into a dance, and I take Bree into my arms. we go through the motions, but she doesn't relax under my touch. Surrounded by the DJ's lights and the sound of the music, all I can think about is our first kiss.

I feel that same intense pull, the powerful draw toward Bree that in that moment had inspired me to pull her clothes and kiss her. I want that again. And looking into her eyes, I can see that she's thinking about it, too. I want it to have an impact, but she makes no move to get closer to me or to show in any way that her feelings have changed.

When the dance ends, Bree smiles at Olivia over my shoulder and takes the opportunity to break away from me and disappear into the crowd of guests. For the rest of the night, it almost feels like we are continuing to dance. We move around each other, not getting too close but not wanting to show that we are actively avoiding each other. That would only raise suspicion. As far as the other guests know, Bree and I don't have any reason to interact with each other. They know that we only met just before the engagement party and that Bree doesn't live in town, so in their minds it would make sense that there's no real bond between us. If it became obvious that we were trying not to be anywhere near each other, that would be the point when people started questioning what might be going on between us.

And while it's not like Bree and I have had a conversation about it, I'm sure we share the sentiment that we really don't need anyone making those assumptions or connections. There's enough difficulty happening between us as it is, we don't need anyone else crawling into the mud pit and flailing around.

But even as we are keeping to ourselves and doing our best not to cross each other's paths, we don't lose track of each other. No matter where I am in the room, I'm aware of Bree. My eyes trail over to her without me even realizing it until I find myself watching her as she talks and laughs, as she stares at the buffet like she's considering whether she really needs something, then inevitably filling another tiny plate, as she turns her head just enough to look back at me.

I know there are people talking to me. A lot of these people I've never met or I haven't seen in a long time, but because they are close to Brandon, they feel like they are close to me. They want to chat with me, to share the excitement of the day with me, even if we don't actually have any connection and it is unlikely we'll encounter each other many times again, if ever.

That's one of the unique things about a wedding. Everybody wants to feel like one big collective, one unit of interlocked relationships anchored by whatever link there is to the bride and groom. People who have never laid eyes on each other are suddenly hugging and at the end of the day there will be a deluge of pictures of people grinning with their arms around total strangers who they've decided to bond with.

But I can't focus on anything but Bree. I try to put my attention on Brandon. I watch him dance with Olivia and give the expected applause when they kiss. I eat and exchange the obligatory commentary about the food with whoever is going through the line with me. Both Brandon and Olivia hate speeches at weddings and absolutely couldn't stand the idea of being thrust right in the awkward spotlight while we waxed poetic about them, so I don't even have that to distract me.

All I want is Bree.

When the reception finally winds to a close, we line up outside with glow sticks and bubbles to usher the new couple out to their waiting getaway car. As soon as they zoom into the distance, I'm ready to call it a night. The staff at the orchard is going to handle breaking everything down and cleaning up for us, so there's no real need for me to stay.

I do a cursory round of goodbyes and check in with Cyrus to make sure that there's nothing I can do. He assures me everything is handled and I slip out to go to the hotel and the room Olivia and Brandon insisted I stay in. I told them I could just go back home after the wedding, but they insisted that it's part of wedding tradition. I'm not so sure that's accurate, but I didn't want to argue with them. This wedding has been stressful enough for them as it is.

I walk into the hotel and go to the front desk. Bree is already there. I didn't see her leaving the reception, but she must have walked out just before I did. I overhear the clerk say her room number and Bree thanks her, then reaches down and picks up the duffle bag at her feet. She turns away from the desk and catches sight of me. Our eyes lock for a moment but she doesn't say anything before sweeping past me and heading up the steps.

I tell the clerk my name and she smiles knowingly.

"The best man," she says. "The couple came earlier to make sure everything was ready and mentioned your name."

I nod. "Ah."

She gives me the number to my room and I realize it is next door to Bree. I can't imagine that Olivia and Brandon would have done that intentionally, but I don't argue. It's only for one night. I take my key and bring my bag upstairs. Bree is already in her room so I let myself into mine.

I immediately notice the welcome bag sitting on the bed. It brings a rueful smile to my face as I remember picking everything out with Bree and packing the bags together. An extra bag is sitting next to it and a card attached is from Brandon thanking me for being a part of his day. Inside is an assortment of our favorite candy and snacks from when we were younger. Some of them I haven't seen in years, and I don't know how he got his hands on them, but they make me happy.

Looking around the room, I start to notice the little details that Bree told me about when I asked her why this place was so appealing to her. As resistant as I was to think of another hotel as being more comfortable or attractive to visitors than one of my properties, now I'm trying to be open and see what she does.

I've heard so much about the little personal touches and the ways that this hotel makes people feel welcome and really enjoy their stay. I explore the room looking for all of it, discovering things I would never have thought of. A night light glowing in the outlet beside the nightstand. A card next to the bed offering a loaned essential oil diffuser with a choice of scents. An extra blanket draped over the back of a chair nestled in the corner.

Through the wall I hear the shower in Bree's room starting up. My stomach tightens. I imagine her clothes falling from her body. Her hair coming loose from the pins that held it up during the wedding. In my mind I see her stepping into the water and tipping her head back to let it stream over her. I try to stop thinking about her. I need to get her out of my mind.

Opening my bag, I get out my pajamas and go into the bathroom. A little basket on the counter holds the bath products she talked about so much. I grab a bottle of body wash and get into the shower. As the water beats down on my shoulders, I think of her hands on my skin. I imagine the warmth of her fingertips and the sweep of her tongue.

It's too much for me. I get out and dress, not bothering to put on shoes before walking out into the hallway and knocking on her door.

CHAPTER THIRTY-THREE

I'VE JUST GOTTEN OUT OF THE SHOWER AND PUT ON MY NIGHTGOWN when I hear someone knocking on the door. I can't imagine who it is. I didn't ask for anything to be brought up by the front desk. Maybe Olivia sent something, or there could be a problem with the room. All I want is to climb in bed and lose myself in the basket of treats that was waiting for me while binge watching TV until I fall asleep.

I go to the door and stand on my toes to look through the peephole. I'm shocked to see Malcolm standing in the hallway. He's looking directly at the door, his shoulders squared, his posture determined.

I could ignore him. I could just refuse to open the door and go crawl in bed the way I intended. I doubt even he would be arrogant enough to stand out there and pound on the door repeatedly when he knows that the rooms up and down the hall are occupied by Olivia and Brandon's guests.

But I can't. I lower myself from my toes and stand with my hands pressed to the door, thinking about the man standing on the other side. I can't bring myself to walk away. Anger is still burning low in my belly, but I can't just ignore him. We're going to have to talk about this.

I open the door and Malcolm's eyes burn into mine. He says nothing. With one step forward he sweeps me into his arms and yanks me against him, crushing his mouth down on mine in a strong, insistent kiss.

I immediately melt into him.

His hands clench my back and pull me in, his muscular chest pressing into me as his tongue slides into my mouth. The taste of him, the buzzing sensation that fills my head when his lips touch mine, is enough to send shudders down my body and I break out in goosebumps despite feeling like my entire body has been set on fire.

He lifts me, hands grasping my ass through the silk nightgown and I wrap my legs around his waist. What little resistance I had is gone, and I am submitting to the carnal need that is churning in my chest. I need him. I need him beside me. Inside me.

He carries me to the bed and sets me down gently, but his lips never leave my skin. They move down my cheek and to my collarbone as I reach for his shirt, yanking it out of where it was tucked in his pants and sliding my hands underneath to trace across his stomach. With one finger, he slips my nightgown down off my shoulder and presses his lips into the crook of my arm, then diagonally down to my exposed breast. Taking my nipple into his mouth, he sucks, sliding his tongue over it and sending a fresh new chill down my spine.

My head rocks back as I release control, sinking into the sensation of his hands and mouth on my body. More forcefully now, he pulls down and I shift my other shoulder so the nightgown slips down to my waist. One hand cups one breast as he pays attention to the other, then switches, making growling, groaning sounds like an animal.

Kneeling, he pulls the nightgown up over my thighs, and I yank it up and over me, so I am fully exposed. He takes just a moment to take me in with his eyes, and I wither in that gaze. I want him so badly, but I can't form words to say. Instead I reach for him, and he clasps my hands together, holding them at the wrist in one of his own before plunging his face between my thighs.

An explosion of light and sensation eradicates my control as his tongue slides between my lower lips. One leg curls around his neck and the other falls over his shoulder, both pulling him tighter as he swirls around my clit, teasing me before applying pressure. My hands slide down to his hair and fill with the strands as one of his hands slides up my stomach and his palm falls over a hardened nipple.

I squeal as a finger is inserted in me, and his grip slides to my hips, crossing over my body as if he wants to hold me down in this position. I don't mind. I revel in the attention his tongue pays to my body, the fullness of his thick finger inside me, the tip brushing gently across the top wall and making me squirm where I lay.

From below, I hear him moan, and the sound of his deep, velvety voice, emitting a sound of pleasure and joy at the taste of me, pushes me past the point of no return. I can feel the wave of a massive climax rushing closer and closer. It arrives so fast, and so forcefully, I can't stave it off. My jaw locks open and I cry out as my body clenches and my legs tremble.

He doesn't stop as I come, seeming to gain pleasure from the way I squirm underneath his grip. When he finally releases me, part of me wants to curl up in a ball and recover, but a larger part of me is desperate for more. I twist as he stands and get my knees underneath me as his shirt flies across the room. He reaches for his pants button, but I push his hands away.

This is my claim.

I yank at the fabric until the button slides out and the zipper unfolds with my guidance. The pants drop ever so slightly down his hips and I reach for the boxer-briefs underneath, pulling them down at the same time as I pull his pants. Slowly, the base of his cock is revealed and I can't contain myself any longer. I press my face forward and await him with an open mouth. When it springs out, I take it gratefully, my lips wrapping around the head and my tongue sweeping underneath and tasting the sweet pre-come.

He groans again and I feel the vibration deep in my core from it. The sound of his pleasure drives me and I take him deeper into my mouth, as much as I can until the head is brushing the back of my throat. One of his hands falls down over my head and gently guides my motion as I suck him, the other sliding between my arms to fill with my breast again.

His thick, veiny cock throbs in my mouth, and I increase my speed. I want him to come, to give him the pleasure he gave me, even if that's the end of it. But I know it wouldn't be. This passionate flame isn't just for one round. It will burn until we are both melted.

Suddenly, he pulls me away, lifting me on the bed until our lips touch again. I can taste myself on his lips, and it drives me mad with desire. He lays me back on the bed as he crawls on, using his knees to separate my thighs and settle between them. As he climbs on top of me, his thick cock slides through my folds and I moan deeply at the sensation.

"I need you inside me," I groan. "Please. I need it."

"Are you ready?" he asks.

I don't even have time to respond.

Suddenly, I am filled with his massive cock, thrusting deep inside me and pushing me to the very edge between pleasure and pain, where the two sensations dance and mix and become one. I clench my eyes shut and stars light up in my vision as he thrusts deeper and deeper inside me. With each thrust, I feel like my body is ripping in half, and yet, I want more. Deeper. Harder.

His mouth buries itself in my neck as he curls over me. My legs wrap around his waist, and he lifts my ass in the air to get a better angle. Slowly, he sits upright, his eyes trailing down my body until it reaches where he is plunging into me. I can see the guttural joy he is getting from watching his cock split my lips apart and bury deep inside me.

Slowly, he raises one hand to his mouth and licks his thumb, covering it in saliva, before bringing it back down to me. I cry out as it slides over my clit, applying gentle pressure as it swirls in a circle over me while he fucks me deeper and deeper with each stroke.

I can't focus, the sensations are so strong and so overwhelming. Pleasure is coming from every direction. His fingers, his cock, the sight of his grin as he pleasures me, the sweat dripping down his muscular chest, the deep lines of the V-shape leading to where he is driving into my body.

It's all too much. I'm going to come again.

My toes curl as I sink into the feeling, my back arching upward as he increases his speed, grunts of effort escaping his lips as he smashes his body into mine. The sound of his primal grunting and my staccato screams mix into a song of passion and lust. I dig my fingers into his back as I lunge forward, my entire body shaking and quivering.

"Turn over," he grumbles as I fall back to the bed, covered in sweat and barely able to function.

I lift one knee to turn, but he grabs me and turns me himself. The last thing I see is a determined expression on his face as he positions me, and then I bury my face in a pillow and present myself to him. He mounts me from behind and instantly, the new position lights my body aflame. All new places inside me that had never been touched before him were being massaged by his thick, hard rod, and I melted into it.

Grabbing my waist in his hands, he holds me in place as he slams into me from behind. With a low, deep growl rolling from somewhere in his chest behind me, and I clench the bedsheets in my hands, leaning into the pressure of his cock stretching me and going deeper and deeper still.

The growl grows louder and he envelops me, leaning down until he can stretch his arms out and hold my wrists in his hands. Pressing me down into the bed, pinning me so I can't move, he rocks his hips harder and harder until I think I might explode. Another, even more intense, powerful climax is building inside me.

Waiting.

For him.

And then, the growl becomes a roar, staring low and building until it seems to take up all the available sound my ears are capable of hearing. It thunders around me, and seems to command my body to obey. As the wave of the most powerful orgasm I have ever felt takes over, he comes deep inside me.

My body milks him, until he is empty and he collapses on top of me.

CHAPTER THIRTY-FOUR

Malcolm

THE MORNINGS THAT I DON'T HAVE TO WAKE UP TO THE SOUND OF AN alarm have always been my favorite. But they have been soundly replaced by the mornings I wake up to the smell of Bree in the sheets and the feeling of her next to me. Add in there not having to hear my alarm go off and abandon the comfort and warmth of the covers way before I want to, and I am an exceedingly happy man.

At least I am until I realize that I can smell Bree there in the bed with me, but I can't feel her. The room isn't equipped with a king size bed, so there shouldn't be enough space on the mattress for her to have rolled completely away from me. I look beside me to where she fell asleep last night.

The other side of the bed is empty.

I touch the sheets. There's no warmth there anymore. It isn't like she just got up to go to the bathroom. I listen for the sound of the shower, but don't hear it. Getting up and tugging on my pajama pants, I go to the bathroom and push open the door. The towel from her shower the night before is still lying on the floor. There's no heat or dampness in the bathroom to indicate that she has taken a shower this morning. I'm walking out of the room when I realize there's nothing on the counter. No toothbrush. No hairbrush. Even the toiletries provided by the hotel are gone. Another glance at the floor confirms there aren't any clothes there with the towel.

I go back out into the room and look around. I didn't exactly pay attention to what was in here last night. There were other things on my mind and I wasn't really focusing on taking note of where her luggage was or if she'd unpacked. But it doesn't take much looking for me to realize I don't see anything that belongs to her. There's no bag. No shoes. No pajamas on the floor. I check the nightstand and the table at the side of the room. I don't see her phone or a charger.

My chest feels hollow as it sinks in what's going on. She's not just not in bed.

She's not here.

The completely irrational thought that maybe she has just gone to get some ice or run downstairs to breakfast flashes through my head. Anything to stop me from having it to you except that she has left without saying anything to me. Maybe she woke up hungry and decided to make the most of her efforts by going ahead and bringing her luggage out to her car at the same time.

I put my shirt on and go back next door to my own room. I get dressed in real clothes and go downstairs to the dining room. I recognize several people from the wedding as they fill their plates and find spots at the table or brave the cool morning air to sit outside. She isn't here. I go to the front desk.

The same woman who checked me in last night smiles at me from behind the computer. "Good morning. How was your night?"

"Great. I was actually just looking for somebody. Bree, the maid of honor. I needed to ask her something."

"Oh. I'm sorry. She checked out maybe an hour or so ago. She said she needed to catch a flight."

I force a smile. "That's right. She did need to get going early this morning. It must have slipped my mind."

I'm trying to sound casual and like it's not all that important that I find Bree, but the look the clerk gives me tells me that she doesn't for a second believe that I knew Bree wasn't at the hotel anymore. I go back upstairs and pack to leave.

"Not going to have any breakfast this morning?" the clerk asks when I'm back at the desk to check out. "We have fresh pumpkin bread this morning."

"That sounds really great, but I need to get going. Thank you. It was a really nice stay."

"Come back any time," she says.

I get in my car in the parking lot and sit for a few seconds just gripping the wheel and staring through the windshield. I'm hurt and angry that she would leave that way without saying anything, but deep down I know the person I'm really angry at is myself.

I'm the one who caused this. I can't blame Bree for feeling the way she does about all of us lying to her, especially after Olivia told me about her father and how much that impacted her, I feel horrible that I did exactly the thing that would hurt her the most. I never thought anything was going to happen between us. If I had, I never would have gone along with not telling her about the challenge.

But that's not an excuse. I shouldn't try to let myself off the hook by saying I didn't tell her because I had no intention of a relationship building between us. That's just a justification and it's truly just bull-shit. I shouldn't have lied. Period. That's the long and short of it. I shouldn't have let her believe I was someone I'm not. And I definitely shouldn't have kept it going when my feelings for her started building and I could tell she was starting to feel the same way.

This is all on me. I can't expect everything to just suddenly be okay, even if that's exactly what I wanted. I would be lying if I said I wasn't hoping that last night was our reset button. I didn't really know how Bree was going to react when I went to her room. I just couldn't stay away from her. I needed to see her. and as soon as I laid eyes on her, I needed to touch her.

And maybe she was going to push me away. Maybe she was going to slam the door in my face. But she didn't. She wanted me as badly as I wanted her, and I hoped that meant we were going to move on. We were going to put it all behind us and just see where this was going to take us.

I shouldn't have been so naive.

I'm still thinking about Bree when I get home and I wake up thinking about her the next morning. But my thoughts have shifted. I'm still hurt. I'm still angry. Only now I've decided I'm not just going to wallow in it. This happened because of me. It happened because of the challenge that Brandon and Olivia gave me, and that happened because of the way I have been doing things.

That hasn't been easy to admit. I haven't wanted to accept that they were absolutely right about me and about the way I've been running my company. Now it's time to change that.

This experience has been far more than I expected it to be. I learned about myself and about other people. Maybe it sounds dramatic, but it was truly life-changing. As I went through it, thoughts and ideas formed in my mind, ways I could make things better, not just for my employees, but also my guests.

That definitely wasn't something I saw coming. Even when I agreed to do this challenge, it didn't cross my mind that I would come out of it finding ways to overhaul how I've been operating my company for as long as I've owned it. But it's time for a change. It's time to admit I don't know everything and everything I've been doing isn't necessarily the right way. I've been successful. I know that many of the things I have done work.

Now it's time to bring it all to another level.

For the next few weeks, I keep my head down, focusing completely on implementing the ideas I came up with during my time living the challenge and even after. While navigating the fallout from the media coverage, I work with my assistant and a close team of advisors to find the most effective ways to implement the changes I want.

I can't say they are all immediately receptive. That's to be expected. They've worked with me for a long time and share so many of my ideas. I'm not willing to compromise, though. I know these are the changes that I want and I'm not going to settle for anything less.

Together we work to change policies and programs to make it a more desirable and beneficial workplace for everybody. I institute raises and plan for bonuses. I overhaul my benefits packages to make sure that anyone who works for me in any capacity will have what they need to take care of themselves and their families.

Much has changed a few weeks later when I get back to the office after a fast lunch and one of the advisors meets me at the door.

"I've been looking over your plans for child care for employees. Are you sure you want to go through with something like this? Do you have any idea how much of an investment it would be to establish dedicated child care centers for your employees in all of your properties?"

"I am very aware of it," I say. "I'm also very aware that it is not just an investment now, but an investment in the future. If I make sure that the employees at my properties don't have to worry about where their children are going to be, who is taking care of them, or how they're going to pay for it, they will be more dedicated and better employees. They won't miss as much time, and I also know that the children will do better. I'm not changing my mind on this. In areas where there are multiple properties in close proximity, we can look at establishing a centralized location, but only if that will not reduce the quality of the care or make it any more difficult for the parents."

"While we are talking about properties, I'd like to set up a time to discuss the new Maple Valley location. I've heard from some of the vendors who are very excited to get started on the project. I know it's ambitious, but I think it would be very exciting and a huge benefit if we could have the hotel open next tourist season."

I shake my head. "No."

He looks baffled as he follows me into my office. "What do you mean no? I thought you had talked about getting open as soon as possible. If we get contracts underway now, we could be ready to welcome guests by early summer. Did you want to aim for something sooner?"

"No," I say again. "No to the whole thing. I don't want to aim to open in the summer. I don't want to aim to open sooner. The project is off the table."

I finish grabbing the things I need out of my desk and head for the door again.

"Off the table?"

"Yes. I'm not going to be building in Maple Valley. But let the vendors know that I will be contacting them shortly with details about other upcoming projects."

He falls into step behind me as I make my way toward the elevator. "I'm sorry. I'm just confused."

"What are you confused about?" I hit the button to bring me back to the lobby. I check the time. I'm cutting it short, but I'll make it. "I thought I wanted to build a hotel in Maple Valley. I changed my mind. It's really that simple. We'll talk about other projects when I get back."

"Where are you going?"

He jumps into the elevator with me so that he can keep up the conversation.

"I am going to be away from the office for the next few weeks," I say. "My assistant has all the details. I'll be working, so I'm reachable anytime by phone or email. I'll be doing meetings over video chat, so if you need to discuss anything with me, just set something up."

"Where are you going?" he asks again.

"I'm going on a tour of my hotels."

I walk out of the elevator without even looking his way. I don't need to. I already know he's staring after me, trying to figure out what I'm talking about, if it's some kind of code. It isn't. I am doing exactly what I just said. I'm hitting the road and the air to visit every hotel and resort I own throughout the country. After that, I'll start planning visits to my international locations. I'm not planning on being at each destination for long.

This isn't an extended vacation. I'm in this for the research.

For the next three weeks I am constantly on the move. I go to each hotel and resort to see how it's running, check out the rooms, and take note of the amenities and service. I take the time to talk to people who work at each of the locations as well as a few guests. I want a well-rounded view of each of these places, what's working and what isn't, how it can be improved.

But it isn't just my properties I'm visiting. In each city I also seek out local artisans and businesses that may be able to provide resources for my hotels. From body products to art to treats, I want to find as many special little details as I possibly can.

By the time I finish my tour back in Maple Valley, I am exhausted but satisfied.

"How did it go?" Brandon asks, bringing me a beer as Olivia finishes dinner. "I barely talked to you the whole time you were gone."

"I know." I take a swig. "I barely talked to myself." I pause and think about that for a second. "You know what I mean. I was constantly on the move. I feel like there were days there when I only slept as long as I could in the car between stops."

"But you did everything you wanted to get done?" he asks.

"I did. It's still going to take a lot of work to implement everything. I have some contracts to finalize and some of the artisans I want to work with are going to be developing products specifically for my locations so that will take time, too, but the ball is rolling on everything. In a few months, there will be a total overhaul."

Brandon shakes his head slowly like he's in awe of everything I'm saying. "That's amazing. Listen to you, making a difference."

"You act like I'm the Grinch," I tell him. "I did already have a heart, you know."

"So did the Grinch," Olivia says, coming into the room with a plate of cheese and crackers that she sets on the coffee table. "It was just a shriveled up little prune."

"Are you saying I have a shriveled up prune heart?" I ask.

"Maybe not that bad," she says with a laugh, picking up a cracker and popping it into her mouth. "But you're definitely making progress."

We all fall into silence. My mind goes to Bree, and I wonder if they are thinking the same thing. I take another sip of my beer.

"Have you heard from Bree?" I ask.

They exchange a quick glance.

"Yeah," Olivia says. "I just spent the weekend with her a couple weeks ago."

"Did she mention me?" I ask.

Olivia shakes her head. "No."

It stings, but I have to accept it. I haven't heard from her and I haven't tried to reach out to her. If we're ever going to find our way back to each other, I can't force it. I have to look at this as maybe the good that has come to my company is what was meant for this all along.

Even if that is far from what I actually want.

CHAPTER THIRTY-FIVE

BREE

THE COLD HAS HIT HARD, AND TWO MONTHS OUT FROM OLIVIA AND Brandon's wedding, all signs of autumn are gone. The Halloween candy is long-since eaten, the turkeys and cornucopias have been tucked away for another year, and it's decidedly Christmas all over the place.

I'm burying myself in as much work as possible and filling the rest of my time volunteering. I've just come home from a volunteer shift and am getting leftovers out of the refrigerator for dinner when Olivia calls.

"You're still coming for Christmas, right?" she asks.

"Of course," I tell her. "I already have my bags almost packed. Three more days."

"I can't wait," she says. "It's been far too long since you've had a Christmas here in Maple Valley."

That's very true. It's been years since I've, as they say, been home for the holidays. "There's nothing like it," I say.

This is also very true. If there is anything that Maple Valley throws itself headlong into, it's nostalgic Christmas. Things start creeping toward festive right after Halloween, with a few people even bucking the spooky season all together and throwing together full-on yuletide extravaganzas while everyone else is still gutting their pumpkins.

Then right after Thanksgiving, the entire town transforms into a midcentury greeting card. Greenery and bows show up on all the street lamps. Everyone has lights on their houses. Cars get bedecked with those little plush antlers and the bright red noses and yards fill up with enough inflatables to create a parade.

"What time is your flight landing?"

"Noon," I tell her. "It's the earliest I could get."

"That's perfect. We'll go straight from the airport to lunch and do some shopping at the new mall in Laurel."

Laurel is the next town over from Maple Valley and what a lot of people still consider "the big city," even though it is by far not a city. It's still bigger and more elaborate than Maple Valley and any time there is a special occasion that can't be accommodated by the businesses in town, we venture to Laurel. Then when inevitably you still need something else, you actually go all the way into Richmond. But we like to stick to the glittery nostalgia of the smaller towns as much as we can.

Talking about Olivia picking me up at the airport immediately makes me think of Malcolm. I haven't heard a single word from him since that night at the hotel. It's a relief in a way, but I'm also surprised. I expected him to call or text. Something. At the same time, I did just get up at dawn and check out of the hotel room. I left him lying naked and asleep, so maybe he isn't feeling terribly charitable toward me.

It wasn't my finest hour. I should have handled it better. I just didn't know what to say or do. I didn't even know what I was thinking or feeling. All I knew was I needed to get away from it.

For a second, I think about asking about him. Just a bit of curiosity. Maybe a confirmation of whether he's going to be with us for Christmas, but I stop myself. I don't need to think about him. I am looking forward to seeing Olivia again and enjoying the festive season.

The airport is completely decked out for Christmas when I arrive and I am brimming with excitement to see Olivia and bask in her total obsession with Christmas. She does not disappoint. I can see her sweater before she even sees me. Its black and neon color scheme might be on the edgy side for the holidays, but the flashing strand of lights and the dancing snowmen bring it right back.

"The jingle bells are a nice touch," I tell her after we hug.

She shakes her ponytail to make the bells ring. "Thank you. I have to represent."

Represent what, I'm not sure, but whatever it is, I'm pretty sure she's doing it.

"Is the traffic bad?" I ask.

"Not really. You picked a good travel day." She grabs my bag from me. "Come on. I have reservations for lunch."

We eat in Laurel and spend a couple of hours at the new mall before ending up back on Main Street in Maple Valley. Holding cups of cocoa from the coffee shop to keep us warm, we stroll down the street admiring the beautifully decorated windows in all the shops. We get to the boutique where I ordered the body products for her wedding, and Olivia points at the door.

"I need to dip in here. Brandon's cousins have mentioned the lotion and bath gel about twenty times. They absolutely loved it so I want to get them some for stocking stuffers."

We go inside and I breathe in the smells again. They are different now. The seasonal scents fill the entire boutique with their personality, drawing me over to a table promising eggnog, gingerbread, and peppermint lines. As I'm shamelessly sampling every one I can get my hands on, the owner comes over.

"Hi," I say, giving her a hug. "It's good to see you."

"You, too," she says. "You aren't here planning another wedding, are you?"

She winks and I shake my head with a little laugh. "No. I'm just visiting Olivia for Christmas."

"Well, that's good, too. How is Malcolm?"

My heart drops a little and I fight to keep my smile on my face. "I don't know. I haven't talked to him since the wedding."

"Oh," she says, sounding surprised. "I just thought…."

"We were just planning the wedding together. That's all."

"Are these your only seasonal scents?" Olivia asks, coming up beside me and leaning down to sniff my wrist where I just spritzed some gingerbread body spray.

"I have a few more. Let me grab them for you."

We leave the boutique laden with bags and when we're a few yards away, Olivia looks over at me. "Do you really think that's true?"

"Do I really think what is true?" I ask.

"That you and Malcolm were just planning the wedding together."

"That's what we were doing," I tell her. "Nothing more."

"You know you told me the two of you slept together, right? You didn't just block that out of your mind?"

"I know. But that was just… cabin fever."

"You weren't in the house enough to have cabin fever."

"PreTSD?"

"Bree."

"What?" She lifts her eyebrows at me, and I squeeze my shoulders toward my ears. "What?"

"How do you really feel about him?"

I don't want to talk about this. I was having such a good time and I don't want to get into this right now. But I know Olivia isn't going to let it go. We get to the car and put all the bags in. We climb in and she cranks the heat in the seats. As we pull away, she gives me a questioning look.

"So?"

"So, what?"

"How do you really feel about him?"

I sigh. "He lied to me, Olivia. He lied and he strung me along and he humiliated me. That's not something I'm willing to deal with."

"But you forgave me," she says. "I was a part of the whole situation, too, and you forgave me."

"That's different. You are still you. I didn't even know who he was. Everything about him was a lie. And I looked up his business and the way he runs it. Haven't you ever seen the complaints about him?"

"I have," Olivia says. "Remember, that's why we gave him the challenge in the first place. That's not the only thing that defines him. I know him, Bree."

"It might not be the only thing that defines him, but it's a big thing. Everything that people have said about him, how secretive he has been…it's just not something I can handle."

"Look into him again," she says. "And…."

She hesitates.

"And what?"

"I was trying to figure out how I was going to bring this up. Malcolm is hosting an event tomorrow night and he invited us. I would really love for you to come."

I shake my head. "No. I don't want to be anywhere near him."

"Just give it a chance. Think about it."

We go to Olivia's house and I settle into the guest room. When I've unpacked, I curl up the armchair with my tablet to look up Malcolm and his company. Olivia seems convinced that I've missed something about him and that it could make all the difference for me.

It doesn't take long for me to see that things really have changed. Rather than all the articles that come up about Malcolm and his company being riddled with accusations and condemnations or wild conjecture about his personal life, they now highlight the enormous transformation that has come over the entire company.

It's incredible to see how much he has changed his company for the better. Interviews with employees gush about how much happier they are working for him and how much their lives have improved. Guests talk about enjoying his properties before, but now really feeling like they are something special and looking forward to the other changes that have been promised, including bringing in more products and services from local businesses.

Reading that makes my heart swell a little. Something came over him. He really did learn. I keep reading and stumble on an article that stuns me. He was planning a hotel in Maple Valley, but the project has been cancelled. Now his focus on the Maple Valley community is all going to the old park he has taken on as his own project and is planning on refurbishing over the next several months–my park, the one I showed him and told him how much I loved it.

He has adopted it and is going to bring it back to what it used to be.

CHAPTER THIRTY-SIX

Malcolm

THE PARK IS EMPTY IN THE COLD WEATHER, BUT I HOPE THAT WILL change soon. I want to park to be a place where the families of Maple Valley can come and enjoy the surroundings all year. I'm planning basic refurbishment of what already exists, but I also have ideas for new features and programs that will hopefully draw in visitors who might not have ventured here recently but could rediscover their love of the park and introduce it to new generations.

I'm here checking up on a few areas that are being prepared for the work that will get started early next year. I don't want any delays in the construction, which means taking the time now to get every-thing ready so as soon as the chaos of the holiday season is over, work can begin at full force. If all goes according to plan, some of the features will be available for visitors early in the spring.

I make a couple of notes about the trail sign I've just checked and turn to go to my next destination. something catches my attention out of the corner of my eye and when I look up, I'm shocked to see Bree standing a few yards down the path, her hands tucked in the pockets of her bright red parka and her neck snuggled down into a thick scarf. She watches me quietly.

Is it possible she just happens to be here? Obviously, I know how much she loves this park. It's my main motivation behind turning it into my project. Maybe she wanted to take a walk and came out here for some quiet.

But she's not trying to avoid me. She didn't turn and head the other direction or duck behind a tree or anything. She's just standing there, looking at me. I think the chances are pretty low that Olivia hasn't mentioned the work I'm doing. She doesn't know the full scope of my plans, but she knows what I've already put into this and that my visit here with Bree is what inspired me.

Did she come because she knew I'd be here?

Hopeful even as I'm trying not to let myself put too much thought into it, I cautiously approach her. "Hi."

"Hi." She glances down at her feet and shifts around a little, not seeming to know quite what she should be doing.

"Fancy seeing you here. You come here often?" I ask.

She looks up at me and chuckles.

I shake my head. "Yeah, that wasn't great."

"Well, I definitely don't come here as often as I'd like. But I really didn't think you did."

It feels awkward between us, like we aren't sure how we should be acting around each other. But there's also a pull I feel in the center of my chest, something I can see reflected in Bree's eyes when she looks at me. It's obvious we missed each other. I know how much I've missed her. How much I miss her even as I'm standing here looking at her. But I'm finally seeing it in her, too.

"I've been doing a lot of things differently recently," I say finally. "It turns out that challenge from Olivia and Brandon wasn't just some ridiculous game. It actually did teach me some things, a lot of things. And so did you. I wanted to take all of that and do something with it, so I've been making a lot of changes in my company. The first thing I did was make sure that I increased pay across the board, especially for those who work so hard to keep all of the properties running but who weren't getting anywhere near the recognition that they should have."

I paused briefly and continued. "The pay increase went into effect the very next paycheck, and all of them will be getting holiday bonuses next week. I'm planning on doing bonuses regularly for everyone and also implementing merit-based bonuses and acknowledgment for years of service. But it isn't just giving them more money. I've been trying to find as many ways as I can to actually improve their quality of life, too. I took a trip around the country visiting all of my hotels and resorts to talk to the people who work there. I found out the things that they need the most and am working on addressing all of them.

"I am building childcare centers for the employees that will ensure all of their children have a place to be while they are at work. That will be included as part of their basic employment benefits, so they won't have to worry about how they are going to pay for it. I'm working on building up a backup workforce of temporary and fill-in staff who will be able to step in when people need time off and for things like holidays when the parents want to be with their families."

"It sounds like you really are making a lot of improvements," she says. "I know that the people who work for your company will appreciate those. That's going to make a big difference in their lives."

"I hope so. They deserve it. It was really eye-opening going and talking to people. They told me about things I never would have thought of, things that just wouldn't have ever crossed my mind."

"It's hard to understand other people's lives when they are so different from yours if you don't take the time to really try to learn," she says.

"I know that now," I say. "But it isn't just about changing things for the employees. I've spent so long just doing the exact same things with all of my properties. With a couple of minor changes from a place to place, they are all basically the same. I thought that was a good thing. I thought people would find it appealing that no matter where they went, they would have the same experience. And in some ways, that's true. They want familiarity and comfort. But there's a lot to be said about adding unique, personal touches that make each destination special."

"That sounds familiar," Bree says with a hint of a smile.

"Yeah. I don't know where I could have heard that before. So another thing that I really focused on while I was visiting all my properties was finding ways that I could make each one special for my guests. Over the next year, I'm going to be totally overhauling my properties to create those experiences. Guests will still get the same level of service and attention, but they will find special little touches that elevate my hotels and resorts above just the basic chains. I want them to see my properties as something special."

"I've been negotiating contracts with local artisans and businesses to provide amenities, art, food, and other little details," I continue. "Management at every location will be put through additional training to help them recognize opportunities to make a guest's stay above and beyond what they expected, personal little details that make them feel appreciated and welcome. I really was inspired by the little hotel you love so much here. I couldn't understand why you would want to stay somewhere like that when there are bigger, fancier options available. But after listening to you and then staying there, I understand it."

"I heard you canceled plans to build your own hotel here."

I nod. "I did. I was going to open a big hotel in town and figured it would draw in tourists. But I don't want to do anything that could compromise business for anybody else. That hotel is part of Maple Valley. People who visit here should get the opportunity to stay there. There are plenty of other places where I can expand. But for now, I really want to focus on taking what I have and making it better."

"And the park?" she asks, glancing around.

"Same goes for the park. It's not mine, obviously. It belongs to the town and to everybody here. I want them to have something wonderful. The way you talked about it, it really sounded like it used to be the heart of the town. It was something that everybody could be proud of and enjoy. I want everybody to have that again. I want to see this place come back to life. So I asked the town if I could adopt it.

They gave me permission, and now plans are underway to refurbish and rejuvenate the whole thing. We're going to fix up the walking trails and add new signs. The playgrounds are going to get all new equipment. There are a couple of areas that I've identified that I think would be great for adding exercise circuits. I want to incorporate some educational programs. I've been talking to the schools about possibly building a greenhouse and doing some agriculture programming for the kids. I didn't even realize how much space there is and how much potential exists in it. Did you know there's a whole campground in the back that hasn't been used in decades?"

"I did," she says. "It's not very big, but I always thought it would be fun to be able to camp out here. It was sad that it was roped off and no one was allowed to camp there anymore."

"Well, they're going to be able to again, starting next year. This whole place is going to be somewhere the community can love again."

"That sounds amazing."

Bree is obviously touched, and my heart warms at the emotion in her eyes. I have to tell her what I'm feeling. It's now or never.

I take another step closer and reach down to pick up her hand. "I've missed you so much. I don't even know how to put it into words. All of this has been with you in mind. I know that I hurt you. I know that I disappointed you. And I'll never really be able to apologize enough for that. But I also know that you mean more to me than anyone ever has and you've changed me in ways I didn't think were possible. I want you in my life, Bree. I promise from this moment on, I will always be honest with you. I'm hosting a gala tomorrow night. Will you go with me?"

She hesitates for a second, thinking about the request. "I'll go, but with Olivia and Brandon. I'll meet you there."

I smile. "That works."

I want to spend the rest of the day with Bree, but as soon as she agrees to go to the event, she tells me she has plans with Olivia and has to go. She squeezes my hand slightly before dropping it and as she walks away, she glances back over her shoulder at me.

The next night the venue at the orchard is glowing. It's a

completely different atmosphere than Olivia and Brandon's wedding, and I'm amazed at just how much the same space can transform. The entire space is filled with lights and greenery. Massive Christmas trees take up each corner, decorated with different themes. A few items are under each tree, the start of what I hope will end up being a large pile of donated gifts by the end of the night.

Preston arrives shortly after guests start streaming in. He comes over to shake my hand and glances around.

"Looks good. I have to admit, I was surprised to hear you would be hosting an event that wasn't at one of your hotels. But this is a great venue."

"It hasn't been open for long, but it's already popular. Hopefully tonight will only boost that more."

We're walking around greeting people when I look up and see Bree appear at the doorway. She takes my breath away. The green gown she's chosen sparkles in the lights, accentuating every curve of her body and making her eyes dance. My growing love for her fills my entire body, making everything but her fall away.

I walk away from Preston and go to her. Without saying a word, I hold out my hand.

She smiles and puts hers in mine. I guide her to the dance floor and twirl her around before bringing her into my arms. Her body rests against mine and her eyes stare deep into me.

Finally, I dip my head and kiss her.

CHAPTER THIRTY-SEVEN

BREE

Four months later...

Spring has officially come to Maple Valley.

The winter has faded away and new warmth has settled over the town, welcoming back animals and bringing new growth to the trees and flowers. Everything is awash with green and pastels and the air smells sweet and fresh. I admire the beauty around me as I drive into town. It's been a long road-trip, but I've finally made it. Glancing into my rearview mirror, I check to make sure the moving truck is still close behind.

Brandon is behind the wheel, bopping along to whatever music he's playing. Olivia is beside him, her head in her hand. We've been alternating between her riding with me and riding with him since leaving my old apartment. Every time we've stopped for a break, she's hopped in the opposite vehicle to make sure she's keeping everybody company along the way. I know she's bursting with just as much excitement as I am.

Finally, after so long, I'm coming home.

It isn't something I thought was going to happen. When I left Maple Valley all those years ago, it was supposed to be for good. I wanted something different for my life. I wasn't going to let what people thought of me and my family define what I could have and what I could become. Even when I was feeling homesick and missed the places I love and being close to Olivia, it really wasn't in my head that one day I would move back.

And then came Malcolm.

Now everything has changed. Since that moment when he kissed me at the Christmas party, I knew that my life would never be the same. We'd found our way back to each other, and I wasn't going to let him go. But that meant things were going to have to be different for both of us. Long distance would have to work for a little while, but it wasn't going to be sustainable into the future. We knew right then we wanted a future, and that meant having to be in the same place.

And there was no better place than Maple Valley.

The plans to move to the town together really started in earnest about six weeks ago. During one of his visits to my apartment, we got to talking about everything and it just occurred to us that there was really no reason I was still living so far away. My career is encapsulated in my laptop. Wherever it is, I can work. I like my apartment and the town I'd been living in, but it doesn't really feel like I have any serious ties to it.

Everything was pulling me back to Maple Valley and into Malcolm's arms.

Then everything turned into a whirlwind. He found a house for us and agreed that while he would keep his house in the city, he'd commute when he needed to go to the office. He didn't want me to feel like I was giving everything up to just step into being a piece of his life. We are building something new together, and that means both of us meeting in the middle.

Olivia has been bubbling over with excitement since we told her I was coming back. She appeared at my apartment the next day with bags of food and later that afternoon, a massive shipment of packing materials appeared. She's been back a couple of times since to help me purge the apartment of everything I didn't need to bring with me and pack up the rest. Yesterday, she and Brandon came to rent the moving truck and take the haul home.

This is the first time I'll be seeing the house Malcolm picked for us. He said he'd send pictures or that I could look at the real estate listing online so I'd know what I was getting into and could tell him if I wanted something else, but I decided not to.

I've been looking forward to the surprise. I knew he would choose something amazing for us, and dreaming about the first time I'll lay eyes on our home has been getting me through the hassle and stress of the move.

Finally we turn down the street that the GPS has directed me to and I pull up the driveway of my new home. The house that rises up in front of me is gorgeous. Surrounded by a wide porch with big white columns and hanging baskets of flowers it is everything I could have ever dreamed of.

Almost.

I climb out of the car and the front door opens. Malcolm walks out onto the porch and smiles at me. Now it is everything I could have ever dreamed of.

"You look well-rested and without any stress," Brandon says as he walks up with me. "Not at all like you've been on a two-day road trip with a moving truck. Oh, wait, that's because you didn't come and help."

Malcolm laughs as he comes down the front steps and gathers me in a hug. "I've had a lot going on."

"We know," Olivia says, playfully swatting Brandon. "He's just salty because I don't like his music."

Malcolm wraps his arm around me and turns us to look at the house. He gestures at it with a sweep of his arm.

"What do you think?"

"It's perfect," I tell him. "I can't wait to see inside."

"Then let's go. I'll give you the grand tour."

"That's right," Brandon calls after us as we head inside. "Don't worry about us. We'll just start unloading everything. Not a problem."

"Come inside," Malcolm shouts back. "I've already ordered pizza, and there's a team of movers arriving in about fifteen minutes to unload everything."

"Oh, thank sweet baby Jesus."

The back of the moving truck slams down and Brandon stalks up the walkway to the porch. Malcolm and I laugh as we climb the steps and he opens the front door.

"Go ahead."

I step inside and the most incredible feeling of being home fills me. It's the first moment I've ever stepped into this house, and yet it's like I was always meant to be here. I can see myself here. See Malcolm here. I know this is where we are supposed to build our future.

"Obviously there's still a lot to be done," he says. "There are rooms that will need more furniture and it's going to need to be decorated and everything, but now that you're here, it can get done."

"I can't wait."

I turn into his arms and kiss him.

The house isn't quite ready for us to stay in it yet, so we are staying at the hotel for the next couple of nights until we can get everything fully in place. I'm looking forward to tomorrow. Arriving back in town today was planned specifically so I can be a part of the grand reveal of the newly refurbished azalea garden at the park tomorrow. I can't wait to see it. Malcolm has been following the progress as the horticulturists brought the garden back to its former glory, and he has told me that it looks incredible.

I wake up the next morning to find Malcolm already up and getting dressed.

"Good morning," he says. "I'm glad you're up. I want you to come with me."

"Where?" I ask, rolling over and stretching.

"To the azalea garden," he says.

"I thought that's what we were already planning."

"The reveal is later. I want you to come with me this morning. You are the whole reason this is happening. You deserve to see it before anybody else. Come on. Let's go down for breakfast and then I'll bring you to see it."

I get out of bed and get dressed, then we go down to the dining room for breakfast. The owner gives us a warm, knowing smile as she finishes putting the final platters of food on the table and walks out of the room. We fill our plates and go outside into the cool morning to eat in the bright sunlight. When we're finished, Malcolm drives us over to the park.

It's the first time I've been back in months. As soon as we pull into the parking area, I can see the dramatic changes that have been made. I can't believe how good it looks and I know the entire community is going to love being welcomed back. There are still some plans unfolding over the next several months, culminating in the reopening of the campground this fall, but the park is alive again and I know this spring and summer it will be bursting with people returning to enjoy it.

We walk hand-in-hand along the paths to the azalea garden. My heart flutters in my chest as we approach. Even from a distance I can see the blooms on the bushes closest to the main path. We turn into the garden and are immediately surrounded by bursts of color. The paths have been smoothed out and the garden beds rebuilt. Bushes are arranged to create pools of color and fully immerse anyone walking through. New benches and picnic tables inhabit alcoves that make the entire space feel enchanted.

"This looks even better than it did when I was younger," I say.

Malcolm smiles at me and we turn a corner. Ahead of me the old gazebo has been completely transformed. It's painted white and extensions have been added so the main part opens out to two smaller gazebos. But it isn't just the building that makes my breath catch in my throat. The entire thing is filled with flowers. Nothing matches. It's just vases, bowls, and baskets overflowing with blooms of all different kinds, reminding me of the flowers at Olivia's wedding.

Malcolm leads me inside and takes my hands. "Nothing in my life has ever been as precious to me as you are, Bree. I never expected you. I always thought I had my entire life planned, that I knew who I was, what I wanted, and where I was going. You changed all of that.

You made me discover things about myself and about this world that I never knew existed and I am so much better because of it. Right now in one of those rom-coms you love, I would probably start talking about how my heart is like this azalea garden, blooming again after being dormant for so long and now it's filled with color and beauty. Or something like that. I tried to come up with something, but it didn't come to me. All I can think of to say is that I love you. I have loved you and I will love you. Always. I want to build a life with you and discover everything that this world has to offer with you by my side. Will you marry me?"

He lowers himself to one knee in front of me and reaches in his pocket to pull out a ring.

I gasp, my head spinning a little as I look at him. I don't need to think about it even for a second. I nod, tears already pouring down my cheeks.

He slips the ring onto my finger and stands up to pull me into his arms and kiss me. I am filled with a happiness and fulfillment I can't even put into words. This is so much more than I could have imagined.

Pulling back to look at him, I smile. "You know what?"

"What?" he asks.

"I think planning a wedding is going to be a lot easier this time around."

ALSO BY BELLA MOONDRAGON

The Alpha King's Breeder series:

Bought by the Alpha: The Alpha King's Breeder Book 1

Loved by the Alpha: The Alpha King's Breeder Book 2

Lost by the Alpha: The Alpha King's Breeder Book 3

Luna of the Alpha: The Alpha King's Breeder Book 4

Legacy of the Alpha: The Alpha Kings's Breeder Book 5

Daughter of the Alpha: The Alpha King's Breeder Book 6

Descendants of the Alpha: The Alpha King's Breeder Book 7

Shadow of the Alpha: The Alpha King's Breeder Book 8

Son of the Alpha: The Alpha King's Breeder Book 9

Spare of the Alpha: The Alpha King's Breeder Book 10

Claimed by the Alpha: The Alpha King's Breeder Book 11

Atonement for the Alpha King: The Alpha King's Breeder Book 12

Rejected by the Alpha: The Alpha King's Breeder Book 13 (coming soon!)

The Luna's Vampire Prince series:

The Culling

The Kingdom

The Conquered

Wolf Shifter Fairy Tale Retellings series

Beauty and the Alpha Beast

Pregnant With Four Alphas' Babies

Chosen As the Breeder

Mated to Four Alphas

Threats Against the Breeder

At War for the Breeder

The Stolen Breeder

Four Alphas, Four Babies

Becoming the Luna Queen

Descendants of the Breeder

Desired by the Devil series

Whispers of the Devil

Banter of the Devil

Murmurs of the Devil

The Mafia Kings series

Indebted to the Mafia King

<u>Loved by the Mafia King</u>

Claimed by the Mafia King

Secrets of the Mafia King

Burned by the Mafia King

Kidnapped by the Mafia King (coming soon!)

Dark Stalker Romance series

Tempted by Sin

Fated by Sin (coming soon!)

Secret Billionaires series

Finding the Secret Billionaire by Olivia Bhelle Kildare

Falling for My Secret Billionaire by Bella Moondragon

Driven by the Secret Billionaire by ID Johnson

Wolf Shifter Alpha Kings series

Ravens and Ruins

Sundrops and Shadows

Snowflakes and Sabotage

The Vampire King's Feeder series

Claiming the Alpha's Daughter

Loving the Alpha's Daughter

Finding the Alpha's Daughter

Stand Alone Novels

One Weekend With the Billionaire

Shared by the Sexy Billoinaire Twins

Alpha of the Western Moon

Writing as B. Moon

The Boy Who Died

Sign up for Bella's newsletter here.

*Or get a free novella from The Alpha King's Breeder series when you sign up here:
The Beta and the Maid*

Follow Bella on Facebook here.

Follow Bella on Bookbub here.

www.ingramcontent.com/pod-product-ccmpliance
Lightning Source LLC
Chambersburg PA
CBHW060259310726
48976CB00007B/2126